Fire Dancer
(A Miranda's Rights Mystery)
Book IV

Linsey Lanier

Edited by
Donna Rich

Editing for You

Gilly Wright
www.gillywright.com

Copyright © 2013 Linsey Lanier
Felicity Books
All rights reserved.

ISBN: 1941191150
ISBN-13: 978-1-941191-15-6

Copyright © 2013 Linsey Lanier

All rights reserved. Without limiting the rights under copyright reserved above, no part of this publication may be reproduced, stored in or introduced into a retrieval system, or transmitted, in any form, or by any means (electronic, mechanical, photocopying, recording, or otherwise) without the prior written permission of both the copyright owner and the above publisher of this book. This is a work of fiction. Names, characters, places, brands, media, and incidents are either the product of the author's imagination or are used fictitiously. The author acknowledges the trademarked status and trademark owners of various products referenced in this work of fiction, which have been used without permission. The publication/use of these trademarks is not authorized, associated with, or sponsored by the trademark owners.

FIRE DANCER

The fourth book in the popular Miranda's Rights Mystery series.

What makes you think you deserve to be so happy?

A honeymoon in Maui in a luxury beachfront resort with your wealthy new husband. Sounds like paradise, right? But this is Miranda Steele we're talking about here. And where Miranda goes, trouble follows.
That lovely honeymoon gets hijacked when Miranda finds the body of a popular fire dancer on the beach. Of course, she has to investigate. What choice does she have? But things get more complicated when she discovers Parker has been keeping some pretty serious secrets from her.

Could those secrets lead to finding Miranda's daughter at last? Or will this Hawaiian honeymoon adventure end in Miranda's ultimate destruction?

THE MIRANDA'S RIGHTS MYSTERY SERIES

Someone Else's Daughter
Delicious Torment
Forever Mine
Fire Dancer
Thin Ice

THE MIRANDA AND PARKER MYSTERY SERIES

All Eyes on Me
Heart Wounds
Clowns and Cowboys
The Watcher
Zero Dark Chocolate
Trial by Fire
Smoke Screen
The Boy
Snakebit
Mind Bender
Roses from My Killer
The Stolen Girl
Vanishing Act
Predator
Retribution
Most Likely to Die
(more to come)

MAGGIE DELANEY POLICE THRILLER SERIES

Chicago Cop
Good Cop Bad Cop

OTHER BOOKS BY LINSEY LANIER

Steal My Heart

THE PRASALA ROMANCES

The Crown Prince's Heart
The King's Love Song
The Count's Baby

For more information visit www.linseylanier.com

WARNING

Stay clear of blowholes. They can lead to death

CHAPTER ONE

The waves washed over him. He could not breathe.

He swam as hard as he could against the swirling dark water, but the current kept dragging him down and under.

The blowhole. He was in the blowhole. The opening of the sea cave, with its mighty roaring gusts.

Panic clawed his insides. His shirt billowed open around him. His lungs burned.

Minutes passed. They seemed like hours.

How much longer could he hold his breath? How much longer could he hold out?

He was young and strong. He had always been athletic, but right now his arms felt like lead.

At last the current reversed and forced him up. He swam as hard as he could, battling the swirling waves. As the water gushed above him like a geyser, his head finally burst through the surface and he gasped in wonderful, sweet air.

He could not see, even in the moonlight. There was too much blood in his eyes.

His head ached where it had been pounded against the rocks. His face throbbed from the beating.

He had left him here for dead.

He should not have come here tonight. He had known it was dangerous. But he had to try. His little brother had to have a chance in life. He could not let him ruin it. The spirit of ohana would not let him.

He threw his head back and once more gasped in air. His vision cleared a little.

Rocks.

Right there at the edge of the blowhole. He reached out for them. Slid.

He reached out again, but the rocks were too slippery.

His hands were numb. He could not pull himself out of the hole. Another wave would come over the lava wall soon. The waves were monstrous tonight, the sea at her angriest.

Refusing to give up, once more he grasped for the rocks.

This time, he found a knob in the formation. Just beyond it was an indentation, forming a sort of handle. The pang of hope in his chest nearly burst his heart. He grabbed onto the knob and struggled to heave himself out of the water.

Part way up. A little more. His chest ached, his arms shook with fatigue. One more tug. Just one more and he would be out.

But he could not do it. The powerful waves had made him too weak.

His arms gave out. His hand slipped. He cried out and slid back down into the swirling water. He could hear the roar of the next wave gathering. His heart pounded.

Think. Think.

He was still wearing his clothes. His open shirt. It might save him. Once again, he reached out for the knobby rock. With the last bit of strength he had, he tied the tail of his shirt around the outcropping.

Would it hold him and keep him from being swept out to sea?

Just as he had secured the cloth, the mountainous wave shot over the lava wall. It rained down on him like a tsunami, forcing him down, down.

The water rose over his head. His shirt slipped off his body—and caught around his neck.

But his shirttail held. He tried to grab onto it, use it like a rope, but his arm was twisted in the sleeve at the wrong angle.

His panic climbed to a frenzied terror. He fought hard. He had to reach the surface again, but his strength was giving out. He struggled to keep swimming. The waves battered against him, weakening him until he felt like an old man.

He could not hold his breath much longer. He thrashed the water with his feet, beat it with his arms. He was so tired. His muscles, his ribs ached like fire. He could not hold his breath.

It was too much.

He fought to keep his mouth shut but his throat spasmed. His chest convulsed. Terror pounded in his eardrums.

He could not do it.

Of their own will, his lips sputtered and his jaw snapped open. He gasped and water flowed down his throat.

His body jerked. He gagged and coughed. He was flailing now, his body convulsing. His head felt light. As if he were in a dream. He tried to wake up, but he could hardly move. Time seemed to stretch out into an endless vacuum.

Mama. Papa. His brother. His sister. He would never see them again. He was going to ohana.

His kicks slowed. His arms began to drift. His efforts to breathe ceased. And then there was blackness. He was still.

It was over.

Still tethered to the rock by his shirttail, his body bobbed in the waves as his life slipped out of him and into the sea.

CHAPTER TWO

Eight hours earlier

Miranda Steele gazed in wonder out the window of the 757 at the expanse of impossibly blue ocean below her. As the green islands took shape under wispy clouds, she wanted to pinch herself.

"I can't believe I'm really going to Maui."

Beside her, Parker took her hand and gave it a tender squeeze that sent a shiver up her arms. "Do you see the part of the island shaped like a human head?" His deep Southern voice echoed with magnolias, mint juleps and delight at her pleasure.

"It's facing that way." She pointed downward. "Looks sort of like the chalk outline of a murder victim."

He chuckled softly. "You would put it that way. That's where we'll be staying. Just along the shore."

"Camping on the beach?"

"Luxury resort."

Of course, it would be nothing but the best for the wealthy and well-bred Wade Russell Parker the Third, CEO of the successful Parker Investigative Agency—where she was now a Level One Investigator.

"Cool," she sighed. But she'd never cared for his money or his status. What had won her over was his heart of gold.

Excitement prickling her insides, she turned to her new husband with a big smile.

Husband.

She could think the word now without the familiar rush of sheer dread.

There he sat in all his Southern gentlemanly glory. The best catch in Atlanta. She still didn't understand what Parker saw in her, but here she was married and going on a honeymoon with him.

Her heart thumped giddily as she took in his dark, neatly-styled salt-and-pepper hair, his mature, middle-aged air of wisdom, the sensual gleam in his Magnum-colored eyes.

His fit, hard-muscled body was casually clad in a pair of dark, straight-leg fashion jeans that he definitely didn't pick up at the dollar store and a form-fitted shirt with a geometric pattern that made the gray of his eyes more intense than ever.

She rarely saw him in casual clothes. But he was determined this honeymoon would be a vacation.

Meaning no work for either of them.

"Has it really been a whole week?" she sighed with the uncharacteristic dreaminess that had crept into her voice since she'd said, "I do."

A flicker of a frown crossed his handsome face. "You mean *only* a week, don't you?"

She cocked her head. "Being married to me is a bore, huh?"

The frown deepened. "You know what I mean, Miranda. As I've said several times, a week is hardly enough time for you to heal."

"And as I've said several times, I'm okay." Though she still had headaches from her concussion and the gash in her leg did ache every so often.

Before she'd taken the plunge with her sexy boss she'd had to use all her strength and skill to fight a crazed killer. Parker had wanted to postpone their honeymoon a few more weeks for her to recuperate from the injuries she'd sustained during that fight, but Miranda found herself truly excited at the idea of going to Hawaii and couldn't wait.

He'd given in.

"Very well," he said on an exhale that told her he'd be guarding her health while they were vacationing.

Parker put her hand to his lips and kissed the old-fashioned Art Deco diamond-and-sapphire engagement ring that had belonged to his mother. That at last had a matching ring beneath it. Satisfied at the sight, he raised his gaze and studied this woman he cherished more than his own life.

Those lush, deep blue eyes with the blackest of lashes. Her thick, wild hair that he adored. He had almost lost her too many times. He would never let that happen again.

He rubbed his fingers over her palm, recalling the calluses from road crew work that used to be there before he'd tempted her to join his firm as an investigative trainee. Her hands were softer now.

As was her heart.

And if all went well with this trip and he accomplished his secret purpose here in Maui without her knowing it, her heart might heal completely at last.

"Tired?" he murmured.

Miranda let herself get lost in his eyes. They were warm with passion and she felt her libido spike. As if it had ever died down since she'd gone down the aisle. "How can I be tired if I'm dreaming?"

"Oh no, my darling. You're very much awake." His smile grew sly as he leaned over and kissed her.

She kissed him back, the sweet delirium of sheer joy coursing through her. She was so much in love.

And yet, even as she ran a hand over his handsome, rugged face, even as her heart did a polka in her chest, she could hear that quiet, nagging voice in the darkest recesses of her brain.

What makes you think you deserve to be so happy? What makes you think this can last?

She pulled away, her mind flashing to her ex-husband's ugly figure slashing at her with a bloody knife. Automatically her fingers felt for the scarf at her chest that she was using to cover the scars he had given her.

Leon.

The monster who had ruined her life and stolen her only child from her. The man who, for the past three months, had been lying comatose in a hospital back in Atlanta.

Where she'd put him.

"Penny for your thoughts?" Parker's tone told her he knew what she'd been thinking.

Miranda cleared her throat and shifted in the seat with an awkward laugh. "Penny? Hey, this trip must have put you back a pretty one. I guess the bill I owe you now is about as big as the national debt."

She'd always insisted on paying him back for all the things he'd bought her. She'd never catch up on the payments. Part of his maneuvering to get her to marry him, no doubt.

"Oh, I'll make sure I'm adequately reimbursed." He took a strand of her long, unruly hair and put it to his lips.

She sucked in a breath. From any other man, that comment would have earned a front-snap kick to the groin. But from Parker, it only made her melt. She was definitely now putty in his capable hands.

As if determined to kiss away her troubles, he leaned forward again and grazed his mouth across her cheek. Shivers skittered down her neck, up her arms, across her solar plexus. Wade Russell Parker the Third had to be the sexiest man alive.

Could you become a member of the Mile High Club in a first class seat? She thought that was usually done in the john.

Her cell phone buzzed and reluctantly she pulled away again to dig it out of the pocket of her new skinny jeans—that she *did* buy at the dollar store—and straightened the bold print top that she'd tied at the waist per the instructions of her new fashion consultants, Coco Hinsley and Joan Fanuzzi, who had been her bridesmaids and had helped her pick out her clothes for the trip.

She looked down at the text message. It was from Wendy.

Geography class is so boooorinng. Why do we have to know the capital of Argentina? Mackenzie's getting ready for the Regional. She's sooo excellent. Miss you.

"That's not work, is it?"

Since Parker had insisted she rest and heal from her fight, she'd only worked a couple of days last week. She'd come into the office over his protests. But she couldn't stay away. Making Level One Investigator was the first accomplishment she'd ever been proud of. Or ever wanted.

She shook her head. "I told Becker and Holloway they were on their own for two weeks."

"As did I."

She arched a brow. Man, he could be bossy. "It's from Wendy. See, nosy?" She held up her phone for him to see.

"I believe you." He frowned at her, then his eyes grew tender. "How is she?"

After her bloody pre-wedding brawl, Wendy's mother decided it was too dangerous for her daughter to hang around Miranda and forbade the teen to see her so much—conveniently forgetting that it wasn't a Sunday school picnic that had brought the two of them together in the first place. Wendy must be texting her on the sly. Miranda missed the kid.

She thumbed a reply, thinking of the time difference. *Stop complaining. Get your homework done and get to bed.*

Parker watched her tenderly. "I'm sorry about what Iris did."

Miranda shrugged. "I'm just glad she's paying more attention to the girl. It's about time."

"Agreed."

Iris was a busy executive. She and her golf pro husband had both neglected their daughter. But that neglect had thrown Miranda and Wendy together and they had forged a special bond. A bond she'd begun to believe could replace the loss of her own daughter. But Wendy wasn't hers.

"It's good she's started classes again."

"Yeah." It had been hard to find a school that would take Wendy after the trouble she'd been in. Miranda hoped she could find some decent friends there. Not snooty girls like Mackenzie Chatham. Even if she was a top-notch figure skater and skating was Wendy's new passion.

"Don't stress over her, Miranda."

"I'm not."

He studied her with those penetrating gray eyes. "I mean it when I said we were both going to relax these two weeks. You need it. And I do, too."

Parker knew how to keep the job from getting to him. That was a lesson she had yet to learn. But he didn't have to be a nag about it. "I know, I know. No work. No murder cases."

"Precisely."

Feeling sassy, she gave him a smirk. "What about my penchant for finding dead bodies?"

"We're going to an island paradise. There won't be any dead bodies."

"Maui doesn't have murders?"

"Not any we'll be involved in. You won't be finding any dead bodies on our honeymoon. I promise."

Her lip curled. "Wanna make a bet?"

His brow rose. "A bet?"

"You know, where each person puts up a stake to lose?"

He gave her a wry look. "If you insist, very well."

She twisted around, eagerly taking his bait. "Okay, buster. What's the ante?"

He looked thoughtful for a moment. "Let's see. If I win, for two weeks…" He stroked his chin.

"Yeah?" A delicious shiver went up her spine. What kind of sexual contract was he dreaming up?

"You'll stop worrying about whether this marriage will work out or not."

She snorted her indignation. How in the world did he do that? She poked him in the ribs. "And if I win, you'll stop reading my mind for two weeks."

"Deal." He chuckled as he pressed his lips to hers, this time hard and strong.

They were almost on the floor when the pilot told them to sit up and buckle their seatbelts for landing.

CHAPTER THREE

A few minutes later, their plane touched down at Kahului Airport. They disembarked, Parker rented a shiny red BMW convertible, and they took off for the Honoapiilani Highway, heading for the west side of the island.

The sun was low in a wide, wispy sky as they rounded the twisty road, passing snatches of yellow and red and purple flowers and the deep, never-ending green of what Parker pointed out as banana trees, coffee trees, and coconut palms.

Her wild hair whipping around her face, Miranda squealed with delight as through gaps in the foliage, she caught glimpses of the bluest body of water she had ever seen. She'd traveled the US, but had never seen the ocean before. And she hadn't had a vacation since…she'd never had a vacation.

The luxury resort turned out to be one of the best on the island. No economy hotel for these newlyweds.

Parker drove to the entrance of a tall, sprawling white building and past a tropical palm-and-rock garden with a babbling brook. At a series of arched columns, he dropped off the car to a valet and led her inside a palatial lobby.

After the bellhop delivered their bags to their eighth-floor bridal suite, Parker swept her up in his strong arms and carried her across the threshold, making her break out in laughter.

"Did you forget you've already done this?" she snorted. He'd carried her over the threshold of the Parker mansion master bedroom every night since their wedding.

"Have I?" He grinned as if he didn't remember.

"It's fun, but isn't this overkill?" she giggled as he bounced her in his arms.

Parker scowled as if offended. "You can't do it too much. The ancient tradition is to keep the bride from being kidnapped, from tripping, from unwanted intrusion of bad spirits."

How did he know all that? Maybe from his first wife who'd been a college English professor. Parker had lost her to cancer over three years ago.

"I don't see how there could be any bad spirits in this paradise. But if there are, I'll just kick their asses."

He chuckled. "I'm sure you will." He spun her around and set her down in the middle of a large, well-lit living room.

Still laughing, she took in the space. Of course this wasn't a simple hotel room. It was a huge honeymoon suite, complete with artwork, glass coffee table and bamboo chairs and couches, all tastefully decorated in chocolates and tans and muted tangerines, all reflecting a subdued island motif. She glimpsed a marble kitchen counter near the back.

Despite the elegant island décor, she intended to make a beeline for the bedroom until the tiki-framed glass doors at the far end of the room caught her eye.

With another squeal, she skipped across the teal Berber carpet, flung open the doors, stepped onto the veranda and gasped at the breath-taking view of the ocean.

Parker came up behind her and laid his hands on her shoulders.

She leaned her head back against his strong chest and sighed. Below her palms trees swayed on a sandy beach that stretched out to white foam and endless turquoise waves. She sighed at the dazzling beauty of the place he'd chosen to delight her with, as tantalizing as the moves he chose to delight her with in the bedroom. "That's amazing."

"Isn't it?" He nuzzled her neck with his lips, and she started to shiver and close her eyes despite the incredible view.

"I guess you're right. I won't be finding any dead bodies in this paradise."

"No, you won't." His mouth moved to her clavicle.

Okay. She'd have to gawk at the view later. "So which way to the bedroom?" she murmured on another sigh.

"To the left. There's something for you on the bed."

"Oh, yeah?" Breaking free of his embrace, she hurried inside, through the door he'd indicated and switched on the light.

What did he have up his sleeve? she wondered. Parker could surprise her like no other man could. Not that any man had ever tried. Except maybe for the bloody lips Leon used to surprise her with.

The bedroom was done in clean tans and hushed greens, accented by mahogany. A huge bed dominated the room. On the tropical print comforter lay a large white box that looked suspiciously like it contained something to wear. Parker loved picking out her clothes.

She ran to the bedside. "What's this? A sexy negligee?"

"You'll see." Parker strolled through the door and leaned provocatively against the post to observe as she tore open the package.

She tossed the lid on the floor and rustled the paper as she reached inside. It was something colorful and—frilly. "Uh oh."

"Uh oh?" Parker echoed, concern in his voice.

She pulled out a long, bright red cotton dress dotted with Hawaiian flowers down the front and back. Layers of ruffles dominated the short sleeves.

She held it up to her and wrinkled her nose. "Are you sure this is for me? You know I don't exactly go for girly girl." All those ruffles on the sleeves would make her look like a Barbie Doll with wings.

He scowled. "That isn't what I ordered. I said sleeveless. Qianna got it wrong."

"Qianna?" She cocked her head. The dress looked handmade by an islander. "You know a seamstress here by first name?" She thought Parker had never been to Hawaii before. She was pretty sure he'd given her that impression.

He ignored her question. "I'm so sorry, Miranda. You don't have to wear it."

He looked so disappointed, she decided to drop the subject of the dressmaker. Turning to the mirror, she held it to her chin and had a look at herself. "I can still wear it to bed."

A slow, wicked grin spread over his handsome face as he moved behind her and stroked her bare arms. "I don't think you'll be needing anything to wear to bed. This is a dress. It was supposed to be for dinner tonight."

"Dinner?" she breathed, tingling sensations dancing over her skin at his touch. "Seems awfully casual for your taste in restaurants." She turned her head and nuzzled her cheek against his jaw. "Why don't we just call room service."

Parker nibbled her ear, pleased at the way she looked, even if the dress wasn't the one he'd chosen for her. She'd made herself strong, her body had always been trim and lean, but in his opinion, she'd lost too much weight since her latest ordeal. As much as he desired her, he was going to make sure she was well fed before the physical rigors he had planned for later on.

"Trust me," he told her softly. "I'll let you have the shower first, but you'll have to hurry."

"What?" Miranda turned around with a scowl. Her hungry husband wasn't in the mood? On the first day of their honeymoon?

Wait a minute. Now it clicked. Her mouth opened in a happy gasp. "Are we going to—?"

Reading her thoughts—again—his eyes sparkled with delight. "Yes. We're going to a luau."

"A luau? In Maui? Hot dog." She didn't know why that made her so happy, but just now it sounded like the coolest thing she'd ever done in her life. Holding the dress in both hands, she did a little dance, then raised on tiptoe to give Parker a kiss. "I'll wear this with bells on my toes."

"Hurry," he chuckled. "We don't want to be late."

"I will," she promised as she scampered into the bathroom.

It was better than an Elvis movie.

On a stretch of lava rock overlooking the ocean, Miranda and Parker were greeted by smiling, scantily clad natives who adorned them with colorful leis of fragrant blossoms. Miranda couldn't help casting a wary glance at the three

Polynesian beauties who swarmed around Parker, giving him more aloha-ness than the average customer.

She couldn't blame them. His well-formed body garbed in a blue-and-white island shirt and dark designer shorts, a demure outfit next to her fire engine red dress, Parker was the sexiest man she'd ever laid eyes on. Still, it gave her a thrill to watch his handsome face turn dark when the grinning, bare-chested young man in the orange-and-white hibiscus-print shorts ogled her in turn as he led them to their table under a row of mango trees.

As the smell of fresh flowers gave way to the delicious aroma of exotic foods and the flirtatious waiter plied them with Mai Tais, Miranda sat back with a smug grin and gazed out at the vast blue ocean and the mountains of the neighboring island beyond.

Absently, she picked up her lei and put it to her nose.

"I knew there was a way to bring out your feminine side," Parker murmured beside her, a smile in his voice.

Turning, she arched a brow. "Pretty expensive outing just for that."

Ignoring her reference to money, he fingered the petals around her neck. "Did you know a lei represents love? And that it's often given with a kiss?" His intense gaze made it sound exquisitely sensual.

"Good thing those greeters didn't try to kiss you. I'd have had to belt them."

Parker laughed and brushed his lips against her cheek. "Ever the dainty one."

Miranda opened her mouth to reply, but before she could, the waiter returned and began placing dishes before her on the white linen tablecloth. "Pohole ferns and heart of palm salad, mahi-mahi with mango sauce, and kalua pig."

Oh yeah? She eyed a small round dish containing something with a muddy, raspberry colored tinge. "What's that?"

"Ah, that is poi. A staple of the islands. Happy dining." And with that, he bowed and turned his attention to the next table.

Parker began heaping food onto a plate for her with tongs. "I thought you would enjoy the more intimate experience of table service over a buffet and this luau serves dishes from all over Polynesia."

She pointed at the plate of meat. "Is that the famous roasted-in-the-ground pig?"

"It is indeed."

She studied the side dish. "I don't know about that stuff."

"It's not a luau if there isn't poi. Try it." He picked up her fork, speared a bite of pig, dipped it in the sauce and held it up to her.

"Anything for love." She parted her lips and squeezed her eyes shut as he slid it in. "Oh my," she said with her mouth full when the exquisite flavor hit her tongue. Moist, smoky pork, melt-in-your-mouth tender. The poi was hardly there and seemed only to enhance the taste. She savored and swallowed. "That's delicious."

"I thought you'd like it, though it lacks the habaneros you prefer."

"For once, I don't miss them." And she dug in.

The mahi-mahi was delicate and tasted like it had just jumped out of the ocean. The mango sauce was delish. The salad had a juicy snap to it. And when they were finished, the waiter brought more. Sea bean duck, lomi-lomi salmon, mussels and scallops, chicken with taro leaf in coconut milk. It was the biggest feast she'd ever had, and she'd had some darn good meals since she'd met Parker.

When she thought she couldn't hold another bite, the waiter—whose ever-present grin was beginning to look a little sadistic about now—brought dessert.

Miranda rubbed her stomach and groaned. "I don't think so, Parker."

"You can't pass up this." He picked up something dark and gooey, held it up to her mouth.

"What is it?"

"Chocolate truffle."

"Oh, Lord." She scarfed it down with a moan of pleasure at the rich satiny taste.

Parker picked up a fork and scooped up a bit of fruit salad. "This is to cleanse the palate."

"My palate's been thoroughly scoured." But she let him shove it in and bit into an amazing coconut and mandarin orange concoction that came with the sweetest, freshest pineapple she had ever tasted.

She took the fork from him and finished it all. "Okay, that's it. I'm ready to fall into bed now." To prove the point, she sat back and closed her eyes.

"You can't sleep now. You'll miss the show."

Her brows shot up. "Show? As in hula dancers?"

His handsome gray eyes twinkled. "You'll see."

The sweet sound of singing and Hawaiian guitars gave her the answer as a row of barefoot, costumed dancers appeared on a stage that ran along the edge of the dining area and overlooked the ocean and sky. Nice backdrop.

"And now, ladies and gentlemen," a deep voice with a light Polynesian accent announced over the intercom, "for your viewing pleasure."

The five beautiful, longhaired women wearing colorful leis and wreaths on their heads and wrists, moved their hands and swayed their grass-skirted hips as they danced to the exotic song in the native tongue.

Miranda stole a glance at Parker and saw delight in his eyes. A streak of jealousy shot through her as she watched the dancers shimmy.

She leaned over and whispered. "You'd better not be thinking what I think you're thinking. Or else."

He raised a brow. "Or else what?"

"Or I'll have to teach you a lesson when we get back to the hotel."

He only grinned. "Looking forward to it."

The audience applauded and the dancers moved off the stage but were immediately replaced by a troupe of men in red-and-orange loincloths and green wreaths on their heads. Chanting, they twisted this way and that, wagging their thighs back and forth in time to a lively drumbeat.

Open-mouthed, Miranda stared.

Beside her, Parker cleared his throat. "Perhaps I'll be the one who'll have to give the lesson when we get back to the suite."

Soon the men were replaced by more women. These wore bold diamond-print outfits and slapped bamboo sticks in time to their song. Then came men and women in spiky headdresses, all in red and black, brandishing noisy gourd rattles. These dancers brought on more gyrating hips and rhythmic drumbeats.

Miranda let herself get caught up in the spell of it. She was as mesmerized as a little girl at the circus. She'd never seen a live show before, except for her singer friend, Coco. Or the time when she was fifteen and snuck out to a Pearl Jam concert—for which her fun-loving mother beat her and locked her in her room for two days.

"And now for all of you honeymooners with us tonight," said the voice over the intercom.

The music slowed to a lovely Hawaiian melody that sounded distinctly like a love song. Parker gave her hand a squeeze as a woman with yellow flowers in her gorgeous waist-length black hair danced and sang. As she sang her hair and body swayed, and the sunset behind her gently evolved into a magnificent swirl of purple and coral.

Miranda sighed with delight. It might have been the prettiest sight she'd ever seen.

The sun went down. Torches were lit and there were more songs and colorful costumes until suddenly the stage went dark and the audience fell silent.

"And now, ladies and gentlemen, the performance you've all been waiting for. The master of the fire dance…Keola Hakumele."

Miranda gripped Parker's hand in anticipation. The drums began to beat again. Louder. Louder. Louder.

Then they stopped and a lone figure leapt onto the stage, a blazing torch in his hand. The audience cheered.

A handsome Polynesian, he looked younger than the other performers, maybe early twenties. He took a long dramatic sweep of the crowd with his gaze, then the drums began to beat. Legs spread, he took a stance and began to move the flaming torch slowly across his body.

Behind his head, across his back, over his arms, between his legs. Then rising, he touched the blaze with one hand and set the other end of it on fire.

The audience applauded and Miranda joined in with enthusiasm.

Like the other dancers, he was barefoot and wore diamond-print shorts—with no dangling loincloth to catch fire—and a string of what might have been shark's teeth around his neck. Around his calves hung what looked like mini grass skirts. His hair was dark and long and as wiry as her own. As he knelt, tossed the torch in the air, caught it again, she worried that hair or the skirts would go up in flames.

The drums went into a frenzy and he began to spin the torch. One hand. Both hands. Over his head as he bent backwards, balancing himself with one hand on the floor of the stage. He touched the flame to his lips and fire shot into the air.

Hoots came from the crowd.

He danced over to the side of the stage and grabbed another baton, this one also with flames at both ends.

He bounded back across the floor, spinning both sticks furiously. The drums went into double time. At center stage, he turned and twisted and played with the torches. Under one leg. Under the other leg. Between his legs. Across his arms again.

He tossed both flaming batons into the air and caught them again.

The crowd was about to break into applause when the drums stopped.

The dancer held both torches above his head as a chorus of men appeared behind him in the shadows. Each of them held a flaming firebrand above his head. Their faces were painted in frightening designs. In unison they chanted a warrior chant of long ago armies.

He Inoa No Kahekili.

He Inoa No Kahekili.

The young dancer gazed out at the audience and spoke in an ominous tone.

"Listen to the story of *Huaka'i Po*. The Night Marchers. They are the ghosts of ancient warriors. They roam the islands. You can know them," he pointed to the flame above his head, "by their torches. They roam the islands, the ancient battlefields seeking, seeking, seeking." He moved across the stage and pointed at various members of the audience.

"If they look you in the eye, beware. You will disappear."

Just then, his eye caught Miranda's gaze.

Terrified and lost in wonder, Miranda gripped the seat of her chair as she stared back at the young man. And then the strangest thing happened.

He seemed suddenly familiar. As if she knew him, somehow. As if she had some kind of cosmic connection with him. His hair, his angular jaw line. She almost felt as if she were looking at her own reflection in the mirror.

Or her own soul.

And then he brushed back his hair and she saw it.

A round, dark spot on the side of his neck.

Cold chills skittered up the back of Miranda's neck. Her hands gripped the seat of her chair. She wanted to gasp, but couldn't utter a sound.

The drumbeat started again. It sped up. The chorus chanted. The young dancer spun his torches faster and faster. Until on a feverish crescendo, he tossed them both into the air at once—and they disappeared.

And the stage went black.

CHAPTER FOUR

Feeling a bit tipsy and still unnerved, Miranda made a show of waltzing into the bridal suite of the hotel. "What a night."

Behind her, Parker closed the door and regarded her with concern. "I don't think that story about the Night Watchers was supposed to be part of the show. It didn't frighten you, did it?"

With a loud scoff, she waved a hand at him. "Who me?"

"Ah. I didn't think so." She knew he knew she was fibbing.

She thought about the dancer and the way he'd stared at her. "He had..." She almost gestured at her neck. "Never mind."

Watching her, Parker frowned. He had seen it too. The dark mark on the young performer's neck. It could be coincidence, but he feared he knew what the mark might mean, though it didn't make sense. Even so, it was too soon for Miranda to deal with it. Her body needed healing. Her soul soothing. He would do all he could to protect her from further pain.

Pushing away the bad feelings, Miranda took off her lei and spun it on her wrist, doing a little dance. "I could do that fire number."

Parker's look of concern melted into a smile. "I believe you could."

She shimmied over to him, slipped the lei off his neck and twirled it around her other wrist. "So what other surprises do you have for me, Mr. Sneaky?"

"A number of things. Tomorrow morning we can eat breakfast, sip our coffee on the lanai, and watch the whales. We can go snorkeling. Or for a walk on the beach."

"We could do that now if we had flashlights. And maybe do something besides walk on the beach." She swayed her hips at him like one of those hula dancers and watched his handsome gray eyes flame hotter than the spinning torches in the show.

"Flashlights are provided by the hotel," he said with desire in his voice. "They're in the dresser in the bedroom."

She wondered again how he knew so much about this place. It was reasonable to check out amenities prior to a trip, but knowing there were flashlights? Well, Parker always knew a lot about everything. She let it go. She had other things to focus on just now.

"We could go out there. Warm sand beneath your skin, the rhythm of waves breaking against the shore." It made her mouth water. She stepped toward him, teasingly drew a lei over his shoulder. "And yet...as fun as that sounds, I don't think I can make it farther than the bedroom."

"Neither can I." In one swift move, he scooped her up in his strong arms and carried her into the next room, making her giggle.

"You walk pretty good for a drunken man," she laughed as he laid her on the tropical print bedspread and began devouring her neck.

"I believe you're the one in the inebriated state." He tugged at the neck of her dress, his hungry lips traveling lower and making desire flame inside her as hot as that dancer's torches.

"Oh, yeah?" She started to pull at the dress then remembered it didn't have a zipper. "How the heck did I get into this thing?"

Parker chuckled. "I'm sure I don't know. But we can both get you out of it."

"Wait a minute." She sat up, grabbed the hem of the garment, pulled it up and over her hips. With stubborn tugging and Parker's help, at last she got it over her head. She tossed it in the air and it landed somewhere on the floor. Her panties followed the dress. She hadn't worn a bra, so that was it.

Taking her in, Parker's gray eyes glistened with desire. "You are so beautiful, Miranda." He reached out to stroke her now naked body. "I do love you so."

And she loved him, too. Delicious sensation rippled through her, making her feel giddier than the Mai Tais. She caught his wrist. "No fair. You have to have a turn." She reached up to unbutton his semi-gaudy Hawaiian shirt.

"Hurry," he whispered, his voice raspy with need.

She undid the first button with careful precision. "You made me wait. Making sure I had a big meal and some drinks first."

His brow furrowed.

"See? I'm not as *inebriated* as you think." She finished the second button.

Parker's hands moved to the bottom of the shirt and he made quick work of opening it. "All the better for what I have in mind for you." He got to his feet, dropped the shirt over a chair and reached for his zipper.

Delicious thrills assaulted her heart as she watched him remove his shorts and the whole length of those gorgeous, strong thighs appeared before her. The sight of him made her mouth water. "Come here."

"I thought you'd never ask." He dove in beside her and his hands began working his wonderful magic on her breasts, her sides, her thighs, between her legs.

"You're driving me insane."

"Just as I intended."

"I want you inside me," she whispered.

"All in due time." He began working his way with his lips to the soft spot between her legs. When he reached it, he snatched a pillow from the head of the bed, shoved it under her hips and attacked her flesh with his tongue, taking his sweet time.

"Oh!" She shivered and groaned in sweet agony as he teased her into sensory overload. Fearing she could stand no more, she dug her fingers into his thick hair. "Hurry."

"Patience," he murmured between strokes.

"You're a cruel one."

"Aren't I, though?" He chuckled, but gave in to desire and sped his caresses.

The pressure between Miranda's legs began to rise and build. She couldn't hold back any longer. "I'm—I'm—"

And just as she thought she'd reached her peak, Parker rose and watched her.

"What are you doing?"

"Drinking you in with my eyes."

"I'm thirsty, too." She wrapped her legs around him and pulled him to her.

Now he was the one who couldn't hold back. He thrust himself into her with powerful, furious moves. She worked her hips against his in mindless passion, sensation heightening, her heart soaring with need and pleasure. Faster, faster, their bodies molded together like waves colliding. And then the spasms came.

"Oh, dear Lord!" she cried.

"Yes!" His chest glistened with sweat and his flesh throbbed inside her.

Her body convulsed with his in pure union, as ancient as the ocean. She cried out in sheer joy, closed her eyes, and sank into a sea of wedded bliss.

CHAPTER FIVE

What makes you think you deserve to be so happy?

Her stomach twisted painfully at the words. Behind her, she could hear waves crashing against the shore. There was chanting. And a drumbeat. An endless, relentless drumbeat.

Huaka'i Po. Watch out. If they see you, you'll die.

In the shadows a face appeared. It was distorted, etched with dark, eerie shapes. Mysterious symbols of voodoo or black magic, signifying…death.

A hand reached out for her.

Her mouth opened in a scream, but no sound came out. Or she couldn't hear it over the drumbeat.

Heart pounding, she pulled away from the clawing hand.

"Help me," a voice cried in the distance. A male voice. It was faint, but somehow she could hear it over the drums.

Don't answer. It's the Night Marchers. Don't go near them.

Where were they? It was pitch black. She didn't know where she was going. In the dark, she felt her way along a jagged, wall-like surface. It felt like rock. A mountain. A volcano. The chanting grew louder. The drumbeat faster.

And yet over the noise, she heard him again. "Help. He's killing me."

Huaka'i Po. She wanted to help, but the Night Marchers were coming for her. Were they after him, too? She moved along the rock, groping, trying to find him. "Who are you?"

"I'm drowning." The voice was weaker that time.

She must be going the wrong way. How could she get to him?

And then a thunderbolt flashed across the sky. She saw she was on a high ledge, climbing along the side of a mountain. She felt her way along the curving rocks and inched around a narrow corner. The lightning flashed again and she saw the tattooed face before her, barring her way.

Its mouth opened. Her heart pounded wildly. And then the face changed. She could see him now. Her breath caught. No. Please, God no.

Leon.

"What do you think you're doing here, you whore?"

"I wanted to see the ocean." She turned and tried to run. But the rocks on the ledge beneath her feet gave way. She tumbled off the precipice and went hurtling down, down. He had looked at her. She was going to die.

Instead she landed hard on a flat surface. Pain jolted through her body. Without getting up, she turned her head. Leon was right behind her.

Slowly, he pulled his belt out of his pants.

"No. Leave me alone."

She was in her old house, crawling across the floor of the living room, trying desperately to get away from him.

He looped the belt in his hand, raised his arm and brought it down hard. "See the ocean? I'll tell you what to want. I'll tell you what to think." His blows fell on her head, her back, her shoulders, her arms. Again and again. Stinging, breaking flesh, drawing blood like a whip.

"Stop it, Leon. Please." Her own begging was worse than the blows.

"Don't tell me what to do." He struck her again, this time against the side of her face. She felt her lip open, her own blood run down her chin. She had to get away before he killed her.

"Where are you going, Miranda? You can't escape me."

She could. She would. If she could just get to the stairs. She crawled and crawled. Finally her fingers touched the bottom step.

She started to heave herself up so she could run, but Leon's hands snatched at her ankles.

"Let go." She lost her balance and fell, smacking her chin on the stair.

In agonizing pain, she gritted her teeth and wrenched herself up again. She scrambled up the steps, her feet inches away from his groping hands.

"You can't get away from me. You'll never get away. It doesn't matter how far you go, Miranda. I'll always be with you."

She heard a baby cry. Amy.

"She's not yours, Miranda. You have no right to her."

"Yes, I do. She's mine. She's mine."

At last she stumbled up the last step. Leon closing in behind her, she broke free and ran to the nursery. She flung the door open and saw her daughter asleep in her crib.

Her face was so peaceful. And on the side of her little neck, that strange black mark. The baby opened her eyes and reached out to her with her little hands.

"Amy," she whispered. "Mama's here for you. Don't cry. I won't let them take you."

But even as she spoke, the chanting began again. And the drumbeat. She watched in horror as dark hands appeared out of nowhere. Horrid arms reached under the baby and lifted her up. Amy's face twisted into a tiny ball of terror and she began to cry. But her wails were drowned out by the chanting and the drumbeat.

Miranda raised her head and dared to look into that crazed, tattooed face. The Night Watchers. They were taking Amy.

"No. No. No. No."

With a jolt, Miranda shot up in bed. Her heart was pounding so hard it felt like a knife had been plunged through it. She sat there a minute, trying to catch her breath.

At last, she ran a hand over her face. "What—time is it?"

Parker turned over, reached for her. "Are you all right?"

She was surprised she hadn't cried out. If she had, he'd have his arms around her now. She longed for that, but he was tired from the long flight and too many Mai Tais. Besides, she didn't want him to question her.

"I'm fine. Go back to sleep." She pulled back the covers, got to her feet.

"Where are you going?" he murmured in a deep, sleepy voice.

"To the loo. Go back to sleep." She watched him a moment until he rolled over and his breathing became steady.

Turning, she trudged to the bathroom, slipping her cell phone off its place on the dresser as she went.

Still shivering, she sank down onto the edge of the tub and thought of Leon. How did that luau show get mixed up in her nightmare? It was ridiculous. She should be laughing. Instead she was shaken to her core.

She'd beaten Leon once, but he kept coming back in her dreams. Her subconscious, as Dr. Valerie Wingate, her shrink, would say. And when he did, she felt like he was right here in the room with her. Still trying to get at her. Still trying to beat her down.

She'd find out if he was still where he belonged. With shaky hands she lifted her cell phone and dialed the number she now knew by heart.

"Brandywine-Summit Hospital. Third floor. May I help you?"

"Uh, yes. I'm calling to check on a patient. I've called here before few times."

"Which patient?" the woman asked tersely. This was a different nurse. Miranda didn't recognize the voice.

"Leon Groth."

"And you are?"

"His sister." She barely winced at her old lie.

"One moment." She put her on hold and Miranda was treated to an eternity of elevator music while she sat taping her bare foot on the fancy tiled floor, hoping she'd get the answer she wanted.

After several long minutes, the voice came back on the line. "I'm sorry ma'am, there's no change in that patient's condition."

Good. "And the doctors don't think he'll wake up soon?"

"I don't believe they think he'll wake up at all." The nurse didn't sound like she was sorry about it, but then Miranda wasn't either.

"Thank you very much." She hung up and released a long, slow breath of relief.

He was still there. He was still in the coma she'd put him in after he'd tried to kill her, and she'd plunged a knife into his back and punctured a lung three months ago.

Thank God.

She sat there listening to the silence for a long moment until she realized she'd never get back to sleep. She stood and wiped her face with her hands, remembering Parker had said something about a walk on the beach.

Suddenly that sounded like a terrific idea.

She opened the door, stepped out of the bathroom and tiptoed to the rack where the valet had placed her luggage earlier. She opened a bag and found a pair of cuffed black jeans, an olive jersey knit T-shirt, cardigan and canvas tennis shoes. Quietly, she slipped them on, then opened the dresser drawer and rummaged around for one of those flashlights. When she found it, she closed the drawer and crept to the bedroom door.

There, she hesitated.

Maybe she should wake Parker up and ask him to go with her. No, she had to be alone right now. She'd send him a text and let him know where she was.

She crossed the suite's living room, opened the outside door and stepped into the dimly lit hallway. Reaching for her cell, she thumbed a quick message.

Went for a walk on the beach. Join me if you wake up.

Then she hustled down the hall and pushed the button for the elevator.

CHAPTER SIX

The air was cool and the stretch of beach along the resort was well-lit. She didn't really need the flashlight. Or her sweater. She took it off and tied it around her waist, dangling the light on her wrist by its strap.

The tide was high and the steady rhythm of the restless waves against the shore soothed her as she strolled along and breathed in the scent of exotic flowers and plants.

Everything was so fresh here. It was just the place to rejuvenate. That's why Parker had brought her here. Nothing but relaxing and fun in the sun.

Except for her dreams.

It must have been that fire dance at the luau that had brought on her nightmare. She recalled the hypnotizing look in the handsome young performer's eyes. The drumbeat, the chanting. All combined, it was pretty spooky.

Huaka'i Po. Night Marchers. What a crock. She wasn't superstitious. And she sure didn't believe in ghosts.

The only ghost she had to deal with was Leon. She rubbed her arms, shivering again at the memory of her dream. It wasn't just Leon. It was Amy. Her sweet little Amy. Leon had taken the baby from her when she was only three weeks old and given her up for adoption.

She hadn't dreamed about Amy in weeks. Tonight it was almost as if she could really see her again. Could actually reach out and touch her. She had smelled that newborn smell, felt the softness of her skin. But of course, that was all a figment of her own imagination.

It was never going to happen.

She kept moving, staring out at the dark, undulating ocean as her heart constricted with fresh pain.

She'd hunted for her daughter for thirteen years with no luck and even Parker, one of the top PIs in the country, couldn't find her. The only option was the courts, and that had turned out to be a disastrous, disappointing dead end.

It had been over a month ago that she and Parker had traveled to Chicago and petitioned the court to open Amy's adoption records. The judge said he couldn't do it without justification. He needed something like a hereditary health condition that the adoptee needed to know about, since it would be in her best interest.

Miranda still remembered Judge Rozeki's question. "Do you have any other close relative who might have a life-threatening, hereditary illness? Your father perhaps?"

She hadn't seen her father since she was five years old. The wonderful Edward Steele had left her and her mother and gone off to God knows where. She'd almost forgotten what he looked like until she'd found a picture of him in an attic in Chicago a month ago.

That photo had brought back a flood of unwanted memories.

Parker had wanted to try to find her father and see if he had a hereditary condition, but Miranda had told him very clearly, very firmly, no.

Not just no, but hell no. And a few other expletives to boot.

She couldn't do it. She couldn't face that man again. Not after all this time. Not after all that had happened to her. Besides, for all she knew, her father could be dead. And if he wasn't dead, he might be if she ever ran into him.

Just the idea of seeing her father again made her feel suddenly sick. Like she had a bad case of swine flu. A *Guinness Book of World Records* case.

Anger rushed inside her as she paced over the soft sand. She hated her father. Maybe even more than she hated Leon. If he hadn't abandoned her to be raised by a cold, cruel, emotionless mother, maybe she wouldn't have married the first guy that came along and gave her a chance to escape. Maybe her life would have turned out differently. Maybe she wouldn't have lost her daughter. Maybe she wouldn't be having nightmares.

But no, until the day she'd met Wade Parker, her life had been bleak and miserable and hopeless. And the resentment she carried for Edward Steele was as deep as the ocean she was strolling alongside. As powerful as the raging waves rolling toward her.

The tide was rising and the waves hitting the sand would have doused her if she hadn't skipped away. The sea was like a living creature, expanding as it ebbed and flowed. She sidled several feet out on the path and kept going, her pace picking up. With the wind in her hair, she broke into a run.

She could never face her father again. Not even if it meant finding Amy. Which it probably didn't. From what she remembered, her father was as healthy as a horse. Just like her mother.

Pain mounting inside her, she ran faster. She wished she could run so far she'd never feel this way again. She ran and ran. It must have been several miles.

The ground beneath her feet began to incline. The sand grew hard and rocky. After a while it was too uneven to run. Her chest heaving, she slowed down and took in the new surroundings. It was darker here, with only the moonlight and lights from scattered torches flickering on the cliffs above.

She came to a stop. A large, jagged structure loomed to one side. Lava, she assumed. Last week she'd read in a guidebook that the whole island chain was formed from volcanic activity under the sea.

Slowly she made her way toward the peak. The sea must be several yards below now, but the sound of water was loud here. Almost like thunder. And there was an odd moaning sound. Curious, she squinted into the darkness.

Suddenly there was a huge gush and a monstrous spray shot from the rocks and spewed into the air, maybe thirty feet high. With that strange moan, it subsided again. But after a minute or two, it shot up once more, this time with a wave from the ocean barreling up to join it.

Mist sprinkled her face and body.

Mesmerized, Miranda stood watching the geyser and the waves dance, as graceful as a herd of wild gazelles leaping into the air.

What was that? A blowhole? She'd read about those in the guidebook, too. It was gorgeous. Amazing. She couldn't wait to see what it looked like in the daylight.

But as she stood transfixed, a strange feeling came over her. A sensation of cold that had nothing to do with the temperature. Her skin prickled as icy fingers snaked up her spine.

Startled she sucked in air. She'd felt that weird sensation before. But how could this beautiful sight give her the heebie-jeebies?

She'd find out.

She crept closer, picked up the flashlight at her side, and shined it on the rocky, pumice-like ground so she wouldn't lose her footing. She came to a sign and held her light up to it.

Warning. Danger.

Better turn back, she thought. The sensation must have been left over from her dream. This place was gorgeous. She'd bring Parker here in the morning and show him what a cool site she'd discovered.

But as she turned to leave, another spray shot from the hole and that icy sensation gripped her again. Now the moan sounded human.

She spun around and peered at the blowhole, shined her flashlight toward the spewing water. It didn't do much good.

And then she saw it.

Her heart stood still. In the darkness an appendage bobbed up and down at the base of the waterspout. A human appendage. An arm.

It was an illusion. She had to be seeing things in the shadows.

But no, propelled by the force of the water there was an arm waving at the base of the hole. She was sure of it. Was somebody out there?

Forgetting about the warning sign, she started over the rocks toward the hole. Moving as fast as she could, she cursed the jagged, uneven ground. It slowed her down, impeding her steps, cutting into her thin-soled sneakers. The rocky passage began to slope downhill toward the sea, making it even harder to keep her balance. It was like traversing a rainy cobblestone street after an earthquake. She stepped in a puddle and her foot got soaked to the ankle, but she kept going.

After what seemed like a lifetime, she reached the blowhole.

Another spray shot up and came crashing down, drenching her and knocking her to her knees. The water was powerful. She grabbed onto one of the boulder-like rocks around the hole and her flesh scraped along the sharp lava. Her leg went into the water. It was all she could do to hold on as the force of the tide receded, dragging her down.

Somehow she managed to keep from being propelled with it and pulled her leg out again. As the water churned and bubbled in the hole preparing for the next gush, she crawled painfully toward the place where she'd thought she'd seen the arm, hoping she hadn't been hallucinating.

She put a hand down in the water and this time instead of rock, she felt something soft. Human.

Her flashlight was still on her wrist. Rising to her knees, she gripped it and shined it on whatever she was holding onto. The light fell on her fingers. There was brown-colored flesh beneath them. She moved the light and saw an elbow. An upper arm. A bare chest. A face matted with long dark hair. A youthful male face.

Oh, dear God. She'd been right. It was a body. A young man.

Without thinking, she tried to get her hands under his shoulders and discovered his shirt was tangled in the rocks. One sleeve on, one off. That must be what was keeping him from getting sucked completely under. But the swirling water was getting ready to gush again.

She had to get him out of here before they both were swept out to sea. "Hang on," she yelled to him. "I'll get you out."

Frantically her fingers found the place in the rock where the shirt was caught. She tugged and yanked, but the fabric wouldn't come loose. In desperation she bent down and tore the material with her teeth. The fabric began to rip. With both hands she tore it in two.

At last he was free.

Now she really had to move fast. She couldn't lift him. She was pretty strong, but she couldn't lift an adult male. She couldn't drag him over these rocks without slicing him to bits. She'd have to go piecemeal.

Summoning all her strength, she tucked her arms under his shoulders and carefully pulled his upper body up and away from the rocks and the sputtering hole. She moved at an angle and then set him down again. She went round to his feet and did the same thing. Back and forth she went, zigzagging, moving him bit by bit, until after what seemed like an hour, they were far enough away from the blowhole.

The water spewed up again and came down dosing her thoroughly.

Ignoring it, she knelt down, pressed her lips to his and breathed. She sat up and put her hands on his chest and pushed as hard as she could.

She breathed into his mouth again. "C'mon." She pushed at his chest. She stopped.

No response.

She put her fingers to his neck and felt. No pulse.

"C'mon," she shouted. He couldn't be—.

There was something wet on her hands. Wet and slimy and it wasn't just water. She groped around on the rocks for the flashlight. She found it, switched it on, shined it on his face. There was a cut down the front of it. She touched the back of his head. It felt like it had been ripped open. He was bleeding all over the rocks. She took off her sweater and wrapped it around his head, tears streaming down her face.

She'd recognized him.

It was the fire dancer from the performance. And when her light fell on his neck, she saw that dark spot she'd seen when he'd stared at her.

Sobbing, her fingers trembling like crazy, she groped in her pocket for her cell phone, pulled it out. She could barely dial, but she managed to press Parker's number.

He answered on the third ring and didn't sound a bit groggy. "Miranda, thank God. Where are you?

"Remember that bet we made on the plane?" she asked in a shaky voice. "I won."

CHAPTER SEVEN

It didn't take long for the police to arrive after she dialed 911. Parker arrived just a moment before the squad cars and the ambulance pulled up.

He stood rigid with a comforting arm around Miranda's shoulders as they watched the officers do their grim work while lights from the squad car beams and emergency vehicles played over the dark scene.

"This is Keola Hakumele, all right," said a tall, thin man with an African accent who was huddled over the body. "I recognize him."

"Everyone knows that face," agreed an officer who was examining the ground with a flashlight.

"He won the World Fireknife Championship in Oahu three years in a row."

A few feet away, another uniform was taking notes. "Works at the Luau Pilialoha. Most popular dancer in Maui." The officer sounded Polynesian.

A stocky, dark-skinned man who looked like the one in charge put his hands on his hips. "Popular with the young girls, Yamagata. My daughter especially."

A skinny woman in crisp blues with her dark blond hair pulled back in a ponytail made her way over the rocky hill that led to the highway beyond. "Found his truck parked alongside the road, Sergeant," she said to the stocky man with an accent that sounded Australian. "White Ford pickup. A little old, but it looks clean. No other vehicle in sight other than ours and the gentlemen's BMW over there." She nodded toward Parker. "Lots of tire tracks from tourists, though."

"Good work, Jones," said the man in charge. "We'll take the truck in and go over it. How are you coming, Dr. Okoro?"

Doctor. The African-sounding man must be the ME.

"Vic's got bruising on the left eye," said Okoro. "Laceration on the right cheek. Could be from the rocks. No defense wounds."

Jones strolled closer to the body. "He could have gotten that shiner earlier in a bar fight or some such." She peered at the face. "He was a looker, wasn't he? Cuts on the head. He may have fallen on these rocks."

"Time of death?" The man in charge wanted to know.

Okoro pulled back an eyelid on the body. "From the look of his eyes, he definitely expired in the water. Skin condition indicates he was in there no more than two hours."

The officer with the flashlight came to a stop. "There's a lot of blood right here."

"Let's give the boys in the lab something to do, Andrews," said the man in charge.

"Yes, sir." He slipped a camera off his shoulder and took a few shots of the spot. Then with a short grunt, he bent down. He had a bit of a paunch and seemed to have some years of experience on him. "Pretty fresh. I'll see if I can get a sample." Andrews sounded like he hailed from New York.

Brooklyn, Miranda decided, thinking of her buddy Joan Fanuzzi back home. The officer was several feet from the body. Had that blood come from the dancer's head when she'd pulled him away from the water? Or had something gone on before he ended up in the drink?

The sergeant scratched at the scrap of dark beard on his chin. "So he fell, got disoriented, stumbled into the blowhole."

And drowned? Didn't sound right.

He turned to Miranda. "Where exactly did you find the body, Ms—?"

"It's Mrs. Mrs. Parker." Miranda had decided to keep her last name for professional reasons, but at the moment the Parker moniker might give her more credibility. "And you are?"

"Sergeant Balondo."

He had a very slight Spanish accent. Filipino, maybe. And a squarish build that made the dark blue shirt of his uniform look like it was still on the hanger. His straight black hair glistened in the beam of the emergency vehicle lights, and the patch of black on his chin bobbed as he spoke. Miranda wondered at the breach of typical cop regulations.

"Can you point out where you found him?" he asked.

"In that blowhole." She gestured toward the spewing water that continued to gush, impervious to the death scene below it. "His shirt was caught on a rock. That must have been what kept him from getting sucked under with the current. I tore it loose and pulled him over here."

"By yourself?"

"I moved half of him at a time. Legs first, then the head, then the legs again."

"That took some effort."

"Yeah. I'm in pretty good shape and I guess I had a lot of adrenaline."

He nodded.

"I didn't notice the condition of his head until I tried to give him CPR and he didn't respond."

"You mean the cuts?"

"Yes."

He rubbed his chin. "Very brave of you." He studied her a moment. "Did you know the deceased?"

Miranda felt Parker tense at the implication, but both of them knew it was standard practice to suspect the person who called in a suspicious death first. "We went to the Luau Pilialoha tonight and I saw him at the show but never before."

The Sergeant's gaze went from her to Parker. "Honeymooners?"

Parker nodded. "We're vacationing here on our honeymoon, Sergeant."

The tall man who was the doctor rose and joined them. "My first guess is accident, sir. Though it's usually the tourists who fall into blowholes."

Sergeant Balondo nodded. "Well, he was a fire dancer. They aren't known for being overly cautious." He turned back to Miranda. "If you don't mind, I'd like you to come into the station tomorrow and give a formal statement, Mrs. Parker. It's just routine." He reached into his pocket and handed her a card.

Accident? That was a pretty quick conclusion. And one her gut told her was a mistake. "Sergeant Balondo, my husband here is Wade Parker. We're with the Parker Investigative Agency in Atlanta. We'd like to help."

"Your statement will do that."

"We'd like to do more. We'd like to help with the investigation." In case it wasn't an accident.

One corner of his mouth turned up. "That's generous of you," he said as if he didn't mean it. "But we can take care of our own investigations. We don't need help from *haoles*." He turned away and headed for the body.

Haoles? Did that mean what she thought it did?

"It means outsider," Parker whispered in her ear. "We should go, Miranda."

Go? She couldn't just drop it. Keola's eyes, the way he'd looked at her tonight during his last performance, still haunted her. She broke free of Parker's embrace and stepped over the rocks to the sergeant. "What if it wasn't an accident? What if it was murder? The Parker Agency has a solid reputation, a long track record for solving murders."

Balondo shook his head. "We don't have many murders on the islands."

She snorted. "You never watched *Hawaii Five-0*?"

"Good night, Mrs. Parker," he said, sneering the name.

Parker watched his wife chase after the sergeant with growing anxiety. If what he suspected were true, he couldn't let her get involved in this case. "Miranda," he said, trying to sound gentle.

She spun around and glared at him. "Are you going to let him get away with that?"

"It is our honeymoon."

Miranda felt as if he'd just slapped her out of a frenzy. She looked into Parker's face. It was weary and riddled with concern. Her heart melted.

"The police can handle it." His voice was a tender plea.

She wasn't sure about that, but she couldn't let this ruin the time he had planned for them here. Though it certainly would put a damper on it. As terrible, as tragic as Keola's death was, she'd have to let it go. The investigation of it, at least.

"Okay," she sighed and turned back to the sergeant. "I'll come in to the station tomorrow."

CHAPTER EIGHT

Miranda sank into the rattan chair in the corner of the hotel bedroom and stared blankly at the rumpled bed.

"You should get cleaned up and try to go back to sleep." Parker took his cell phone out of his pocket and plugged it into the charger on the dresser.

In a daze, Miranda looked down at herself. Her new jeans were torn and bloody. There was a rip in her shoe. She didn't move.

"Are you cut? There's a first aid kit in the bathroom."

"I'm okay." She didn't care if she was cut.

"Do you want a drink?"

She shook her head. "Those Mai Tais gave me bad dreams."

"You had a nightmare?"

She gave a short nod, still staring into space.

He crossed to her and reached for her hands.

She held them up to stop him.

"You are cut," he said, concern in his weary gray eyes. "I'll get the ointment."

She waved him off. "I'll get it in a little bit." She wasn't bleeding any more. Just a little sore.

"Was it Leon?" he asked quietly. He meant her dream.

She gave another nod. "He was coming after me with his belt. He drew blood."

"Good God." He knelt to hold her.

"I couldn't fight him off. And I saw Amy. She was reaching out to me. It was as if…she was begging me to rescue her."

He stroked her hair with a gentle caress. "I'm so sorry. Is that why you went out alone?"

She nodded again and they both fell silent.

After a long moment, Parker murmured so softly, she almost missed it. "Would you like to resume the search for her?"

She snapped out of her daze and stared at him. "For Amy?"

"Yes."

She knew what he meant. Look for her father. "I can't do that, Parker."

There was an odd look in his eye and she wondered if he was conjuring up some overpowering argument to change her mind.

"There was something else," she said before he could voice it. "In my dream."

"Tell me."

"Drumbeats. Chanting. Like in that show tonight. The Night Marchers. They took Amy away so I couldn't get to her."

"I wish I'd never taken you to that luau." He disappeared into the bathroom and came out a moment later with the first aid kit. He opened it and began applying salve on her hands, ignoring that she'd said she'd take care of it.

It felt good, but as he rubbed and put a few bandages on her, her mind went back to her dream.

It had been Leon who had taken Amy away. Not the Night Marchers. The luau didn't change reality.

Her head began to clear and she remembered it all. "I was lost on a mountain somewhere. It was dark. I couldn't see anything. As I groped along, feeling my way, I heard someone calling out to me. 'Help me,' he said. 'He's killing me.' 'I'm drowning.'" She sat straight up and glared at him. "It was him, Parker. The fire dancer. He was sending me a message. He *was* murdered."

Parker stiffened. "You're concluding that from a dream?"

"Not just a dream. An impression. A darn strong one."

He studied her a moment, then gave his head a quick shake. "As good as your instincts have proven to be, we have to let the police handle this case. If it is murder, they'll figure it out and find the killer."

"I'm not so sure."

"They're laid back here, but they're competent."

Her eyes narrowed. "How do you know that?"

Ignoring the question, he rose, returned the first aid kit to the bathroom and began to unbutton the navy tailored shirt he must have thrown on when she called. "I understand you were upset, but the next time you go out on your own in the middle of the night, I'd appreciate it if you let me know." His tone held just a touch of a gentle chiding.

She scowled. "You were asleep."

He moved to the closet. "I woke up a few minutes before you called. I couldn't find you anywhere."

Guilt flooded her. He must have been worried. Crap. She was trying to be a decent wife to him, even with all her baggage. "Wait a minute. I did let you know. I sent you a text."

"I didn't get it."

"I sent it." She distinctly remembered pushing the button. Had she sent it to someone else by mistake? Maybe the servers were slow here. Maybe he just didn't notice it. Not like him, but he was worried and it was the middle of the night.

Frustrated, she got up, crossed to the dresser and picked up Parker's cell. She'd prove it to him. She brought up his messages and began scrolling through them. Her message was there. He just hadn't seen it.

She opened her mouth to tell him when a text from someone named Detective Nakamura caught her eye. That sounded like an island name. Why would Parker be in contact with another detective here? Curiosity—and apprehension—getting the better of her, she opened it.

I will do my best to locate your target.

Target? What was that about? Next text.

Good news. Your target is here on the island.

Her heart began to pound and her throat went dry. She scrolled to the last text before hers. It had come in just before they left for the luau. Parker must have gotten it while she was getting dressed.

Confirmed. Edward Steele currently resides in Lahaina. That was a nearby town.

Edward Steele?

All at once, her whole world tilted off its axis. Her stomach lurched so hard, she thought she'd barf. Her knees buckled and she reached out for the dresser to steady herself, ignoring the sting it sent through her palm.

"What the hell is this, Parker?" Her voice was a low rumble in her chest she didn't even recognize.

Parker came out of the closet in his stone washed jeans and bare, muscled chest, a sight that normally would have made her knees weak for a different reason. Just now, she was too angry for that.

He saw the phone in her hand and his face went white. "Did you find the text you sent?"

"Yeah. And this one, too." She raised the phone and read, her voice trembling as much as her hand. "*Confirmed. Edward Steele currently resides in Lahaina.*" She glared at him in disbelief. "You've been looking for my father? After I told you not to?"

His mouth hardened. "You did not tell me not to look for your father."

"Yes, hell I did."

"No, Miranda. You didn't."

"Of course, I did. I told you in no uncertain terms that I can't face him. That I don't want to face him."

"That's why I'm handling it."

"What?" He was twisting her words to suit his own purposes. "I don't want you to handle it."

He let out a slow, frustrated breath. "Sometimes, Miranda, you don't know what's good for you."

"What?" she gasped again. That sounded like something Leon used to say to her. Suddenly all her fears and doubts and apprehensions about this marriage exploded and came rushing back to her with the force of the blowhole she'd seen tonight.

She turned to glare at the bed. She couldn't sleep here. She couldn't stay in this room. She couldn't breathe.

She laid Parker's phone back on the dresser and somehow her fingers found the car keys. Her mind reeling, she grasped them, spun on her heel and headed for the living room.

Parker followed her. "Where are you going?"

"Out of here."

"Tell me where," he demanded.

"I've got an investigation," she sneered.

He stepped in front of her, blocking her way. "Miranda, be reasonable."

She pulled her messy hair out of her eyes and bared her teeth at him. "Oh no, I can't be reasonable. I'm just a female, remember?"

His face turned to stone. "I didn't say that."

"You implied it."

"I did not."

"I haven't got time to argue about it." She stepped past him.

"Don't go out there." He reached for her arm, a little too brusquely.

Was he going to hit her? Reflexes kicking in, she spun and jabbed at his biceps with her fist.

His reflexes were faster. Always were. He blocked the jab and threw her off balance. She stumbled a bit and he reached for her arm to keep her from falling over.

She wrenched out of his grip. "Leave me alone, dammit."

"Don't go," he repeated, anger flashing on his face.

"Don't tell me what to do."

Fury tightened his jaw, made his eyes almost black. She'd never seen him so mad. "I thought our marriage would end this reoccurring pattern."

How dare he? "Must be in my genes," she snarled.

He reached for her again. "When are you going to stop running away and face your problems, Miranda?"

That was a good one. She pulled out of his grasp again, turned and glared at him. "I'm facing this one. I never thought this marriage would work out and it looks like I was right."

And with that she spun, yanked the front door open and left, slamming it behind her.

Parker stood staring at the door, its slam ringing in his ears.

Stubborn, impetuous, irascible woman.

How could she be so talented and still so blind at times? He ran his hands through his hair and sank down onto the couch. It was no good going after her. Not now. That would only prolong the fight. He'd have to give her time to calm down. To think reasonably.

He stared out through the glass doors at the star-filled sky, the inky, undulating ocean beneath it.

She'd said he could read her mind. Usually he could see through her, but he hadn't this time. He should have realized how strongly she would feel about his attempt to contact her father. But, dammit, she wasn't supposed to know about it.

He rose, moved to the wet bar and made himself a Bacardi on the rocks.

Then he plodded back into the bedroom and picked up his cell phone. He thumbed to her message and winced. He should have believed her when she said she'd texted him. Then this argument wouldn't have happened. He scrolled to Ryo Nakamura's message and smiled despite the pain in his heart.

His former student had done well with the assignment he'd given him. He should. After serving in the Navy, he'd become one of the best trainees the Agency had produced. Parker was sorry when after two years of service with him, Ryo decided to return to his homeland. But he was proud his trainee had become the lead detective with the Lahaina police.

That would make him Balondo's boss.

He set down the phone, finished his drink, made his way to the bed and sank down into it. He'd have to try to get a few hours' sleep and then get to the station when it opened in the morning. He turned off the light, lay down and forced his eyes to shut.

If Miranda was determined to investigate Keola Hakumele's death, and he was sure she was, he'd better pay a visit to Nakamura as soon as possible. She was also one of the best trainees he'd ever had and he couldn't risk her finding out any more.

CHAPTER NINE

Telling herself the sting in her eyes was from the wind, Miranda pulled her hair away from her face as she sped down the empty Honoapiilani Highway in Parker's rented BMW on her way to Lahaina.

She glanced at the GPS, into which she had programmed the police department address on the card Sergeant Balondo had given her. She'd be there any minute now.

She'd had a computer, but she'd never used fancy things like cell phones and GPS's before she met Parker. The stray thought made her grunt.

Who cared how or when she'd learned to use a bunch of gadgets? Wiping something away on her cheek that must have been condensation from the moist air, she turned down the street indicated on the small screen.

She found the Lahaina police department across from the ocean—of course—just off Kaaahi Street. It was a snug one-story building with a plain tile roof and a whitewashed façade that had the look of a strip mall. Except for the emergency trucks and the boat parked in the open docks in the back. She guessed police and rescue here would need a boat.

She got out of the BMW, crossed the lawn under the shadows of decorative palm trees and strolled through the glass doors.

The reception area had that utilitarian look that all police stations shared. The floor was plain off-white tile that looked like it had been laid in the early seventies.

Against the back wall was a row of those hard cafeteria chairs with metal legs and a small, unadorned coffee table with magazines scattered over it. The walls were standard eggshell and looked like they could use a paint job.

A small alcove led to a door where, no doubt, the offices were. In opposite corners sat a couple of potted palms, which Miranda thought was overkill with all the foliage outside.

Through the rectangular hole that made up the front counter she could see the top of an officer's head behind a magazine. She made her way there and found a large man behind a laminated desk.

She cleared her throat and the officer raised his gaze from his reading material. Its cover sported a surfboard and a well-endowed blonde in a bikini.

"May I help you?" he asked in a low, steel wool voice.

"Sergeant Balondo asked me to come by and give a statement."

"I don't believe the sergeant's here right now."

She might have known he'd gone home already. She tried to smile. "Can you check?"

The officer exhaled, as if annoyed she'd interrupted his busy schedule. "Name?"

"Parker. Mrs. Parker." She wished she'd used her real name.

He picked up the phone and pressed a number. "There's a Mrs. Parker here to see you, sir."

"Will do." He set down the phone. "The sergeant will be with you in a moment, ma'am."

"Thanks." She was in luck. He was still here.

"You can have a seat over there." He nodded toward the chairs and picked up his magazine.

In the plush accommodations? But no sooner had she set her butt on the hard plastic than a side door opened, and Balondo appeared, a notebook under his arm. Under the neon lights with his straight hair a tad mussed and dark circles under his dark eyes, he looked even grumpier and more suspicious. "I thought you said tomorrow, Mrs. Parker."

And I'm happy to see you, too. Miranda got to her feet and shrugged. "I couldn't sleep."

Balondo's squareish chest expanded a slow, weary sigh. "Come on back."

He led her down a narrow hall, past a stingy cube bank to a small room. Inside he offered her a seat in another one of those ultra-comfy chairs, sank down across from her and took a pen out of his notepad.

Miranda rubbed her arms. She hadn't been in an interrogation room since she'd first gotten to Atlanta.

"Cold, Mrs. Parker?"

"I'm fine. Go ahead."

He began in a routine, sing-song tone. "You found the deceased at approximately 1:25 this morning, correct?"

"Yeah, I guess." She hadn't looked at the clock.

"May I ask what you were doing on the beach at that hour?"

"I was restless and needed a walk."

He narrowed an eye at her. "Do you often get restless and go out in the wee hours of the morning?" Miranda couldn't tell if that suspicious air was real or just habit.

She forced herself not to smirk. "Only when I've had too many Mai Tais."

That earned her a dark scowl. "Where are you staying?"

"The Ashford-Grand."

He nodded and made a note. "You ended up pretty far from the hotel."

"Actually I ran part of the way."

"So you're a runner?" Now the suspicion in his tone seemed genuine.

"I keep in shape." She blew out a breath. She was getting tired of this routine. She knew Balondo didn't think she was a suspect. He'd just wanted to harass her for coming here at this hour. "I stopped when I saw the blowhole."

"And?"

"I stood there watching it. It was, you know, majestic. Beautiful. One of the reasons why people come to West Maui, right?"

"I suppose so."

"I stood there watching the water spew into the air for a while. That was when I saw the arm."

Balondo's face went somber. "Arm?"

"Bobbing around at the base of the blowhole. Like this." She raised her arm above her head and tried to imitate what she'd seen. The action made her a little sick. "It was hard to make out in the dim light, but I thought it was human. I thought someone needed help. So I went to see."

She went through the details again. She found the body in the water. The blowhole was about to suck both of them under. She spotted the tail of the dancer's shirt caught on the rock. She ripped it off. She dragged him in halves away from the danger. She attempted CPR.

When she finished, the sergeant sat back with a grim look that didn't tell her anything. He laid his pencil down. "That's very thorough. Thank you for your time, Mrs. Parker." He started to get up.

"That's it?"

"Have you told me everything?"

"No, I haven't. I've haven't told you my impressions. I don't think it was an accident."

He sat back down and almost groaned with unconcealed impatience. "Mrs. Parker. Apparently you're unaware that tourists fall into blowholes all the time. Just two weeks ago we had to airlift a woman out of that place."

"But Keola wasn't a tourist."

"No, he was a temperamental artist. So you're right. It might not have been an accident. It could've been suicide."

"His head was ripped open." She still had his blood on her hands, her clothes.

"People slip and fall on those lava rocks. He could have hit it on the jagged edge of the hole. He could have jumped from the cliff overhead."

Rubbing her arms, she recalled the towering crags around the blowhole that she'd noticed when the emergency vehicles flashed their lights. Would be pretty hard to jump off and hit the blowhole in the dark. Okay there was no real evidence that pointed conclusively to murder, but that didn't mean there wasn't one.

"I still think that young man was murdered, Sergeant. And I want to help find his killer."

"You can help by staying out of our way."

She ignored the jab. "Have you found anyone with a motive to kill him?"

"Goodnight, Mrs. Parker." He rose from his chair.

She should've known better. It took time to build a relationship with the police. She found herself wishing for Officer Chambers, her buddy on the Atlanta force. She sat back and cleared her throat. "I don't mean to pry, Sergeant. I just want to make my services available to you."

Giving her a patronizing smile, he opened the door of the interrogation room. "I'll let you know if we need them, Mrs. Parker. I'll see you out now."

Swallowing a curse, she got up and followed him.

"Through that door." He gestured to the sign marked *Exit* when they were halfway down the passage. "Thank you again." Then he turned and disappeared down a side hall.

Miranda didn't head for the exit. Instead she stood eyeing the path the sergeant had taken. Maybe she'd pacify her frustration with a little snooping. If Balondo caught her, she could always claim she was bad at directions.

She listened a minute, trying to detect a door closing. Hopefully to his office.

The whole station was as quiet as a morgue. Well, she guessed they did have a morgue back there. But the office area seemed empty. Maybe everyone had gone home. Maybe Balondo had snuck out the back. Wouldn't hurt to check it out, right?

Steadying her nerves, she took a deep breath and dared to step into the passage the sergeant had used.

A row of closed doors stood on one side, an open area on the other. No sign of Balondo. She peered around the corner.

Cube bank.

Tangerine colored dividers sectioned off several small spaces, each cubbyhole complete with metal desk, filing cabinet, computer.

Hmm. Might be worth it to sneak a peek at one of those systems. Before she could decide, a noise came from the back. Startled, she glanced up just in time to see a shadow flit across the tiled ceiling as a door scraped open. Footsteps. Voices.

Heart pounding, she ducked back into the main hallway and plastered herself against the wall.

"Well, that was fun," groaned a man with a Brooklyn accent. Sounded like Officer Andrews from the crime scene tonight.

"And pointless." That was Officer Jones' Aussie accent.

More footsteps. They were coming this way. Miranda held her breath and hoped the officers were heading for their desks and not for this hallway.

"I hate when they pull that pidgin Creole crap," Andrews said. "'Ho, brah. Da same like I just say. I don't know nuteen.'"

"She was playing dumb for us cops," Jones smirked.

"I ought to be used to it after ten years on the job, but it still gets on my nerves." Something squeaked and Miranda let out a breath as she imagined heavyset Andrews easing himself into his desk chair.

"I've been on the job two years and I know I'll never get used to it."

A drawer opened.

"Hey, who took my Spam and pineapple sandwich?"

"You already ate it."

"Did not."

"Did too. You wolfed it down before Balondo sent us to that luau owner."

Luau owner? They'd gone to see the luau owner? Miranda listened harder.

All she heard was something that sounded like the moan of a wounded bulldog.

Jones gave a defeated snort. "What a whiner you are, Andrews. Okay, you can have some of my Onion Crunchers."

"I prefer Barbeque Rings." Despite the complaint, a bag rustled and was followed by copious munching noises and the sound of keyboards clicking.

Miranda wondered if chip crumbs were getting lodged between the keys. That always happened to her.

The keys stopped. "Okoro's already made a report." Andrews said. "Tox is clean. Preliminary COD drowning."

"Doesn't say accidental."

"Nope. Maybe tonight wasn't so pointless, after all. Minoaka did give us a motive."

"Sure did," Jones agreed. "She fired the fire dancer."

Keola had been fired tonight? Why? He was terrific.

"And he took it really hard."

"He was devastated. Enough to kill himself, you think?"

Andrews sighed. "It's looking like it." He uttered a sad chuckle. "If I had to work for Mary Minoaka, I'd want to kill myself, too. What a bitch."

"That's why her name is Minoaka—smile."

Despite the grim topic, Miranda had to smile, too. Both at the cop cynicism and the tidbits she was picking up. This Mary Minoaka had to be the person in charge of the show at the Luau Pilialoha.

"You know what the headwaiter called her?"

"What?"

"Bloody Mary."

Jones cackled. "Good one." There was a pause. "Well, I'm finished with my report. Should we wait to concur with Yamagata?"

"No, he's going home after he's done with his assignment."

"He sure drew the short straw tonight. Having to tell Keloa's family."

Miranda's throat tightened. The family. Of course, the dancer had family. What they must be going through right now.

"Yeah, we definitely got the better of the deal. Let's call it a night and start up again tomorrow." The chair creaked again and Miranda sucked in her breath.

"I'm with you, Andrews."

There was packing-up and shutting down noises and then more footsteps as Jones and Andrews began to move. But their voices faded. They were going out the back.

"Have a good night."

"You, too."

The back door closed. Miranda blew out a breath. The coast was clear, but she didn't need the computers now.

Straightening her clothes, she headed for the *Exit* sign, slipped out the door and past the clerk at the desk, who seemed to be nodding off.

When at last she was in the parking lot, she let herself breathe again. Hot damn. A lead already. If she were lucky, the office for the Pilialoha Luau would be near the place where she'd had dinner. And Bloody Mary would be working late.

She hopped into the BMW, revved her up and steered the car toward town.

Ten minutes later, she sat staring up at a darkened building on Front Street. This was the place all right, but everyone had gone home.

Crap. She'd have to come back in the morning.

So now what?

She couldn't go back to the hotel. Her mind started to reel again as the things Parker had said came back to her.

Sometimes you don't know what's good for you.... I thought our marriage would end this reoccurring pattern.... When are you going to stop running away and face your problems?

Renewed fury pounded in her temples. She couldn't believe it. Yes, she could. He'd always had a domineering streak. She'd always let it pass before.

How could he look for her father behind her back? How dare he? Fresh anger washing over her, she scanned the street for a cheap place to stay and realized she'd been so mad, she'd left the hotel without her wallet or even a change of clothes. Crap.

Well, good thing the weather was nice here.

She pulled out onto the road and drove around for awhile. Finally she found a beach park and turned into the lot.

She picked out a cozy spot near some picnic tables overlooking the ocean, pulled the car into the space and turned off the engine.

This was nice. This was just perfect. Gorgeous view. Gorgeous night. She'd get some sleep and figure out her next step in the morning.

She adjusted the seat back a bit and watched the waves rolling in.

Maui was a beautiful place. Maybe she'd open up shop right here. She wondered what the license requirements for private investigators were. No, her father was in this town. She could go to one of the other islands. Or maybe New Zealand.

She rubbed her neck. If only she had a pillow. She'd even left the hotel without her sweater. With a groan, she shuffled this way and that, trying to get comfortable. While the leather bucket seats were cool for sitting, as a bed they left something to be desired. She tried the glove compartment for a towel to roll up. Nada.

Just as she was considering ramming the car into a mango tree to defuse the air bag for a mattress, her cell buzzed. She yanked it out of her pocket. Parker calling to apologize?

No. Another text from Wendy. She glanced at the dash. Three in the morning. It was nine in Atlanta. The kid must be on her way to a class.

How's ur honeymoon? I'm headed for Algebra. Yucko. Mackenzie was so cool last night. Her pirouette is incredible and her Biellmann spin takes your breath away. She's going to win the Regional, I know it. Even Jordan thinks so and she's always hard to convince.

Miranda stared down at the screen. It was risky if Wendy's mother was checking her phone, but she decided to take a chance. She thumbed a message back. "Who's Jordan?"

Jordan McFee. She's in my class. She's kind of a nerd, but she's nice.

McFee. As in Chatham, Grayson and McFee? Mackenzie's father's law firm? Probably.

Kaylee swears Mackenzie will win, too. She'll believe anything, but this time, I think she's right.

Once more. "Who's Kaylee?"

Kaylee Hayden. She's in my class, too. She's best friends with Jordan.

Miranda thought back. Edward Hayden was an investment banker at CK&G. Wendy's father was one of his clients. All in the well-to-do family. At least these girls sounded nice and Wendy was making friends. That was good. Very good.

If Mackenzie does win, she'll go to the Junior Interstate. I hope my mother will let me go. Oh, Mackenzie even let me shine her blades yesterday. Way cool, huh? Gotta run.

Shine her blades? Please. Miranda wanted to tell Wendy not to let that girl push her around, but she didn't have the right. And she knew the kid wouldn't listen to any unsolicited advice from an adult. Instead she thumbed, "Yeah. Way cool. Have fun."

No response. Wendy was gone.

That familiar sense of loss came over her as she stared out at the ocean. The crashing waves echoed the waves of pain washing over her heart. Wendy would never be hers. And now she had lost Parker as well. Such was life. Her life, anyway.

She stared at the moonbeams playing on the ocean. She thought Parker had chosen this place for her—for them. Instead, it was all for his ulterior motives. How could he hunt down her father without letting her know?

She closed her eyes, trying to will away the hurt.

Instead, a memory stole over her heart from somewhere deep within her subconscious. She saw herself as a little girl in a pretty dress, dancing with her father in the living room of their home in the Chicago suburbs. A song from some old musical played on the phonograph. Something about trying to find an island that was calling you. *Bali Ha'i.* She started to hum it, then stopped herself.

Oh, for heaven's sake. She couldn't deal with any of this now. She was too exhausted. With a grunt, she opened the door of the BMW, climbed into the backseat, curled up in a ball.

And with the sound of the relentless waves in her ears, at last she fell asleep.

CHAPTER TEN

Parker stirred and reached across the mattress for his wife.
Gone.
He opened an eye and scowled at her spot on the bed. Empty. On an irritated growl, he rose and made his way into the living room. He stared at the couch.

Also empty.

He'd half-expected her to sneak back into the suite and curl up here. The rational part of his brain knew her better. Investigate a murder. How far did she think she could get in the middle of the night?

He turned and plodded into the bathroom for a shower. She might be in the lobby or in one of the restaurants. If she wasn't, he'd rent another car and track her down. It wouldn't take him long to find her. As soon as he assured himself she was safe, he'd take care of his business and then fetch her. He'd do whatever was necessary to soothe her ruffled feathers.

He had no intention of leaving her on her own here for long. Or of spending his honeymoon alone.

Forty minutes later, Parker was rapping his knuckles against the office door of Detective Ryo Nakamura.

"Enter."

He couldn't help grinning at the look of shock that greeted him as he stepped inside.

"Parker! I didn't expect a visit from my old mentor so soon." The tall man in his mid-thirties rose and came around the desk.

Parker's heart warmed at the familiar sight of the neatly trimmed, jet-black hair, the high-set cheekbones and straight jaw that gave his former student a threatening appearance that could make the most hardened street thug shiver in his metallic Adidas. Ryo wore a white, button-down dress shirt, silk tie, and coordinating slacks. Parker was pleased his own clothing habits had rubbed off on Ryo.

"I didn't realize you were in town."

"Just got in yesterday. It's good to see you, again, Ryo." He took the detective's hand in his, relishing the warm handshake.

"Have a seat. Coffee?"

"No, thanks." Parker settled into the plain chair before the equally plain desk.

"How about some of my oolong tea?" Ryo strolled over to a small table in the corner and poured amber liquid from a colorful pot into a ceramic cup.

"I'd forgotten your preference for tea." Two things his former student had been almost fanatical about. His tea and his martial arts moves. "But no, thank you. I'll be having something later."

Ryo blew on the hot liquid in the cup and eyed Parker quizzically. "I didn't realize you were coming to Maui personally."

"I apologize for not mentioning it." Ryo had already provided the information he needed. Parker hadn't intended to visit his former student, at least not in an official capacity, until last night.

To divert the subject, Parker gazed at the photos and commendations lining the inexpensively paneled walls. "Five years out of the Parker Agency and you're already Assistant Chief in the Investigative Services Department here? I didn't think you'd end up in a desk job."

Ryo set his cup down on the desk and took a seat behind it. "I do miss the field, but sometimes you have to make sacrifices to make sure things are done right." The detective leaned back with an authoritative air that suited him well. Parker had to smile at the insignia on the cup of the Maui Police Department. Ryo was all cop.

"I know what you mean." Parker could relate to that. Of course owning his own company, he could have the best of both worlds. One of the many reasons police work had never suited him.

Ryo grinned a shy, almost boyish grin. "I'm hoping to be appointed Deputy Chief next year."

"Excellent. I'm proud of you."

Ryo's eyes sparkled. "So is Elise."

"Elise?"

"My wife."

"You're married?"

"Three years now. No kids yet."

"Congratulations."

Ryo gestured to the certificates on the wall. "I owe a lot of those to you. And not just for my training at the Agency."

Parker rubbed his chin and thought back. "Four years ago now, wasn't it?"

"My first assignment. I still can't thank you enough for your help. I couldn't let pride keep me from asking for help from you. I had to make sure that one didn't get away. I couldn't take any chances."

"Yes, it was a wise decision," Parker agreed. But Ryo had never been prideful. When his team had to go after a notorious drug dealer and gunrunner and he found himself short of manpower, he didn't hesitate to call on Parker. His old boss had been only too glad to make the trip and to help bring down a dangerous career criminal with contacts to gangs in Oahu.

The suspect had been hell-bent on bringing as much corruption to West Maui as he could—and profiting nicely from it.

Ryo and Parker had been hell-bent, too—on bringing the man in. But it didn't go smoothly. There was an altercation. Shots were exchanged. Parker was nearly hit, but he managed to return fire first. And had ended a life.

Not something he was proud of. Especially when he learned the suspect had a son. But the man had chosen his own path. And now the island was free of that plague.

"Well, that was some time ago." Now it was Ryo's turn to change the subject. "What brings you to the station so early? I just got in myself." It was just past six.

"Still an early riser who likes to get to the office before it opens, I see."

"Old habits die hard. Did you get my text last night?"

"I did."

"Since you're here in person, that target you're looking for must be important, but he didn't have a rap sheet. What is he? A deadbeat dad?"

Parker sat back and steepled his hands. "In...a manner of speaking."

"I haven't had time to dig up any more on him. Except that he goes by the name Pumehana. He owns a tiki bar on Front Street."

"Pumehana. Tiki bar," Parker repeated, filing those details away. "The confirmation you sent is sufficient. I have the home address. Actually, I'm here to discuss another matter."

"Oh?" Ryo sat back, his bright, dark eyes expectant.

Parker studied Ryo's desk. Embossed cup of oolong tea, phone, printer, papers piled in an in-box. A glass jar half-filled with the watermelon candies his student had been fond of. He knew this man. He could trust him. He took a deep breath and plunged ahead. "Last night the body of a fire dancer on the island was found on the beach. A Sergeant Balondo is in charge of the case."

"Yes. I need to check on that, if you don't mind." He turned to his keyboard and began to type. "Terrible incident. Sounds like it's hit the news already. Keola Hakumele was a popular figure in our little town."

"I know. My wife found the body."

Ryo stopped typing and stared at Parker in shock. "You're here with Sylvia?"

As one of his prodigies at the Agency, Ryo had been invited to the house for dinners and get-togethers. He'd met his first wife several times.

"Sylvia passed a few years ago."

His brows drew together in genuine sympathy. "I'm so sorry to hear that."

"I've recently remarried."

"Well. My condolences and my congratulations. I'm sorry I haven't kept in touch."

"I'd say that's my fault." Parker had fallen apart when Sylvia became ill. Since then he hadn't kept in touch with many people from his past. She had been the love of his life. But now Miranda had come along and stolen his heart all over again. She made him feel happier, more alive than he had in years. That was, when she wasn't exasperating the hell out of him. "My new wife is an investigator at the Agency," he explained.

Ryo gave him a sad smile. "Keeping to your own kind this time?"

"Something like that. She's good. Very good. Very…persistent. A lot like yourself."

"I'll take that as a compliment."

"It's her opinion Keola was murdered."

Ryo rocked back in his chair again. "Is it? Unfortunately such accidents are too common here."

"Nonetheless, she let the sergeant know she wants to help investigate the case."

Ryo chuckled and took a swallow of tea. "I'll bet Balondo loved that. He's pretty headstrong."

"He didn't seem enamored of the idea."

He set the cup down, studied it thoughtfully. "I'll have a word with him."

"That's not why I'm here."

With a puzzled look, he raised his palms. "All right. I give up. Why are you here, Parker?"

"Do you recall the photo I sent you of the man I'm looking for?"

"Yes. It was taken over thirty years ago, so you said." Ryo hit a few more keys on the computer.

"Did you notice anything odd about the man? An unusual characteristic?"

"Not particularly."

"On his neck?"

He stopped typing again. "Oh, yes. There was some sort of dark spot. I thought it might be from a smudge on the lens."

"It was a birthmark."

"Should make him easier to identify." Ryo studied his computer screen.

"Keola had the same mark on his neck."

Ryo turned to him, eyes wide. "That doesn't necessarily mean…"

"But could you check?"

"Next of kin should be listed in Balondo's report here." Once more his fingers danced across the keyboard, paused, danced again, then stopped as he read. "I see that your wife came in to make a statement last night."

"Yes." He might have known this was the first place she'd go.

"She tried to save the deceased. Must be a gutsy lady."

Parker heard the admiration in Ryo's voice and felt a pang in his heart. That gutsiness was one of the things he found irresistible about her. "That she is."

Ryo read a little more, then blew out a breath. "You're right. This Pumehana is the next of kin."

Parker suppressed a shudder. He'd desperately wanted to protect Miranda from any more pain and instead he'd plunged her headlong into a steaming vat of it. "As I said my wife is very persistent."

"Yes."

"Even though Balondo refused her help, she's investigating the case herself."

Ryo's expression displayed surprise and approval. "I'd love to see what she comes up with."

Parker nodded. "But what I need from you, from your men, especially Balondo, is that she doesn't learn what you just told me."

"About the next of kin? Why don't you want her to know that?"

Parker drew in a breath. "Because my wife's father is Edward Steele."

"So Keola would be—"

"Her half brother." The mark on his neck indicated he was a blood relative.

Ryo picked up his tea, put it down again without taking a sip. "Well, then. You had better hope no one discovers any evidence of foul play. If they do, your wife will be a person of interest."

One of the things he was here to clear up. "She doesn't know who Keola is."

"Oh?"

"Her father abandoned her and her mother when she was five. She hasn't seen him since."

"I see."

Parker gave his former student a hard look. "To the best of your ability, Ryo, make sure my wife doesn't discover who that young man is."

Suddenly Ryo looked very uncomfortable.

"Is there a problem?"

"Actually, yes." An apologetic expression spread over his face. "I'm sorry, Parker. If I had known you'd be in town, I'd have made other plans, but—"

"What?"

"I'm leaving on vacation in a couple of hours. I only came in this morning to review this case and tidy up a few things."

Parker's stomach plunged. "Oh? Where are you going?"

He shrugged. "Los Angeles. My wife wants to see Hollywood. You know, Rodeo Drive, Beverly Hills. All the places ladies like to see. She's so excited. I haven't taken any leave since I started here."

Parker straightened his shoulders. "You're overdue then. Glad I caught you."

"I admit I had second thoughts when this case came up last night."

"Second thoughts?"

"It's the first time I'm leaving Sergeant Balondo in charge, and to be honest I have some reservations. Don't get me wrong. Balondo's a good man, dedicated, hardworking, methodical." He paused.

"But?" Parker prompted.

Ryo blew out a breath. "But sometimes he lacks that ability to put all the pieces together. He gets there. It just takes him longer than others."

The phone on his desk rang and Ryo glanced at the number. "It's Elise. She'll be wondering how long I'll be. She has her heart set on seeing Hollywood. I can't disappoint her or I'd—"

Parker held up a hand. "I understand, Ryo. Really, I do."

"I'll get a message to Balondo about Pumehana. He'll take care of it. He'll do all right on this case. Besides, you have to cut the umbilical cord sometime, right?"

"Absolutely." Ryo would do what he could to help. Parker couldn't very well ask him to cancel his plans in order to baby-sit his sergeant.

Parker got to his feet, extended his hand as Ryo picked up the phone. "Thank you for your help, Ryo. It was good to see you again. I hope you enjoy your vacation."

"Keep in touch, Parker."

"You, too." And with that, he turned and made his way to the door.

His jaw tight, his mind in overdrive, Parker left the police station. Ryo might do his best to handle Balondo, but despite his friend's promise, the detective couldn't guarantee Miranda wouldn't discover who Keola was. And with her stubborn persistence, Parker didn't have long before she did just that.

The best course of action was to ascertain the information he'd come for, fetch his wife and leave the island. Not the way he had planned their honeymoon. Not easy to pull off, either. Especially with Miranda's temper so raw right now.

Nonetheless, he would execute the new plan as quickly as possible and move on. With a little luck, Miranda would never learn the truth.

He sat fidgeting on a bench hidden behind a kona tree across the street from the police station, watching the officers file in and out.

His sunglasses, Bermuda shorts and Aloha shirt made him look like a *haole* tourist, though no one who knew him could mistake him for one. Still he had to be here. He had to watch. Hadn't his father taught him to cover all the bases? To find out what the pigs knew?

And after that business with Keola last night…He'd heard on the news someone had found the body. The police were looking into it but thought it was an accident. Body.

Keola was really dead.

Gently, he rubbed his fingers over the bruise on his jaw where the asshole had smacked him. No way the cops could tie the fire dancer's death to him. He'd made sure there was no evidence. Except the body. He shook his head. Still, no way. There was no evidence. It wasn't like he'd shot the bastard. It would all blow over in a day or two.

He didn't often feel sorry for the things he did. He was his father's son, after all, as his mother—may she rest in peace—often said. Maybe if she hadn't died the way she had, he'd be more like her instead of him. But he wasn't. Still, he didn't like what he'd had to do last night.

Keola should have stayed out of it. Should have minded his own business. But no, he had to stick his nose in. For *ohana*. Family.

He didn't know what it was like to have family. He didn't have a brother or a sister. His father and mother were dead. He had no one except his grandfather and that old scumbag didn't count. No, he was on his own and he'd made his way the best he could. The only way he knew. The one his father taught him.

And he was making such good headway now. His business was picking up steam. If he could keep it all going, it wouldn't be long before he'd have what his father had wanted. An empire. He couldn't let Keola Hakumele get in the way of that.

Rubbing his arms, he peered across the street through his sunglasses again. He didn't see anything unusual around the building. No, the dumb cops couldn't pin anything on him. Still he didn't like that they were investigating around that blowhole. Too close for comfort. Best to cut back on business, to lay low for a while. That pissed him off.

He looked up and saw a tall, good-looking white man come out of the front door of the station. Not an officer. He was dressed in a polo shirt and jeans. A lawyer maybe? Most of them wore suits. Business man?

Wait a minute.

The man's features came into view and the hair on the back of his neck stood straight up. Every muscle tensed. Was that—? Was he going crazy? He lowered his sunglasses to get a better look.

It was *him*.

He was sure of it. It had been four years, but he still kept the newspaper clippings. He remembered the TV reports like he'd seen them yesterday. That face had been everywhere back then. They called him a hero. The man who saved the county from a plague—meaning his father. He even remembered the man's name.

Wade Parker. The fancy detective from the mainland. What fucking business did that *haole* have coming here now? It couldn't have anything to do with Keola, could it?

He could feel his heartbeat in his ears as he watched Parker move to his car and get in. Fancy car. Maybe he'd steal it. No, that wouldn't be smart. And it wouldn't be enough. It wouldn't begin to be enough to pay for what Wade Parker had done.

Slowly he got to his feet, his mind racing as fast as his pulse. Of course. Now he got it. Now it made sense.

This was Fate. Destiny.

If it weren't for Keola, he might not have been here watching the police station just now. He might not have seen the fucking detective. Keola's death was going to bring him the revenge he thought he'd never have. He had no idea why Wade Parker was here in the islands, but he would make sure it was his last trip anywhere.

The car cruised by. He glared at the license plate, quickly memorized the numbers. He'd find out where Wade Parker was staying. He'd find a way to get to him. And he'd make sure that bastard got what he deserved.

A slow, painful, agonizing death. Huh. Even that was too good for the man who'd killed his father.

CHAPTER ELEVEN

Parker drove through the narrow streets of Lahaina's residential section, recalling with warmth the way the scenery in this area flowed so smoothly from seashore to suburb to farmland to mountain. He passed the modest homes and yards that reminded him of certain sections outside of Atlanta, though there were palm trees here instead of Georgia pines and surfboards in the boats instead of merely rods and reels.

Finding the address he'd ascertained for Edward Steele, he pulled his car across the street several yards down and turned off the engine.

He studied the house. A homey two-story bungalow in blue stucco. Single car garage. The yard was smallish, as were the neighbors', but nicely decorated with palm trees and long-leaved shrubbery bearing bright yellow blossoms. A hedge ran to the backyard where he thought he caught a glimpse of lawn furniture.

No activity. The house was quiet. It was early. The family might still be asleep, getting what rest they could after the dreadful news they'd received last night.

Though if Edward Steele was still as irresponsible as he was thirty years ago, it may not matter to him. Keola was Polynesian. Or half Polynesian. He didn't look much like Steele. If it weren't for the telling mark on his neck, Parker would have concluded the young man was not Steele's natural son.

A compact station wagon passed him and pulled into the driveway. After a moment the doors opened and a young Polynesian woman got out. The woman opened the rear door and a little girl emerged. She couldn't have been more than five or six. The other rear door opened and a boy got out. He didn't look much older than the girl.

The woman leaned inside the car. She must have said something to the boy from inside because he nodded and carefully closed the door. A moment later the woman extracted herself from the rear of the car. She had a baby in her arms.

At that moment, the door of the house flew open and an older Polynesian woman ran out and threw her arms around the younger one and her child. Both of them began to weep openly. Keola's mother? And sister?

A figure appeared in the doorway of the house.

He wasn't a tall man. He had a round, Santa Claus like face and an equally round girth. He was dressed in a novelty T-shirt, shorts and flip-flops. His dark, wavy hair had grayed, but he was the man in the picture Parker had.

Edward Steele.

He moved toward the weeping women. As the children looked on, he took them all in his big arms and began to cry with them, his wails as piteous as a shrieking sea lion at the loss of a cub.

Parker's gut wrenched with compassion for them. For the mother he didn't know. For the sister. For this man he'd never met before. This man he had carried a deep resentment for since the day he'd learned of his existence. He had hated this man for the grief he'd caused Miranda. But Parker had seen too many needless deaths. No one deserved this kind of pain, this kind of loss.

He exhaled and stared at his own hands on the steering wheel. He'd intended to meet with Edward Steele under some plausible pretense, to engage him in small talk, and to tease enough detail out of him to determine the state of his health.

Now wasn't the time for such a conversation.

He watched the family turn and slowly plod toward the house, heaviness in each step. He kept his gaze on them until they went through the door and shut it. He stared at the door.

Hugging, weeping, bonding in common sorrow. This wasn't the behavior he expected from a man who had abandoned his family thirty years ago. Perhaps Edward Steele had had a change of heart. He certainly appeared to have a new family.

Parker had no intention of letting the man know his motives. But if his actions were as genuine as they seemed. If he was as intuitive as his daughter. If he suspected she was alive and looking for him, no matter what the reason. No doubt he'd want to see her.

Was this what Miranda was afraid of? What she didn't know how to deal with? Parker thought of the tension he'd had with his own father. It was minuscule compared to this, but he wouldn't have wanted someone meddling in it no matter what their intention was.

If he hadn't understood before, he did now. Now he saw why she was so upset last night. He had fairly rammed the decision down her throat. He hadn't given her a choice at all.

All right, Miranda. We'll do it your way. As difficult and disappointing as it would be to give up the search for her lost daughter, he would have to. For her.

He turned the key in the ignition and drove away from the mourning house.

CHAPTER TWELVE

The first sound Miranda heard when she opened her eyes was the same one she'd fallen asleep to a few hours ago. The whoosh of never-ending ocean waves against the shore.

She lifted her head—which was sticking out of the side of the convertible—and pain shot through her neck and into her skull.

Ouch.

She tried to move and her temples started to throb. Great. A stiff neck from sleeping outside in an awkward position. A hangover from too many Mai Tais. And a relapse of the concussion she'd sustained a week ago—all at once. The fun never stopped.

As she steadied herself before trying to sit up, a deep male Southern voice fluttered in her ears. "You look like you could use a massage."

Now the perfect moment was complete. With effort, she turned her head.

Over her bare foot, which was poking out of the other side of the car's backseat, Parker stood as arrogant as ever.

"Or perhaps a doctor." His gaze moved slowly from her foot, up her leg to her crotch. Then it traveled upward and settled on her face.

He was wearing a polo shirt the color of crème de menthe, with a tiny navy logo over the breast. A pair of black fitted jeans only enhanced his muscular build. But she couldn't mistake the fury in his eyes for desire.

She scowled at him. "I don't remember calling a private investigator."

"Good morning to you, too," he said dryly.

She sat up and reached for her spinning head. "Ow."

"Actually, I'm the one who needed an investigator to locate my stolen car."

She gave him a sour look then glanced past him and saw another BMW convertible parked a few feet away. This one was cobalt blue. Might have known. He had the bucks to rent a whole fleet if he wanted to. Her gaze returned to his face.

She studied the distinguished lines, the wisp of salt-and-pepper hair the wind had blown over his forehead. His gray eyes had their usual intensity but there were shadows under them. He seemed weary. Like he hadn't slept much. In his hand was a paper bag.

She sniffed and smelled coffee. And food. "What's that?"

"Breakfast. Would you like some?"

Did he think he could make up for what he'd done so easily? "No, thanks."

"Very well, I'll just eat it here. In *my* car." He opened the driver's door and took a seat behind the wheel.

Irritation bubbling inside her, she watched him set the bag down on the spot between the bucket seats. He opened it, took out two Styrofoam cups and placed them in the cup holders. He took the lid off one and took a sip of it. The rich smell of fresh coffee filled her nostrils and made her mouth water.

"Hmm, that's good." He set down the cup, reached inside the bag and drew out something wrapped in paper. It smelled heavenly.

That was just plain mean.

With a huff she shoved open the back door and stomped around to sit beside him. She half-slammed the passenger side door and turned to him in disgust.

"Sometimes you don't play fair, Parker."

"No, I don't." He gave her that wry Parker smile, pulled the wrapper down and took a bite.

The saliva in her mouth was contending with the ocean tides. "Is that a breakfast burrito?"

"Hm-mm." He reached for a napkin and dabbed his lips as he swallowed. "This one has extra spice." He took the open bag and turned it toward her. "I'm willing to share."

Giving him a death scowl, she stuck her hand in the bag and pulled out the burrito. She echoed his movements, pulling down the wrapping and digging her teeth into the soft spongy delight.

Oh man, it was wonderful. A delicious, warm tortilla filled with fresh veggies and eggs, gooey with cheese and snapping with spice. She'd be in Heaven if she weren't so furious with this man.

"Coffee? It's black, just the way you like it." He handed her the cup.

She put down the sandwich and took the cup from him, being careful not to touch his hand. She removed the lid, took a sip and suppressed a sigh. It tasted freshly ground and as good as the fancy stuff Parker had imported back home. Why did he have to know all her weaknesses?

She munched away, staring out at the ocean, the palm trees swaying overhead.

Parker did the same.

She got about halfway through the burrito when she remembered the message she'd found on Parker's phone last night. She stopped eating, wrapped up the burrito and put it back in the bag.

She leaned her head against the seat, waves of pain and humiliation shooting through her. "When were you going to tell me you were looking for my father?" The softness of her own voice surprised her.

Parker swallowed his last bite and tossed his wrapper into the bag. "I wasn't going to tell you." His voice was equally soft.

She snorted. It was just like him to keep secrets like that.

"I merely intended to ascertain the data we need."

"You mean find out if he has a terminal disease that could be hereditary."

"Exactly. And if he didn't have one, you'd never have to know I contacted him."

She closed her eyes and shuddered at his audacity. "So just leave me in limbo, huh?"

She felt him tense beside her as he scowled at her. "I was under the impression you wanted it that way."

He just didn't get it, did he? She spun around and glared at him. "Not by pulling strings behind my back. By my choice, Parker." She slapped at her chest. "If I wanted a man who told me what to think and feel, I could've stayed with Leon."

His nostrils flared and his dark brow grew more set as he glared back at her. "That's low, Miranda."

She brushed crumbs off her T-shirt. "Well, you married a lowlife. It's about time you realized that."

Once more they sat in silence, staring out at the waves, tempers seething.

Parker forced himself to breathe slowly and remain silent. This wasn't going to be easy. With Miranda, nothing came easy. At last, he heaved a sigh. "Why don't you come back to the hotel and get some rest?"

"I've got a case to solve."

"Did someone hire you?"

She gave him a sneer. "You always were one for technicalities. This is pro bono."

"Miranda, the police believe Keola's death was an accident. They know the area."

"Shows what you know. Now they think it could have been suicide."

That shut him up.

"By the time they work their way around to murder, I'll know who the killer was."

He nodded, doubt in his eyes. He thought she was chasing shadows. She'd show him. She'd show everyone.

He reached for her hand. "I don't think—"

She pulled away. "Don't tell me what to think."

It was no use to fight her. Better to let her wear herself out. "I was merely going to say that if you're going to interview a suspect, you might want to be better attired."

Miranda glared at him then looked down at herself. She was still dressed in her jeans and T-shirt from last night. One knee was torn and there were blood smears everywhere. Things were casual on the island, but not quite that laid back. She wouldn't get much information out of Keola's boss looking like she'd stepped out of a horror movie. Why did Parker always have to be right?

With a grunt, she folded her arms over her chest. "Okay, then. I'll have to go back to get my things."

"And a shower." Parker started the car.

Miranda sat up. "Hey, I didn't say you could drive me there."

"No, you didn't." But he was doing it anyway. With a smug look that really got on her last nerve, he pulled out of the parking lot and headed back to the hotel.

CHAPTER THIRTEEN

Miranda didn't speak to Parker at the hotel. Why should she? There was nothing more to say.

She took a quick shower, rubbed some fast absorbing ointment on her cuts and changed into khaki dress slacks and a pale blue top. Ignoring the memory that it was an outfit he had picked out for her, she ran her fingers through her thick, unruly hair.

Parker stood silently watching her as she grabbed her suitcase, which she hadn't unpacked. The lines on his face seemed deeper and there was visible pain in the way he regarded her.

That almost made her melt but stubbornly, she fought back her weakness. It wasn't going to work out between them, no matter how much passion they had together, no matter how much they thought they loved each other. She could see that clearly now.

This time, she made sure she had her wallet. She snatched it out of the suitcase, shoved it into her pocket along with some of her business cards. Then she snapped the case shut, picked it up and made her way to the bedroom door.

"Where to?" Parker asked.

"None of your business." She stepped into the living room, with its classy tropical décor and was immediately accosted by the memory of Parker carrying her over the threshold yesterday in honor of that silly wedding tradition. Her lip quivered and she bit back the swell of feeling.

With a casual air, Parker strolled up beside her. "Whom are you going to interview?"

"I don't have to tell you that." She made a move for the door.

He blocked it. "Or perhaps you're going to a job interview. Good thing you changed."

She gave him a flat smile. "If you're really that interested, you'll follow me like you always do." The sneak.

"Would you like some company, instead?"

"No, thanks." She set her suitcase down, pulled her wallet out of her pocket and counted the cash. Sixty bucks. That would do for now. She shoved the wallet back in her pocket and picked up the case again.

"A second pair of eyes?"

Was he starting to believe Keola's death wasn't an accident? No, he was just keeping track of her. She blew out a breath of frustration. "I can handle it." She stepped around him.

"How about a chauffeur?" He held up the keys and jangled them.

She stopped. Okay, it was his car. But she didn't need the BMW. She could find her own ride. Any clunker would do. Or she'd take a cab. But that could add up, and sixty bucks wouldn't get her very far in this pricey area. She might have to dig into her bank account. No way she was running up a credit card bill he'd be more than happy to pay off for her.

Grinding her teeth she glared at him and his smug expression. Okay. She could be the adult here. Certainly, she respected Parker as an investigator. How could she not? He was one of the best in the business. He had trained her, after all. Maybe it wouldn't hurt to have that second pair of eyes. She was professional enough to admit that.

Straightening her shoulders, she took a deep breath and forced herself to sound emotionless. "All right, Parker. I'd appreciate a ride to the Pilialoha Luau office."

A wide grin spread across his dazzling face. "At your service."

But his look of triumph as he opened the door and made a grand gesture for her to precede him almost made her change her mind. In fact, her reflexes wanted to respond with a roundhouse kick to the groin.

Instead she tossed her head at him as she went through the door. He didn't know how lucky he was she had so much self control.

The sun was bright and happy as they drove in silence past the ferns and coffee trees and coconut palms that lined the tourist-centric main street of the town. Past the brightly colored shops and buildings. Past jewelry stores, an art gallery, a T-shirt outlet, a dolphin gallery. Some of the structures looked like captain's houses with second-story porches decorated by fanciful railings, with the commercial twist of signs beckoning tourists to stop and browse the wares.

At last, Parker pulled along the curb and Miranda got out of the car and strolled up to a frame edifice painted in bright blue with a gaudy orange trim. A sign read *Pilialoha Luau Office*. Can't get much plainer than that.

She crossed the porch and tried the door. Open. She stepped inside. Parker was right beside her. Oh, yeah. That second pair of eyes she'd invited along. But he'd better not interfere.

She made her way to a counter along the wall bearing a sign marked *Tickets*. A clerk in the ubiquitous Aloha shirt with a lei around his neck smiled a greeting. He looked young. Like not-even-out-of-high-school young.

"Aloha, ma'am," he said in a voice that hadn't changed yet. "How may I help you?"

Fire Dancer (A Miranda's Rights Mystery)—Book IV

"Hi, there. Is this office for the Pilialoha Luau?" Might as well start with the obvious.

"Yes, indeed." He smiled an eager-to-please smile, showing a row of straight white teeth. "Our next show is tomorrow night at six-thirty. How many tickets would you like?"

"I've already seen the show. I'm interested in speaking with the manager. I believe her name is Minoaka?"

His smile disappeared. "Is something wrong? Perhaps I can handle it for you." He looked like he'd do anything to keep a disgruntled customer from speaking to his boss. She must be a real terror.

"I'm a private investigator." She dug into her pocket for one of her cards and gave it to him. Good thing she thought to bring them along. "I want to see Minoaka about the death of one of her employees."

Eyes wide, he stared at the card, then at her.

"The employee was Keola Hakumele. He was found on the beach last night."

"Oh, yes." His mouth turned down as he bowed his head. "I heard about the terrible accident this morning. I feel so bad for the family."

"Did you know Keola?"

"No, I—I just started here a few weeks ago," he babbled. "Of course, I'd heard of him. He was very popular. But I never met him. I thought what happened was an accident."

It was probably just nerves that had him so rattled. Still she made a note of the name on his tag. Jimmy. "We're just covering all our bases, Jimmy," she told him. "Can I talk to Minoaka now?"

He looked as if one of his buddies at school had just pulled his pants down in the locker room. "Sh—she's very busy," he squeaked. "She doesn't like to be disturbed."

So that was it. "I won't take much of her time."

His mouth dangled open. He looked totally helpless.

Miranda leaned on the counter, invading his space a tad. "Surely, Jimmy, you wouldn't want to impede the investigation of a fellow employee's death."

The implied threat was enough to push him over the edge. He held up his hands like she was robbing him and nodded vigorously. "Okay, okay. Wait here. I'll see what she says."

He hurried around the desk and trotted down a hall.

Miranda didn't wait at the counter. She followed him into the hallway. Parker was right behind. So far, he'd kept quiet but that might not last. Besides, she felt like he was grading her. She decided to pretend he wasn't there.

By now, Jimmy was halfway up a wooden staircase at the end of the hall. As Miranda reached the bottom stair, he turned back, his mouth open, as if wanting to remind Miranda that she should wait at the counter. Then he shook his head and pressed on. Must be saving his courage for his boss.

She and Parker creaked up the staircase and down another long hall, to a wooden door where Jimmy was standing. The young man knocked timidly. No answer.

Miranda could hear shouting inside.

Looking as if he might cry, the clerk bit his lip and knocked again, this time a little louder. Still no answer.

He turned back to Miranda and lifted his hands in a helpless gesture. "See? She doesn't want to be disturbed."

"Let me try." Miranda stepped past him and opened the door.

"Hey, you can't do that."

"Just did." She advanced another step and entered the room.

As she took in the place, she heard Jimmy's footsteps scampering away. The high-ceilinged office was large and plain, all wood, painted in a dull color that looked like it could use a new coat or two. It had the musty smell of an attic.

Along one wall colorful island bric-a-brac was displayed. Feathered gourd rattles, bamboo sticks, a grass skirt. Beside the artifacts hung several awards for Best Luau in Maui. Then came photos of a large woman posing with what looked like various members of the show. She wasn't smiling in any of them.

Miranda turned to the tall, gothic-shaped window overlooking the ocean. In front of it the woman in the photos sat at an old desk that looked like it was built in the forties. She was dressed in a blood red shirt. Her wavy, jet black hair was cropped short and unstyled. In one nostril she wore a tiny gold ring.

Her jowls quivered as she shook her head and pounded the desk. "I told you buy ten cases tequila for thousand," she screamed in a thick Polynesian accent. "I told you no go over my price. You think I'm running a charity here?"

Glancing behind her, Miranda saw Parker step inside to lean against the doorpost, amusement dancing in his gray eyes. He wanted to see what she'd do with this one.

"I don't care what mark-up is," the woman screeched. "And bartenders can be replaced, you know. They dime for dozen." She paused to listen but only for a moment. Then her voice got louder. "Refuse delivery. I go to Petani's instead." She slammed down the receiver, looked up and squinted at Miranda as if she hadn't seen her before. "What de hell you doing in here?"

What a sweetheart. So this was what Andrews and Jones had meant by "Bloody Mary."

Miranda took a step forward. "Are you Minoaka?"

The woman bared her teeth. "Who wants to know?"

"My name is Miranda…Parker." She resisted the urge to look back at the man who really carried that name. Might as well keep using it, if it could help.

But Parker was not one to be ignored. The large woman pointed at him. "Who dat?" Her voice was a tad softer. Parker had that affect on women. All women.

"My partner," Miranda said quickly. "He's just observing. We're looking into the death of Keola Hakumele."

The woman's thick nose wrinkled in a snarl. "I already talk to police last night."

Miranda folded her arms. "You don't sound too broken up about the incident."

The woman's black eyes flashed. "I plenty broken up. We all grieve in our own way. I still have business to run. I'm busy. You go away now." She waved a chubby hand toward the door.

Miranda ignored her. "Did you know Keola well?"

"I don't know any employee well. Not good business to get too close." She opened a manila folder and studied its contents.

"You didn't know anything about the most popular fire dancer in town?"

Minoaka slapped the file shut. "I know he could be a pain in de ass."

A nibble. "Pain in the ass? What do you mean?"

"I don't mean nothing. I don't know nothing. You go now." She rose, picked up the file and lumbered over to a cabinet along the wall, her red shirt billowing over tight black slacks, her black sandals scuffing along the wooden floor as she moved. At the cabinet, she pulled out a drawer and stuck the folder into it.

Miranda studied her nails. "Sure, Minoaka. I can leave. But it sure would be a shame to shut this place down if we can't get the information we need."

The woman slammed the drawer shut and turned, eyes blazing, nostrils flared. With the nose ring, she reminded Miranda of an Iberian bull about to charge its matador. Too bad she hadn't brought a red cape.

"You wouldn't dare," she spat.

Miranda cocked her head. "Try me."

Her eyes looking like they might incinerate the place any second, Minoaka stomped back to her desk and plopped down. "What you want to know? Make it snappy. I got work to do."

Cooperation at last. Of sorts. "You can start by telling me why you think Keola was such a pain in the ass."

Minoaka gave her a sour look, scrunching her lips in a childish pout. "I hear it from Wainani all the time."

"Wainani?"

"Dominic Wainani, de stage manager, Keola don't like de lighting. Keola don't like de tempo. Keola don't like dis, Keola don't like dat. He temperamental performer. Moody. Know what I mean?"

Miranda nodded.

"And all dose girls following him all de time. Dey bad for business."

"Sounds like the type of guy you'd like to get rid of."

She slapped herself on the chest as her voice went up a notch. "I no pooshover. His head was getting too big for his britches."

"You mean he had an ego?"

"The size of Oahu." She began stamping papers on her desk as she talked. "He say he's artist. Baloney." Stamp. "Night Marchers. Phooey." Stamp. "I tell him not to put dat nonsense in the show. I tell him not to scare de customers with those stories. He do it anyway." Stamp. Stamp.

Now that was interesting. "You mean the Night Marchers thing wasn't part of the show before last night?"

She stopped stamping. "Heck, no. And when he did it, I tell him he can march his night ass right out of here."

Just like Andrews and Jones had said. "You fired him?"

"Darn straight, I did."

"But he was the headliner."

"Bah. Fire Dancers. They dime for dozen." Stamp. Stamp. Stamp.

The cantankerous woman reminded Miranda of a couple of bosses she'd worked for in her travels. She felt even more sorry for poor Keola. "You have someone to replace him already?"

"Of course. I have Justin Nahele. He been waiting for months. He beg Wainani, he beg me all de time. 'Put me in the show. I'm better dan Keola.' So now he got de job."

Now that sounded like a motive. "Where can I find Nahele?"

"He downstairs practicing with Wainani." She looked up from her papers and waggled a chubby finger at Miranda. "Don't you dare disturb them. They have to be ready for tomorrow night."

Miranda put on a smile as sweet as a freshly picked mango. "I wouldn't think of it, Minoaka. Thank you for your help."

Minoaka only scowled at her. "You tell dat Balondo I already said all I got to say."

"I'll do that." She turned to go while the getting was good.

On the way out, she brushed past Parker, who was still lingering in the doorway. He hadn't said a word and his expression seemed full of admiration. The kind he used to give her on her first cases with him. A rush of tenderness swept through her. Good Lord, he was making this hard. Why couldn't he argue with her about her methods instead? It sure would be easier to stay mad at him.

But then it wasn't her methods he objected to. It was the whole investigation. She knew he was just waiting for her to get it out of her system. Hah. What she needed was to get him out of her system.

Apparently, that wasn't going to happen. As she hustled down the hall, he stepped up beside her and murmured in her ear. "A temperamental artist would be prone to suicide after being fired from a job that meant a lot to him."

"Only means I haven't dug deep enough yet," she hissed back.

"Perhaps. Perhaps not."

"Well, I'm going for another shovelful. You don't have to come with if you think it's so pointless."

But stubborn mule that he was, Parker followed her as she made her way back downstairs and past the clerk, who pretended not to see them.

Ignoring her good-looking shadow, she slipped out the front door.

CHAPTER FOURTEEN

Outside, the sound of a lone drumbeat greeted her ears. With Parker still on her heels, she followed it across the wooden porch and around the building to the dining area.

Under the morning sun the place stood vacant and lonely. There were no linen tablecloths. No fancy china or silverware or colorfully-garbed greeters. Rattan chairs were piled atop empty tables. In the far corner, a lone worker swabbed the floor.

On the stage, a young man in cutoff jeans danced to the drumbeat, an unlit torch in his hand. Another man, who was tall and looked much older than the dancer, stood at the edge of the stage watching him intently.

Suddenly, Miranda felt her eyes grow moist. This was where she'd watched the show with Parker last night. Her blissful honeymoon. Keola's last performance. Her heart swelled at the memory. What a difference a day makes.

She shook herself.

"I'll stay out of your way," Parker murmured, sadness in his voice as he moved to the bar to wait for her. His thoughts must be going in the same direction.

She watched him pull a stool down and perch on it. Oh, for Pete's sake. There was no time for emotional stuff now. She had a murder to solve.

Straightening her shoulders, she turned and made her way through the tables, heading for the stage.

"Step, stomp. Step, stomp. That's right," the tall man cried out.

As she neared Miranda saw he was lean and lanky with wavy gray hair that receded a bit at the temples and was caught up in a braid that fell down his back. He was wearing sandals, dark jeans and a form-fitting black shirt.

"Step, stomp. Step, stomp," he repeated, clapping his long, bony hands in time to the drumbeat.

His thin bare chest gleaming with sweat in the sun, the dancer shuffled to the left then back to the right.

"Good. Now turn and toss."

The dancer spun and flung his flameless torch into the air. As it came down, he reached for it but his fingers fumbled and the wooden baton clattered onto the stage.

"I'm sorry," he cried, nerves in his voice. "I'm so sorry, Wainani."

The man slapped both hands against his forehead in a dramatic gesture. "No, no, no, Justin! Never let them see you've made a mistake. Just keep going. Smooth. Smooth." He moved his hands in the air like a conductor directing an orchestra.

"I'll try. I'll do better. I promise." The dancer picked up the torch and dropped it again.

The older man made a grunting sound and shook his head.

"I'm so sorry. I'll try harder. Please."

The man lifted his gaze skyward as if asking why he had been so cursed. He raised a hand. "Stop. You're tired. Just take five."

The dancer nodded, picked up his torch and, this time managing to hold onto it, scrambled from the stage. In the absence of the drumbeat, ocean sounds took over the now silent stage.

The older man turned on his heels with a huff, about to make a beeline for the bar.

Miranda stepped in front of him and cut him off. "Doesn't seem to be much of a replacement for Keola, huh?"

"What?" The tall man glared at her. She saw his black shirt was open at the neck, revealing a mass of graying hair covered with several gold chains. Must take the stage manager job seriously.

"You're Dominic Wainani, right?"

He made a sound like barking seal and rolled his eyes. "How did you get in here? I don't do interviews. You'll have to talk to our publicist." He brushed past her.

"I'm not here for an interview, Mr. Wainani. I'm looking into the death of Keola Hakumele."

He stopped in his tracks and slowly turned back, giving her the once over with a pair of wary green eyes. "And you are?"

"Miranda Parker. I'm a private investigator." Once more she dug in her pocket and handed him a card. "May I have a moment of your time?"

He looked very uncomfortable, but he nodded. "Minoaka said someone would come round to talk to us about that, so I suppose I'll have to give it to you." He folded his arms over his thin chest. "What do you want to know?"

"You're the stage manager here?"

"Creative Director."

Excuse me. "Tell me about Keola."

He shrugged. "He was a great talent. His loss is felt deeply by all of us here at Luau Pilialoha."

Now that she was close to him, she saw red circles under his eyes that he'd tried to cover up with makeup. Maybe he really did feel the loss. Or maybe he'd been crying because he was terrified of being caught for a serious crime.

"Minoaka didn't seem to think he was such a great talent. She indicated he could be easily replaced."

He coughed and rubbed a finger under his long nose as his face became animated with an array of emotions. Mostly disgust. "Let's just say Minoaka is difficult to work for. She doesn't understand the art of the fire dance. All she cares about is the money. Keola was special. We will all miss him very much."

"Sounds like you were close."

"In the creative sense. He was an artist." He waved a hand in the air. "Oh, he got on my nerves sometimes. I'm an artist, too. But Keola was one of a kind. No one can replace him, contrary to Minoaka's opinion."

"What about the guy I just saw? What's his name?" She gestured toward the stage.

"Justin Nahele." Wainani shook his head and rolled his eyes. Must be a nervous habit. "The boy's trying hard, but he'll never match Keola. Keola had raw talent. An innate sense of the moves. A natural grace."

She pursed her lips and took a step closer. "Why was Nahele picked as replacement then, Mr. Wainani?"

He almost rolled his eyes again, but stopped himself. "Justin's been begging Minoaka to let him fill in for Keola for months. He wants more than anything in the world to be a fire dancer like Keola. He worshiped him."

Oh, really? This was getting more and more interesting. "Sounds like he might have been a little jealous of him."

Wainani laughed as if he were talking to a child. "We're all a little jealous of each other in the artistic community. Just as we all deeply admire each other. Outsiders don't understand."

"I see." Artistic or not, jealousy could make you want to destroy a rival. She'd seen that before.

"Is that all, Mrs. Parker? I have work here, as I hope you can see."

"Just a few more questions." She leaned her butt against the stage. Might as well get comfortable.

He drew in an exasperated breath. "Very well."

"What about a girlfriend?"

He frowned as if she'd said something in Bulgarian. "What do you mean?"

"Girlfriend. As in, did Keola have one?"

He lifted his hands. "He was a local celebrity. Young women hounded him. He could have had his pick of any of them."

"And did he? Perhaps one of them had a boyfriend. Perhaps Keola got on a boyfriend's nerves."

Wainani narrowed his eyes at her. "Are you saying there was foul play in Keloa's death? I thought it was an accident."

"We're trying to determine that."

With a stunned look, Wainani ran a hand over his forehead. "Keloa was dedicated to his art. He gave himself over to it. He spent hours practicing. He didn't have time for a girlfriend."

"So he was a loner?"

"I would say so. Many of us are."

"Sounds like you're one, too."

He looked at her as if she were the rudest person he'd ever met. "Your point?"

Maybe Wainani was the jealous one. But what would he and Keola be doing at the blowhole in the middle of the night? She decided not to press that now. "What was this thing about the Night Marchers?"

He blinked as if it were difficult to follow her change of topic. "Huaka'i Po. Keola's latest obsession." He waved a dismissive hand. "A silly island superstition some parents use to frighten their children into behaving. I didn't like it. I didn't think he should put it into the show."

"Did you argue over that?"

"We argued over a great many things. But yes, we argued. Our show is supposed to be happy and romantic, not…spooky. He went over my head and did it anyway."

"Minoaka agrees with you."

His face showed that he suddenly understood what she was implying. "I made a mistake. I shouldn't have complained to her. She was livid. She called Keola into her office and screamed at him with that horrid screeching voice of hers." His face went dark as he drew in a ragged breath. "Then she told him he was fired and that he'd never work in Lahaina again."

"He took it hard?"

"He was devastated. Absolutely devastated."

"So you think he was in the state of mind to…"

He blinked at her. His green eyes grew turquoise with moisture. "End it all?" Slowly, he nodded. "Yes. Perhaps. He could brood with the best of us. It took all I had sometimes to get him out of one of his funks." Now his eyes began to glow with trepidation. "Do you think that's what happened to him? Oh, God. Was it all my fault?"

This guy was either a really good actor or he cared about Keola. But if he'd just wanted the kid out of his hair, it didn't make sense to kill him after he was fired. She pressed on.

"Do you know where Keola went after Minoaka let him go?"

He frowned as if trying to remember. "I'm not sure. Earlier he told me he was going to see his little brother after the show. He might have still done that. He was worried about him."

"Why?"

Wainani stared out at the sea. "His brother has been in trouble lately. Hanging out with a bad crowd. Rebellious teenager. His mother kicked him out of the house."

"I see." She was getting closer. She could feel it. Maybe this little brother knew exactly what happened to Keola. "Do you think he met his brother at the blowhole?"

"I really can't say. But I know his brother is staying at his father's bar."

Her heartbeat picked up. "His father owns a bar?"

"Yes, a tiki bar."

"What's the name of it?"

"Coconut Rum. It's on Front Street. Near Wahie Lane, I believe."

Another good lead. She'd have to check it out. "His father's name is Hakumele, I assume."

Wainani scowled again. "No, that's Keola's middle name. Let's see. Let me think. Oh, yes. His father goes by the name Pumehana."

Well, that was confusing. Good thing she'd asked. "Pumehana?"

"It means warmth and affection," he said softly. "His place is a lot of fun, I hear. Or it used to be...until last night."

Parker sat on the barstool, his gaze fixed on the pair standing before the stage. The director seemed surly, but Miranda looked lovely and fresh in her pale blue blouse with the backdrop of the blue sky and sea complementing her. He smiled at her casual pose, the confident way she posed her questions. He could hear only vague snatches of their conversation, but he knew she was getting all the information she needed out of the man.

She'd always had inborn instincts. And inborn drive and determination. But now, she also had skills. She had come a long way since she first swaggered into his office back in Atlanta. She had grown into a fine investigator. Pride rippled through his chest. It was mingled with frustration. It took a tremendous amount of self-control not to interfere. To sit back and let her work it through.

As he leaned on the bar and summoned another round of patience, a troubling thought struck him. He may have trained her, but she really didn't need him or the Agency any more. She could strike out on her own, if she chose. And knowing her, she was thinking of just that. He couldn't let that happen. He couldn't lose her again.

She turned and he took in the expression on her face. She'd learned something.

The bottom dropped out of his heart. Had she discovered the fact he'd been trying so hard to keep from her? No, she'd be furious if she had. And upset beyond words. It was something else. Something that would spur her to dig deeper, as she had put it. And he'd been so sure her investigation here would only confirm the Keola Hakumele's death had been a tragic suicide.

What if she were right? What if it wasn't suicide?

There'd be no whisking her away in short order then. She'd follow the trail until it led her to the killer. He tapped his fingers on the bar. Time to change tactics. The only way he could control how much information she had was to join her investigation instead of merely observe it. If only she'd stop being so prickly.

He watched her shake Wainani's hand and leave him to his work. She strode toward him with a brusqueness that made his heart ache. He slipped off the stool and put it back in place.

"Excellent work," he murmured when she reached him.

"Thanks." She kept going. Her eyes didn't meet his and the twitch in her mouth spiked his irritation with her.

He stepped to her side. "Have you reached any conclusions?"

"I've got a nibble or two." She moved swiftly through the open entrance to the porch.

He quickened his pace. "I was thinking. What you're missing is physical evidence to prove what happened to Keola was neither an accident nor a suicide."

Closing her eyes, she stopped just before the steps leading to the walkway and spun on her heels. "If you think this is such an exercise in futility, Parker, why don't you go back to the hotel? I can manage without a 'chauffeur.'"

Her testiness inflamed him, yet the fire in her deep blue eyes reminded him of the first time he saw her. When she'd been falsely accused of murder and had so eloquently told him to "get lost." He wanted to shake her. He wanted to bury his lips in hers. Instead, he would do his best to tame those ruffled feathers.

"You misjudge me, Miranda," he said as calmly as he could.

She folded her arms and glared at him. "Oh, yeah?"

He drew in a slow breath. "I was going to suggest we examine the scene in the light of day."

Miranda had to blink at that one. Had she heard him right? He wanted to look for evidence? Or did he have some trick up his debonair sleeve? What was she thinking? He always had some trick up his sleeve.

She turned away but didn't go down the steps. Parker had a point. Some solid physical evidence would be a lot more convincing to Balondo than just her gut feeling. And it would be pretty hard to examine the area around the blowhole by herself.

She turned back and tilted her chin at him. "You're saying we should go there now?"

"No time like the present. Besides, the tide isn't at its peak yet. We'll be drier." He gave her that trademark sex-appeal grin.

She forced her feelings into a wall to block his charm, not too sure if it had worked. She had such a weakness for him. A good reason not to examine the crime scene with him. Besides she needed to question Justin Nahele. And she wanted to check out what Wainani had told her about Keola's little brother.

She tapped her foot on the wooden floor of the porch. She was a professional. And with Parker's status in her profession, no doubt she'd consult with him in the future from time to time, no matter where she ended up. He seemed to be familiar with every place in the world, after all. She ought to get used to working around him. Examining the area where she'd found Keola would be good practice. Her other two tasks could wait an hour or so.

She gave him a quick, professional nod. "Okay, James. Take me to the blowhole."

His sexy gray eyes twinkled. "I'd be delighted, m'lady."

CHAPTER FIFTEEN

Her "chauffeur" drove in silence for a long while. Miranda bided her time counting the ferns and the flowering hibiscus plants and the avocado trees and the coconut palms they passed along the Honoapiilani Highway. She watched the ocean disappear behind an elaborate apartment building and wondered how much dinero it cost to live in this pretty place. They probably charged by the sigh.

After several minutes, Parker made a turn into a residential area, drove past a shopping center, then through a wooded area where the trees hung over the railings shading the pavement.

"It looks as though you learned something significant from the stage manager at the luau," he said blandly.

"Actually, he's the creative director."

"I see."

Miranda gave him a sidelong glance. He hadn't eavesdropped on her conversation with Wainani? Almost too good to believe, but he had stayed at the bar the whole time. And now he wanted to discuss what she'd learned?

What was up with this new approach? He might be playing games, but he was still one of the best investigators ever born. If he wanted to help—even for ulterior motives—it would be silly not to avail herself of his skills. If that second pair eyes was good, so was a second opinion.

She decided to loosen up a little. "I learned the creative director didn't want Keola to put that Night Marchers stuff in the show."

"Interesting."

"Wainani argued with him about it. And when he did it anyway, the director went to Minoaka and complained."

"And that was when she dismissed him?"

Miranda nodded. "She went ballistic and fired Keola on the spot. Even told him he'd never work in this town again."

Parker's face lined with anger at that news. "That's no way to treat a valued employee. That could have driven him to suicide."

"Maybe. He took it awfully hard, according to Wainani. But I also learned that the kid who replaced him wanted his job. Bad."

"A jealous rival?"

"Could be. Might be a motive for murder." She braced herself for his protest.

Instead he nodded in that pensive way of his. "Mmm." Was he coming around to her theory?

Feeling excited for the first time since last night, she turned to him in her seat. "And you'll never guess what else Wainani told me about Keola."

"What?" Parker pulled the BMW off the road and onto the dirt shoulder.

Miranda scowled. "Why are you stopping?"

"We're here."

She shielded her eyes with her hand and scanned the grassy hill. "I don't see a blowhole."

"It's over that rise." He gestured ahead.

"If you say so." She got out of the car and shut the door as Parker came around to her side.

"What were you going to say?"

"I'll tell you later." She didn't want to lose any more time. Plunging ahead, she made her way through the tall grass with Parker keeping in step beside her.

At the top of the crest, she stopped and sucked in her breath.

Jagged lava cliffs loomed on either side of a large basin-like area, a massive stretch of ashen rock as sharp and spiky as shark's teeth. Crammed with rough crevices, shallow spots and puddles, it looked like the surface of Jupiter. Except that it was all framed by a sea of heartbreaking blue. In the middle of the twisted mass, the blowhole sputtered, shooting its spray into the air.

Miranda shook her head in amazement. "How did I get over there in the dark?"

At her side, Parker shaded his eyes with his hand. "I wondered that myself."

She continued down the mossy slope about twenty yards until the earth became slabs of cracked rock and the soil between the slabs grew muddy.

No sign the police had ever been here. The yellow markers were gone, too. Crap. "This area is huge."

"Yes. Too bad we don't have a team from the Agency."

"You could fly a few people over."

He gave her a wry look. "Shall we get started?"

"Guess so."

It was hard with no equipment, and you really had to watch your step, but she began picking her way over the boulders, head down, studying the crust at her feet, while the wind played with her unruly hair.

She was surprised at the colors. Most of the rock was ashen gray, but some was mixed with shades of rusty reds and steely blues, reflected in the watery pools that were scattered about.

She didn't see anything unusual. No dark discoloration from bloodstains. She looked up and gazed at the surrounding mountain of dried lava. It looked like the teeth of a huge dinosaur. With a gush, the blowhole shot forth its spume.

"I think I'm in the wrong place."

"Oh?" Parker raised his head. He'd been examining a spot along a jagged wall that ran along the northern edge.

"I had to come in from there." She pointed in the opposite direction. "And I ended up there." She pointed at the blowhole. Then she took off for the geyser.

"Don't get too near," Parker warned, anxiety in his voice.

"I'll be careful." She would be. She was lucky she hadn't been swept out to sea last night.

Slowly she strode toward the sputtering fountain, feeling her clothes moisten as she neared. When she'd come as close as she dared, she studied the ground. "Keola was bleeding from his head."

"From hitting it against the rock around the blowhole, according to Balondo."

"Maybe. But if my theory is correct, he might have been bleeding before he got to the hole."

"Someone fought with him and forced him into it?"

"Yeah. If you have a fistfight on these lava boulders and you get knocked down, you're going to get sliced up. Everything's so sharp." The cuts on her hands and knees proved that.

"And if you hit your head, it could kill you. It might have been a different kind of accident." Parker strolled in her direction. "By the way, how are your injuries?"

"I'm fine." Her head had even stopped hurting now that she was on this case. She squatted down, peered hard at the wet surface. "But if someone got you down and bashed your head against these rocks—"

"There'd be blood left. You couldn't clean it up."

"Not unless you were where the ocean would wash it away."

"Possibly."

She raised her head and regarded the waves splashing up playfully from below. "So you have a fit of temper and you accidentally kill your friend. To cover it up, you stick him in the blowhole." It seemed to fit.

Parker was silent, no doubt trying to find the flaws in that explanation.

"Wait. What's this?" Still squatting, she squinted at the rock between her feet. It had a dark red splotch. "I think I just found blood. It's farther out than where I dragged the body."

Parker came to her side and scrutinized the spot. "It does look like it."

She rose, took a few steps toward the direction she had come from last night. She gave a little yelp. "Here's another one."

Scowling Parker followed her. "Surely the police found these spatters and swabbed them."

"I could call Balondo and ask. I'm sure he'd tell me." If she pried it out of him. "There's another one." She was at the spot where she'd first seen the blowhole last night, almost to where the ground was less rocky and began to slope down again. She looked up and saw the back of the warning sign. Her heart froze at the sight.

"Bingo," she murmured.

Parker hurried to her side. "What is it? Oh, dear Lord."

Two bloody handprints were smeared along the bottom half of the sign. Not one. Two. Miranda stared at them, her mind racing. Someone had reached out for the sign, maybe to steady himself. Someone else had reached for him.

"He tried to get away. But his killer stopped him."

"Balondo's team had to notice this."

"Even in the dark last night?"

"Surely they must have come out here again this morning."

"I'll find out." She dug her cell out of her pocket and punched in the direct number on the card the sergeant had given her.

He answered on the second ring. "Balondo here."

"This is Miranda Parker."

"Good afternoon, Mrs. Parker." He sounded as thrilled to hear from her as a phone solicitor.

"I'm at the crime scene."

"Crime scene?"

"The blowhole where Keola Hakumele was found. We found blood on the rocks."

His sigh rippled through the phone. "We did, too, Mrs. Parker. My team was out there earlier this morning. Rest assured, everything is being properly analyzed."

Man, this cop could be annoying. "Good to know. Did you find the handprints on the back of the warning sign?"

There was a pause. She could see him rubbing his soul patch as he processed that one. "What are you talking about, Mrs. Parker?"

"You know, the sign that warns us *haoles* about the blowhole? There are two bloody handprints on the back of it. If you use a little black magnetic powder and casting silicone, you might be able to lift them."

There was a long pause. And an odd sound. She thought he might have a bulldog in the office with him. At last he replied. "We didn't go that far out. I'll get a team on it." Another pause. "Oh, and Mrs. Parker?"

"Yes?"

"You're not leaving town, are you?"

She looked down at the phone. This guy didn't suspect her now, did he? If he did, he'd change his mind when the fingerprint report came back. "No, of course not."

"Good. Don't. And keep in touch." He hung up.

"He's sending out his people," she told Parker.

"We should wait for them to get here." He sounded unusually grim, even for this situation.

Should they? Miranda shoved her phone back in her pocket and folded her arms. She wanted to talk to Keola's brother, but she wasn't ready to go yet. Something was still missing.

She stared at the area, so beautiful and bleak. The blowhole went off again. "Where did the murderer come from?"

Parker considered the question a moment. "He could have come from anywhere along the highway."

"The police didn't find any vehicle besides Keola's truck."

"But there were tracks."

"Mingled with dozens of other tracks from visitors to the site."

"We should have a look at them." He started for the road.

She frowned. Parker knew they couldn't discern which tracks belonged to the killer. "Why did Keola come here?" she called, trying to steer him in another direction.

He stopped and turned back, raised his hands. "To meet someone? Or so your theory would say. It might have been someone he knew."

"But why here?"

"It's isolated."

"So's a back alley in town."

His gaze swept the landscape and stopped short at the opposite cliff. He stood staring at it and she felt an odd twinge in her gut. He took off.

Now she followed him, once more negotiating her way across the rocks and boulders, heading for the other side. "The killer could have come from that trail beyond the warning sign that leads to the beach." She waved a hand behind her. "Maybe he took Keola by surprise."

He waited for her to catch up, as if he were guarding her. "Because he lured him out here to kill him?" She couldn't tell if that was conviction or skepticism in his voice.

"Maybe."

They reached the opposite wall. She examined the incline and found enough of a foothold to climb it. She put her shoe in the space, took hold of a rock with a grip that wouldn't cut her hands and hauled herself up.

"Be careful, Miranda."

"I'm okay." She continued upward. She heard Parker grunt from below and follow her.

It didn't take long before they were at the top of the rise.

She took in the high, jagged wall of the coast. A steep drop to the ocean below, the waves gently beating against an equally jagged shoreline. It was a breathtaking sight. And there, right where the wall curved, an opening. From here, it looked like it could be as tall as a house.

If you were careful, you could negotiate your way down there, but you'd have to know the terrain like the back of your hand. Like an islander would.

That strange prickly feeling slithered along the back of her neck like a salamander. "Is that what I think it is?"

Parker peered over her shoulder, scanning the rocky surface. "A littoral cave," he said at last, as if lost in thought.

"A what?"

"A sea cave. They're formed over time by the erosion from the waves. They occur when there's a weak spot in the lava. The force of the sea weakens the rock and creates fissures. Openings. The water and air in them is compressed and build to tremendous force."

"Resulting in blowholes?"

"Exactly."

"So the blowhole might lead down to that cave."

"Possibly. Or there might be another cave under the water that feeds it."

"Thanks for the geology lesson, but I'm wondering if there's a different kind of connection."

He nodded, his stern expression telling her that his mind was traveling the same course as hers.

She pointed to the opening below. "A cave like that could be a nice little hideout for someone who just killed somebody."

"Or it could be a place to store...all sorts of contraband."

Her blood went cold. "Maybe Keola was into something that didn't have anything to do with getting fired from the luau." She thought of that brother of his. The one who'd recently been in trouble. Exactly what kind of trouble was that? Had to be big for his mother to kick a teenager out of the house.

She needed to talk to that kid. Now. She lifted herself off the craggy hill and turned to climb back down.

Parker glared at her in surprise. "Where are you going?"

"Back to town."

"You don't want to wait for Balondo and his men?"

"They can handle it."

"I really think we should wait."

She shook her head. "Sorry. Right now, I've got something more important to do."

CHAPTER SIXTEEN

They were already past the spot where Miranda had spent the night in the car and nearing the restaurants on the north side of town when Parker could no longer ignore the feeling of apprehension churning his insides.

He stopped at a light. "Are you going to tell me why we're headed back to Lahaina?"

Miranda had that faraway look in her eye that told him she was concentrating deeply, putting the pieces together. He hoped to God they weren't the pieces he was thinking of. "Wainani told me Keola has a little brother who's been in trouble."

Parker's gut clenched. There was a brother? "What kind of trouble?"

"He didn't say, but it was bad enough that his mother kicked him out of the house. Apparently, the dancer was worried about the kid. Wainani thinks Keola might have gone to see him after the show."

"And you think that might be the reason Keola went to the blowhole?"

She pushed her lovely, windblown hair away from her face. "That's my hunch. I'd like to talk to the brother and find out."

"How are you going to find him?" Was she going to talk to the mother? Surely Wainani didn't give her Keola's parents' address. He hadn't written anything down for her. But perhaps Miranda had gotten the address from Balondo.

"The brother is staying at the father's tiki bar. I guess the father's a soft touch. His name is Pumehana. It means warmth and affection."

No, not the bar. That was far worse. She could come face to face with him. And she knew that nickname. Parker's mind raced through the options. There were only two. Talk her out of this or tell her the truth. The truth would only hurt her. If he could save her from that agony, he would.

A horn blared behind them.

Miranda pointed up. "The light's green."

He took his foot off the brake, made a right turn and pulled into the first parking lot he saw, which happened to be that of an apartment building, shaded by coffee trees. He was glad for the privacy.

He turned to her, trying to sound gentle. "I'm not sure this is a wise move, Miranda."

She turned to him, irritation on her face. "What's not a wise move?"

"Going to see Keola's brother."

"Why not?"

"I can think of a dozen reasons. A young boy. Unreliable testimony."

She frowned at him in disbelief. "We're not in court yet."

He'd better come up with something better than that. "What if the brother was involved in Keola's death? He won't give you the straight facts."

Now her dark brows knit together in mingled confusion and annoyance. "Uh…didn't I learn how to handle that in the Interrogation Methods class I took at your Agency?"

Patience. He'd think of something convincing in a moment. He dared to lay a hand across the back of the car seat but didn't let himself touch her. "I'm just saying it might be better to pass the information onto Balondo and let him and his team handle it."

Her breath grew measured. Her hands clenched. She was angry and visibly insulted. He didn't blame her. "Balondo and his team will be busy at the blowhole getting the fingerprint and blood smear evidence."

His arguments weren't working at all. They didn't even make sense to him. He had to try a different angle. "The boy is grieving."

That softened her expression. "Yeah, the whole family must be going through hell. Especially the father."

He almost winched. "It's not a good time."

"Of course, I hate to bother them right now, but I need answers. And I figure they'll appreciate what I'm trying to do."

He was slipping. He tried again. "What if the brother was involved in the murder? What will that do to the family on top of everything they're going through right now?"

She stared down at her hands while she contemplated that. But then she shook her head. "That will be rough. Really rough. But what if he's not involved? What if he knows why Keola went to the blowhole? Who he was meeting there? C'mon, Parker. We're wasting time. Let's go."

He reached for her hand. "You can't do this, Miranda."

Those blue eyes flashed at him. "Are you getting all macho again? I don't really need your permission, you know."

He gritted his teeth. He couldn't seem to stop making her angry when it came to this matter. "I'm simply trying to interject some rationality."

"I'm being plenty rational. It's you who's going bonkers. This is how you investigate a case, right? Or did I just dream everything I learned at the Agency? Are you going to take me to the tiki bar or not?"

"I can't do that." If she asked him why, he'd tell her. He'd have no choice. But she didn't.

"Okay, I'll get there on my own." Her face aflame, she got out of the convertible and slammed the door. Then she reached into the backseat for her suitcase.

"What do you intend to do? Walk there carrying that case?"

She strolled to the front of the car and gave him a sarcastic smile. "I'm not too frail to do that. But there is such a thing as a taxi. It's not that primitive here. I think they have them."

"Miranda."

Ignoring him, she glanced past the coffee trees to the street corner, pointed toward it. "In fact, I'll call one from that place over there. It's a restaurant. Imagine that."

"Miranda, please don't do this."

"Leave me alone, Parker."

His whole body froze behind the steering wheel as he watched her walk away. He should jump out, run after her. He should take her by the shoulders and blurt out the harsh truth. But he couldn't. There was still a chance he could save her that pain. The tiki bar would be closed, wouldn't it?

Almost to the restaurant, she spotted a taxi cruising down the road and hailed it. It pulled over to the side and she leaned in to speak to the driver. After a moment, she got inside.

Parker put the BMW in gear and followed the cab. Maybe he'd think of something more convincing on the way.

CHAPTER SEVENTEEN

Miranda was still shivering with anger when the cab pulled up to the curb in front of Coconut Rum.

What in the hell did Parker think he was doing? He was treating her like a child. Worse than when she started at the Agency. It was obvious he had no respect for her abilities at all. He was too arrogant. He thought he knew everything. Thought he knew how to handle a case better than anyone. She'd show him.

She'd find Keola's killer, see that he was locked up and give the all-knowing Wade Parker the boot.

The thought made her stomach sink, but she shook it off.

Reaching into her wallet for some cash, she handed it to the driver, glad the ride had only been a few blocks and didn't cost all she had. She climbed out of the cab with her suitcase and headed for the bar.

The wind rustled through palm fronds on the roof and the sun made the lacquer on the bamboo exterior glisten. On either side of the entrance two of those poles with the strangely carved faces stood guard. Just under the roof a set of unlit neon letters spelled out the establishment's name. Below that hung a red sign stating, "Sorry, We're Closed."

She ignored the sign and strode through the open entryway.

A bamboo divider separated the lobby from the main room. She set her suitcase down and stepped around the divider to take in the place.

Inside it was silent and dark except for the sunlight streaming in through open blinds along the far wall. The luscious view of the ocean from the tables must bring in a lot of business. The walls were decorated with painted wooden pineapples, starfish and, of course, coconuts. Thick support columns sported masks and grass skirts and leis.

Past the hostess stand, a pineapple-and-coconut fountain bordered with surfboards stood in a corner. It was dry. A nearby chalkboard boasted the best Bikini Martinis on the island. Over the bar a palm canopy featured coconut-breasted hula girls and a sign that declared, "Life is better in flip flops."

Just what you'd expect a place in Maui called Coconut Rum to look like.

She scanned the bar and saw no one until her gaze focused on a dark corner in the back. There stood a broad-shouldered, heavyset man in a bright blue flowered shirt. He had his back to her.

She stepped up to a barstool and took a seat.

After a moment, she realized the man was standing at a grill. From the counter beside it, he took a patty, unwrapped it and tossed it onto the hot surface. It began to cook, filling the noiseless place with its sizzle and the delicious aroma of seared beef.

Miranda cleared her throat. "Excuse me?"

It took a moment for him to answer. "We're closed," he called over his shoulder. She noted his voice was deep and bassy and lacked the Polynesian accent. That was curious.

"I know. I was wondering if I could speak with the owner."

"We've had a death in the family. We're not open for business." He picked up a spatula and turned the patty over. Steam rose over his head.

"I understand that."

"Then go away. Please."

A flash of sympathy flooded her, more powerful than before. "I'm sorry for your loss," she said, meaning it sincerely, though the words were trite and never did much good.

"Thank you. Now please leave. We won't be open again for...a while." His voice broke and took her heart along with it.

"Are you Pumehana?" she asked softly.

"Who wants to know?" He took the patty off the grill, laid it carefully on a bun that sat on a small plate, then turned off the heat. He turned to a small sink to wash his hands.

She had to say something that would get his attention, make him talk to her. She decided to go for blunt. "Pumehana, I'm the woman who found your son on the beach last night."

He turned off the water, dried his hands and turned to her. The shadows still hid his features. "What?"

"Late last night I went for a walk on the beach. I ended up at the blowhole about nine miles north of here. I saw something that didn't look right. I went in to see what it was and found a young man in the water. I thought he was alive, so I pulled him out. I tried to save him, give him CPR. But he was already gone. I called the police."

He stood there a while, as if he was having trouble taking in her words. He was probably still in denial. "Thank you for trying to help," he said at last, his voice a harsh croak. Something in it sounded vaguely familiar. He ran a hand through his hair. "But what do you want from me?"

She picked up a coaster from a stack and turned it over in her hands. "I'm a private investigator. I'm trying to find out what happened to Keola."

He took a step closer, but his face remained in shadow. "Aren't the police already doing that?" He sounded like he was from the mainland. The Midwest.

She flicked a nail against the surfboard on the cardboard coaster. "In my experience, sometimes the police don't act quickly enough. I know it seems strange, but I felt a sort of…connection with him."

He folded his arms. "You want money?"

"No. I just want to help, if I can." She put the coaster back on the stack.

"My son is gone. No one can help that." He stepped out of the shadows with a sad laugh.

That laugh. She knew that laugh.

She could see his face now. She sat stock-still and took in his features. As her mind processed them, the jolt she felt was like an electrified punch in the gut.

Round cheeks, round nose. Thick, wavy black hair that was now going gray at the temples. He'd grown it to his shoulders. His skin was dark and tan, and the furrows in his face were deeper than she remembered. He was the right height, too.

His body was still bulky, though more muscular. But other than that and a little aging, he was just like the picture she'd found in that attic in Chicago. And then she saw the mark on the side of his neck.

It was him, all right. Pumehana, her ass.

They stared at each other awhile, as her heart thumped away in her chest, aching more with each hammering beat. Her gaze fixated on the side of his neck. That birthmark. Like the one her baby Amy had been born with.

Like the one on Keola's neck—the one she'd forced out of her mind. Her stomach roiled. She felt dizzy. She wanted to throw up.

"Keola was…Polynesian," she managed to get out.

He frowned at her, as perplexed by her change in tone as by the question. "Part Samoan. Part Hawaiian."

"You're not either. Was he adopted?"

"No, my wife's part Samoan and part Hawaiian."

Wife, he had a wife.

"Why?" He studied her as if he hadn't seen her before.

She gripped the bar as every muscle in her body went taut. It felt like rats were gnawing the lining of her stomach. Oh my God, she thought. Keola was…her brother.

Half brother. Half brother, she told herself, forcing herself to breathe. As if that made a difference.

She thought of Parker and how he'd demanded, begged her not to come here. *He'd known.* She'd used the nickname—Pumehana. He'd known about that, too. No wonder he'd been acting so weird.

She took another couple of deep breaths and her mind started to clear. So far, "Pumehana" hadn't recognized her. If she hadn't found that picture of him recently, she might not have recognized him, either. And she'd grown up since he'd last seen her. Maybe she could get out of here before he figured out who she was.

But she couldn't drop the case. Not now. Brother. She needed to talk to Keola's brother.

"You have another son?" she forced herself to ask.

"Yes and a daughter. What do they have to do with anything?" He sounded defensive now.

A daughter, too? A half-sister. And the other son, another half-brother. The room started to swirl. Stubbornly she cleared her throat and pressed on. "The creative director at the luau where Keola worked said he was going to see his brother after the show."

He stared again, mulling over what that might mean. Then he took a step toward her and peered at her again. She eyed his thick, muscular arms. Strong arms that used to swing her up and into the air, making her giggle uncontrollably.

She watched his eyes study her. Blue eyes that had always had a smile in them, now red and swollen with grief. They moved over her face, her frame, then back to her face.

His expression turned to disbelief and suspicion. "Do I know you?"

She could lie. But he'd probably figure it out in a minute or two. She'd never thought he was stupid. Irresponsible and reckless, but not stupid. Might as well get it over with.

"Is Pumehana your real name?"

"No. It's a nickname. Why?"

"I'm sorry. I forgot to introduce myself." She took a deep, cleansing breath to steady herself and held out a hand. "My name is Miranda Steele."

She watched him stare at the gesture. He didn't take her hand. "My…last name is Steele."

She forced out the next words in a whispered croak. "I know, Dad."

His eyes went wild. "Miranda?"

"So you remember the little girl you left in Chicago?"

"Miranda?" he said again, coming closer. "Is it really you?" He opened his arms.

She held up her palms. The last thing she wanted was a hug. "I didn't come here for a reunion. I meant what I said. I'm here to investigate Keola's death."

He came around the bar and she saw he was in Bermuda shorts and flip-flops. The style fit him. "My little girl grew up to be a private investigator?" There was a smile on his face now. That big, gregarious smile she used to love so much, though it was still tinged with sorrow.

She turned her palms toward him before he could reach her. "I need to speak to your son. I was told he's staying with you."

Resignation in his eyes, he stopped and his face went grim again.

Parker sat staring at the "Sorry, We're Closed" sign, gripping the steering wheel of the BMW so tightly, he thought he might break it in two. He tried in vain to concentrate on the sound of the everlasting sea in his ears. The rising tide, the trade wind that was picking up.

He'd arrived just in time to watch Miranda slip into the bar. His heart filled with dread, he'd jumped out and rushed to the door.

At the threshold, he'd forced himself to stop. It was too late now.

She wouldn't want him barging into the place, trying to save her. She wouldn't understand. And perhaps she was right.

He had to stop smothering her. He had to stop trying to protect her. She didn't want that. She wanted to call her own shots, to be the one to deal with the consequences. He had to respect that.

He had gone back to the car. He'd wait for her. Perhaps she'd let him comfort her when she was finished in there. If she'd still speak to him.

But she'd gone in a good fifteen minutes ago. That couldn't bode well. It took all the strength he had to just sit here.

She was suffering. He could feel it. And he ached along with her and longed to hold her in his arms and soothe her pain. Perhaps he could stroll in, pretending to be a tourist in need of a drink. Lord knew he did need one. He considered going round the side to peer into a window.

Another urge came over him. The urge to rush into that tiki bar and give the man who'd deserted his wife as a child the beating of his life. But how could he attack a man who'd just lost his son? Who was now seeing his daughter after thirty years?

He studied the bar's exterior, wishing he could have bugged the place. The building was dead still. If he knew Miranda, there was no tearful reunion going on behind those walls. And yet there was no rumbling, no earth tremors. The bar's roof hadn't blown off. If he knew Miranda…she was sticking to the job. Even through this. Admiration for her swelled in his chest. What a woman she was.

He had to let her be. He had to let her handle this on her own. That's what any reasonable adult would want. He should have seen that from the start. He should have laid his cards out on the table to begin with. He never should have tried to find her father behind her back. He'd been too sure of himself. So certain he could make it all work. Blind to what might happen if something went awry.

In sum…he'd been wrong. And it might cost him dearly.

If she gave him another chance, if she came back to him, he'd never hide anything from her again. No more secrets.

He took his hands off the steering wheel and laid them in his lap, fisted. It was time he gave her the space and the respect she deserved.

And that meant all he could do right now…was wait.

CHAPTER EIGHTEEN

Miranda watched Edward Steele, a.k.a. Pumehana, ease his heavy body onto a barstool a few seats away from her. He looked like he didn't know what to make of the situation any more than she did.

"You want to talk to my son, Mikaele?" he said at last, still eyeing her in disbelief.

Her stomach felt like lead. She hadn't gotten a name. "Do you have any other sons?"

"No, just Mikaele and another daughter."

Once more, her mind reeled. Three children. Two half-brothers and a half-sister. And a step-mother. None of which she'd known existed. Anger bubbled up in her throat like witch's brew. Swallowing, she forced it back down. Suck it up.

"I think your son might know why Keola went to the blowhole last night."

Fresh pain washed over his face as he nodded. He straightened and called toward the back. "Mikaele. Your burger's getting cold."

Nothing stirred.

"I let him sleep here," he explained.

"I heard he was in trouble."

"He's a good kid, but he's fallen in with the wrong crowd. His mother won't let him back in the house. I don't know what we're going to do about school."

"School?"

"He's been suspended."

"How old is he?"

"Sixteen." He shook his head. "One son in trouble, the other dead. I guess I've never been much of a father." He eyed her sadly. "I don't suppose you'd contest that."

Miranda shifted her weight. Now there was an opportunity to let loose with all the anger and resentment that had built up inside her since she was five. Just when she thought she couldn't hold it in a second longer, a door opened in the back and a figure shuffled out.

The scrawny, bare-chested young man dressed in baggy swim trunks moved over to the counter and picked up the plate Pumehana had prepared for him. He turned to take it back to his room without a word.

"Mikaele, there's someone here to see you."

The boy glanced back without enthusiasm. His black hair was short in the back, but fell over his eyes in the front. "Who?"

"Come over here and see."

He half rolled his eyes as if it was all too much effort and sauntered toward the bar.

"This is, uh—"

"Miranda Parker of the Parker Investigative Agency. I'm looking into your brother's death." No need for messy explanations.

Her father stared at her again. "You're married?"

"Yes." *Yes, I married the boss*, she wanted to sneer at him.

Mikaele set down his plate and eyed her through strands of his dark hair. His face had the same angles hers had. "Why do you want to talk to me?" There was distrust in his tone.

She forced a pleasant look and softened her voice. "I heard Keola came to see you last night. Is that true?"

Wriggling with discomfort, he turned to his father. "Do I have to talk to her?"

"Answer the lady's question, son."

With a sullen look, the boy picked up his burger and took a big bite. To give himself time to think of a good reply, Miranda surmised. She was onto something here.

"Can I have a soda?"

The big man grunted, got up and came around the bar. He retrieved a glass from under a counter, pulled a few handles and filled it with ice and frothy liquid. He set the drink down in front of his son. "Now answer the question. Did you see Keola last night?"

Mikaele wiped his mouth with the back of his hand. "I don't know. Maybe."

Pumehana reached for the young man's shoulder. "You don't know if you saw your own brother before he died?"

Guilt washed over the boy's features. He looked as if he might cry. "Okay, I saw him. But only for a minute."

"Was it at the blowhole?" Miranda asked.

"Yeah, but I wasn't there very long." He pulled out of his father's grip.

"Where did you go after that?" his father demanded. "You haven't been hanging out with that Ha'aheo guy again, have you?"

"No, Dad," he sneered.

Instinct pricked at Miranda's heart. "Who's Ha'aheo?"

"Jonathan Ha'aheo," the father told her. "An older kid. He's in his early twenties, actually. He was arrested for causing a ruckus on Front Street with his buddies a month or so ago. He told the police Mikaele was with him that night."

"I didn't do anything."

Pumehana looked like he didn't buy that at all. "We'll make sure you won't."

The kid rolled his eyes.

Miranda scooted up to the bar and used her gentlest tone. "I'm not here to get you in any trouble, Mikaele. I just need information. What was Keola doing at the blowhole last night?"

His head down, the boy lifted and dropped his skinny shoulders. "I don't know. I think he was meeting someone."

"Who?"

"How should I know?"

"Because you were there." She gave the gentleness a bit of edge. "Maybe for longer than you want to admit? Did you have something to do with what happened to your brother?"

He glared at her. "No. Hell, no."

"Don't use that kind of language in here, son."

"It's a freaking bar, Dad. Why are you picking on me? I'm in mourning, too." Defiantly, he brushed back a strand of hair and Miranda spotted a mark on his arm.

She grabbed his wrist and turned it over.

"Hey, lady. What do you think you're doing?"

"What's this?" She pointed to the design.

It was a tattoo of a fiery torch with eerie, ghostly flames shooting from it. It reminded her of Keola's show last night.

"It's nothing. It's to honor my brother."

Pumehana stared at the mark in alarm. "When did you get that?"

"Last night." That much was true. The skin was still red and swollen around the edges.

"Is that what I think it is? Is that Huaka'i Po?"

Miranda frowned. "The Night Marchers?"

Pumehana nodded. "They're a local gang. They've taken the name of that ghost legend. We think Ha'aheo's involved with them."

Mikaele's eyes grew wide. He pulled out of Miranda's grip. "Leave me alone."

"Son, tell us what happened last night."

"I don't know what happened. And I don't have to talk to her. She's not the cops." With that, he turned and sprinted to the back of the building, leaving his burger unfinished and slamming a door behind him.

Pumehana ran a hand through his hair. "I don't know what I'm going to do with him."

"I'm sorry."

"I'm sorry for his behavior."

"I have enough to work with." She pushed off the barstool and stood. "Thank you for your time." She turned to go.

"Miranda."

She turned back. "What?"

"I'd like…"

She braced herself. "You'd like what?"

"I was wondering if you'd like to come by the house while you're here. You could meet…everyone."

Meet his new wife? His new family? "I don't think that would be a good idea."

"I'd really like them to meet you."

The boy never gave a hint of recognition just then. No doubt her father had never mentioned his *other* daughter to his new family.

So now she should just come waltzing over and get to know everyone just like that? All cozy and happy? Like nothing had ever happened? He had to be out of his mind.

She shook her head. "Sorry, Dad. I can't do that."

"Okay, maybe that was a bad idea. But maybe you could stop by here later? So we could talk again? I can hang around a while."

It was only her stubbornness that kept her from bursting into angry tears and cussing him out. She'd worshiped the man when she was a little girl. He was her whole world. And then one day, he was gone and her life had been hell ever since. How could he think a smile and a hug could undo all the damage he'd caused?

She drew in a breath and straightened her shoulders. "If I learn anything further about the case, I'll let you know. But I have no intention of having a relationship with you."

And with that, she turned and walked out.

"Miranda," she heard him call out as she picked up her suitcase from its spot in front of the bamboo divider. She ignored him and kept going.

She stepped out into the sunlight and blinked as her whole body began to throb with shock. How she'd kept it together this long, she had no idea. She had to get away from here.

A cab. She needed another cab. She scanned the street and spotted the shiny red BMW convertible parked along the curb. Parker sat behind the wheel watching her.

As if on automatic pilot, her legs moved to the car. "How long have you been here?" It couldn't have taken him more than a few minutes to tail her here.

"I pulled up just as you went inside."

"And you sat here all this while?"

He nodded. "That's right."

"You knew who the owner of that bar was, who Keola's father was, didn't you?"

"Guilty as charged." His eyes were full of pity and apology.

"You didn't rush in and try to rescue me?"

"No." His voice was more somber than she'd ever heard it. Sitting here and waiting must have been hard for him. He was used to running things. He studied her. He had to see how shaken she was. "Are you all right?"

She blew out a breath. "I've been better. But I'll handle it."

"Miranda, I'm sorry. So sorry."

"For?"

"For everything. For going behind your back to look for your father. For taking you here to Maui and pretending it was only for a honeymoon. For hiding the truth from you. Will you forgive me?"

She stared at him, her heart melting. No man had ever apologized to her before. Her life had been hell since her father abandoned her. She'd married an abusive jackass. She'd lost her only child. She'd spent years roaming the country, hopping from one meaningless job to another. And then she'd gone to Atlanta and met Parker.

And suddenly, her life had gotten better.

As if programmed, she lifted her suitcase and put it in the backseat. Then she opened the passenger door and got inside. "When you put it that way, I guess I'll have to."

Relief washed over his face. "Where to?" he asked, watching her snap her seatbelt with trembling hands.

"Any place but here."

CHAPTER NINETEEN

Parker steered them past the quaint shops on Front Street, past the storefronts and restaurants on Papalaua Street. After they'd turned onto the Honoapiilani Highway and were beyond the shopping centers and residences, Miranda put her hands to her face and wondered if she would ever stop shaking.

She turned her head inland, stared at the silver blue mountains in the distance and reminded herself this was far from over. She still had to find Keola's killer. She had to keep it together a little while longer.

"We have to go back to the blowhole," she murmured in a robotic tone.

"Why is that?"

"Keola's younger brother was there with him last night. We have to reexamine the scene in the light of that."

Parker glanced at her with shock. "You spoke with him at the bar?"

She nodded. "His name's Mikaele."

"What was he doing at the blowhole?"

"He wouldn't say. And he wasn't there long, if you can believe him. He's sixteen. A rebellious kid who's been kicked out of school."

"That's not good."

"No. He had a tattoo on the inside of his wrist. He said he got it last night. It looked fresh."

"What sort of tattoo?"

"A torch. All fiery and angry. He said it was in honor of his brother. But—Pumehana," she didn't know what else to call him, "thought it was a gang tat."

Parker noted the use of her father's nickname. They obviously hadn't made amends while she was in the bar. Not that he had expected it. "What gang?"

"The Night Marchers. Huaka'i Po. Remember the story? A hoard of dead island warriors carrying torches and wandering about, who can kill you with a single glance?"

"That's the gang's name?"

"That's what he said. Guess it makes them sound frightening and powerful. And now it sort of makes sense that Keola put the story in his show. He was sending out some kind of warning to protect his brother. He was popular enough that word of his new act would spread to any gang member in the area and let them know he knew who were they were. And he'd be watching. That's my theory, anyway."

"Quite plausible. A gang," Parker said darkly, as if he took the information personally. "Did the brother give you any names of the members?"

"No, but Pumehana knew about one. A twenty-something named Ha'aheo. He's got a record. Was arrested for stealing valuables from cars about a month ago. Sounds like it fits."

Parker gripped the steering wheel and forced himself to focus on the traffic in front of him before he ran off the road. He'd better pull over before he had a wreck. The highway ran along the beach front here. He spotted the park where he'd found Miranda this morning. He turned into the entrance.

There were more vehicles here now. People were eating lunch at picnic tables or playing on the beach. The second BMW was gone. He'd called the rental company earlier and they'd already fetched it. He pulled into a semi-secluded spot under a palm tree and turned off the engine.

Miranda glared at him, alarm in her eyes. "What's the matter?"

"What was the gang member's first name?"

"Jonathan. Jonathan Ha'aheo. You know the guy?"

The son. Fifteen years of private investigation forced his jaw to clamp shut, but his heart threw down a different gauntlet. No more secrets. He'd promised himself that. It was time he started living up to it.

The sound of the crashing waves in her ears, Miranda watched the tension lining Parker's face. Behind his gray eyes she could see he was reliving something. She knew it.

No wonder he knew so much about this place. "You've been here before, haven't you?"

It took awhile, but at last, he nodded. "Yes. It was my last big case before Sylvia became ill."

Sylvia. He paused again and Miranda braced herself. This sounded like it was going to be painful. Well, painful memories seemed to be on the menu today. "Go on."

"There was a young student at the Agency. Ryo Nakamura."

She knew that name. "The one who sent you those text messages?" The messages she'd found on his phone.

"Yes. He was one of the best graduates the Agency had. I wish he had stayed on, but he chose to return home and follow in his father's footsteps with the police."

Police? "Here in Lahaina?"

"Yes."

Parker knew someone on the police force here personally. She'd assumed Detective Nakamura was private. The punches just kept coming. "Do you know Balondo, too?"

"No."

That made it a little easier. "Okay. So you've got an in with the department here. That's a good thing. This Nakamura can help us cut through some red tape, right?"

"No. He's on leave as of yesterday."

"Leave?"

"He and his wife are in California. It's the first vacation he's had in four years."

"Oh." Just her luck. "So what about this Ha'aheo guy?"

She watched him steady himself, gather his thoughts. Parker never liked to talk about his past cases. Whether because of some distorted sense of humility or because they were too painful, she could never tell. But this time it was different. After a long moment, he drew in air and began.

"Four years ago Ryo was working a big case. A gang had taken root here in Lahaina and he was after the leader. The suspect was dealing drugs, running weapons, gaining power, growing more dangerous with every week that passed. Ryo felt the job was beyond the manpower he had. He couldn't get help from Oahu or Hawaii at the time, so he turned to me. I agreed to help. Judd came with me. After some investigation, we managed to track down the suspect in a ramshackle house on Kuhua Street."

She watched fierce storm clouds form on his face. She'd seen that look before one night when they dealt with a wife beater.

"We thought we had the house surrounded, but he climbed out a window. He ran across the street and over a fence into the yard of a warehouse. We followed him. I was the closest. I had him in my sights. I shouted to him to surrender. He didn't."

"He got away?"

Parker shook his head. "I went around a corner and he was standing there, a .38 in his hand. Aimed at my chest."

Miranda's stomach tightened. "What happened?"

"My weapon was already drawn, of course. I tried to talk him down, tell him the rest of the force would be here any second. We had the evidence to put him away for years and it would be wise to cooperate. But he just cussed at me and insulted my intelligence for siding with law enforcement."

Cussed? Insulted his intelligence? That had to be the cleaned up version.

"Ryo caught up with me. I heard him come around the corner behind me. I thought his appearance would convince the man I hadn't been bluffing. But the suspect panicked. I saw the flash of his gun. He turned it on Ryo. Before he could get off a shot, I took aim and fired. He went down. It all happened in a split second."

"Oh, my God. Did he—"

"Not right away. I hit him in the abdomen. An ambulance came and took him to the infirmary. He lived long enough to be taken to prison in Oahu. Eight days later, he died from the wound I gave him."

Miranda watched Parker inhale, exhale. He took such things to heart. "He was a criminal," she told him. "You stopped him from peddling drugs to young kids and Lord knows what else."

He nodded, as if he'd told himself that a thousand times. "Afterwards, I learned he had a wife. She committed suicide shortly after he died."

"No." Her voice was a whisper now.

"And there was an eighteen-year-old son. His grandfather would be taking care of him now. I'd made him an orphan. I sent a check to the family after I returned to Atlanta. It was never cashed. I would have followed up, but then Sylvia came home from the doctor with those bad test results." He drew a hand over his face.

Miranda's heart went out to him. She knew Parker had been through hell back then. "Who was he?"

"The suspect? His name was Robert Ha'aheo."

She stared at him, her stomach quivering at the name. "You think...he was the father of Jonathan Ha'aheo? That Jonathan was the eighteen-year-old son?"

The lines in Parker's face deepened. "Yes. That was the son's name. And it sounds like he's following in his father's footsteps."

All the more reason to act. "We need to go the blowhole, Parker. We need to get inside that sea cave we saw."

"Because?"

"Because of what you said. Contraband. There's no telling what we might find in there."

Parker considered the idea. "That sea cave might not have a thing to do with Keola's death."

But she'd felt something when she'd climbed over that volcanic cliff and stared at that cave. The sensation had been unmistakable. The same one she'd felt just before she'd found Keola's body. She wondered for an instant if she were psychic or something. But her strange feelings didn't prove anything either.

She lifted a shoulder. "You're right. On the other hand, that whole area could be where the Night Marchers conduct business. It's remote. At night it's pretty secluded. We won't know anything more until we get inside."

Parker rubbed his chin, shaking off the bad memories of the past. It was part of the job, after all. He stared out at the ocean. She followed his gaze.

The waves were rough now, angrier. The wind was kicking up sand and strong enough to blow her hair away from her face.

"We'd need a boat to get inside the cave."

Miranda waved a hand. "Ought to be easy for you to get one."

Parker was still hesitant. "Even if we did find evidence of gang activity in the cave, it would hardly prove Jonathan killed Keola."

She listened to the laughter of children playing on the beach. A beach ball flew into the air. Several swimmers were out on the water. Someone was trying to tame an obstinate wave with a surfboard. "You never know. There could be some sort of evidence."

"There was no murder weapon."

"So?"

"So that means an outside chance of finding circumstantial evidence."

She frowned, frustrated by his skepticism. But he sounded more convinced Keola was murdered now that a gang member—one whose background he knew—might be involved. "Circumstantial evidence is better than none. Besides, Mikaele saw his brother at the blowhole last night. He said Keola was waiting for someone."

"Will he testify to that in court?"

She blew out a breath. "Probably not. I had a hard time getting that much out of him. But we're wasting time. How fast can you get that boat? You know how to drive one, don't you?"

"I do, but it might not be a good idea right now."

"Why not?"

"With the rising tide and the trade winds, it could be dangerous."

"I'm not afraid of a little danger. Are you?"

He gave her a wry look. "If we drown ourselves we won't be much good in helping to find Keola's killer."

She had to smile at that. He did believe her. Point taken. She knew enough about boats to know you had to be careful or you could end up in Davy Jones' Locker. "Okay. When is a good time?"

"The tide won't be low again until it's dark. Early in the morning is our best bet. Before six."

"Long time to wait," she sighed.

He turned to her and brushed back her hair. "You must be exhausted after what you've been through."

His sudden touch made her flinch. He put his hand down.

She thought about seeing her father again after all these years. Learning he had a family she wasn't a part of. Discovering Keola was her own brother. As was Mikaele and the unknown young woman who was his sister. It felt like her whole world was tumbling down around her.

She rubbed her face. "Yeah, I am exhausted. But I need to work off these bad feelings."

"There's a fitness center at the hotel." There was tenderness and understanding in his voice.

"Fitness center." Not the same as going to that sea cave, but it might do the trick. "Do they have gloves and punching bags?"

Parker gave her an apologetic frown. "I think they lean more toward Pilates and Zumba classes. Elliptical bikes?"

She shook her head. "I need to hit something."

"We could spar in the room."

Go back to the hotel with him? To the room she'd walked out of? But right now, that seemed like years ago. Right now, she had a boiling vat of emotion churning inside her. She had to do something or she'd go stark raving mad.

She'd risk it. "You're on."

CHAPTER TWENTY

By the time she stepped into the tastefully decorated island honeymoon suite with Parker carrying her suitcase behind her, Miranda's temples were throbbing so hard, she thought her head might erupt and start spewing lava down her face.

It wasn't just tension or the pounding concussion flaring up. It was anger. A dark, purple rage of fury that was like a rabid leopard clawing her insides, desperate to get out.

Parker set her case in the corner. "Are you sure you want to do this? You're not fully recovered from—"

She glared at him with a growl. "You chicken, Parker?"

His face went dark. "Not at all." He moved to the coffee table, pushed it toward the glass doors, then headed for the chocolate-and-rattan sofa. "We should try to find something for gloves."

She couldn't wait that long. She had to do something. Taking two long strides, she spun and threw up her leg in a roundhouse kick.

Parker barely had time to snatch a cushion off the couch to pad his chest before her foot landed square against a dark brown palm tree on the fabric with a whoof.

Staggering a bit, he couldn't help but grin. "You've improved since the last time we did this."

"Yeah, well my *fudoshin*'s pretty off today."

That day they had first sparred in the Agency gym, he'd accused her of letting her emotions take over when she fought. Since then, she'd learned to control her feelings, channel them when she needed them. But not today. Today they were just as wild as a tsunami. Going with the tide, she came at him again, landed a sharp right jab that bent the palm tree's fabric fronds into themselves.

Impressed, Parker absorbed the shock and shuffled to the left. "Excellent move."

His praise used to mean everything to her, but just now it didn't do a thing to soothe the pain.

Prancing past the sofa to pursue him, she jabbed at the cushion again. "How could he do that? How could he abandon us and start another family?"

Parker held the pillow steady, pivoting away from her. They danced past the chairs, the kitchen area, the hallway, and ended up at the couch again.

Right, left, right. She slugged as hard as she could, but it wasn't enough. "He went halfway around the globe to get away from me and my mother," she shouted, still walloping the poor, defenseless cushion.

The tears started now. Angry tears. Outraged tears. She tried to hold them back, but the pain and humiliation washed over her. Like what she used to feel at Leon's hands.

Suddenly she stopped swinging as a revelation hit her.

Leon had made her feel worthless. Every blow he'd given her had made her feel more and more worthless. For years she'd just let him. She'd done nothing about it. Nothing at all because…she'd been just as worthless to her father.

Well, she thought, wiping her cheek with the back of her hand. Wouldn't Dr. Wingate be proud of her for coming up with that? But when she remembered her father reaching out, trying to hug her today, she wanted to tear something apart again. "And now he wants to pretend he's happy to see me? How dare he?"

Parker stood holding the cushion, quietly watching her meltdown. "People can have a change of heart."

"Change of heart, my ass," she growled. "Why did he leave me with her? I was no more to my mother than a servant. I hate him, Parker. I know I shouldn't, but I can't help it. I truly hate him." She let go and pummeled the cushion again with both fists.

"I know, I know." Parker gritted his teeth. Her punches were like bullets shooting straight to his chest. It was because of him she was in such pain. Because he'd thought he knew what was best for her. He wished he could turn back the clock. Yet he doubted he'd have taken a different course. Perhaps it was Fate.

Exhausted, she finally stopped.

Miranda put her burning knuckles to her face. She thought of the fury and bitterness that drove her after she left Leon. The long hours of martial arts training. The low-level construction jobs she'd taken to make herself strong. To show up men. The bar fights she used to get into.

What had she been trying to prove? That she was good enough? That her father should have loved her? But he hadn't. Not enough to stay. She stood there, grinding her teeth, fighting back another round of tears. She hated to cry and seeing her father again had turned her into a blubbering waterfall.

"Finished?" Parker asked, his low voice almost an echo in her head.

She looked up and gazed into those steady gray eyes. That rich mane of salt-and-pepper hair, that incredible physique. She thought of that day in the company gym when she'd gotten her first good lead. The day she'd first sparred with him in the ring. The day she got her first kiss from him. She remembered the fire of it. The thrill of it. The desire it inflamed.

She studied his mouth. Warm and luscious and inviting.

And then she couldn't help herself. She tore the cushion out of his hands, grabbed his face and pulled him to her.

Her lips slammed against his in a wild, ravenous frenzy. He stumbled back, fell toward the couch and caught himself, with her on top of him, their lips still locked.

He pulled away for a breath. "Lord, how I've missed you."

"Me, too."

She was about to attack him again, but he beat her to it. He came at her, taking the lead, his mouth eager and hot, devouring her with the hunger of a starving man. He reached around her. They slipped, tumbled off the couch and onto the teal Berber carpet.

They rolled.

Over and over until they hit a chair against the opposite wall. He pivoted them back and they ended up somewhere in the middle of the room.

His hands were all over her now, touching, stroking, probing. Arms, sides, breasts. Oh, yes, breasts.

"Don't stop," she grasped, breaking from his mouth for another instant.

"Don't worry, I won't." He took a quick breath and plunged back in.

Their tongues entangled, he tugged at her top, got it to her ribs. She jerked his polo shirt off him, got stuck at his arms.

He broke away to raise his torso, pull his shirt over his head, and hurl it into the hall. She echoed his movements. Raising herself on one elbow, she yanked one arm out of her blouse, then the other. She tossed the pale blue garment into the air.

Her gaze fixated on the designer logo on the fly of his jeans. She went for it like a shark goes for a lure. Her fingers fumbled at the waistband while he struggled to find the zipper of her khaki dress slacks.

"Why don't they put them in the front?" he grumbled.

"You're the one who picked this outfit."

It seemed like an hour, but at last, both pairs of pants went flying. They hit the sofa, making a nice throw to decorate its arm.

And now for the underwear.

That didn't take as long. In two seconds, her bra was off and soaring toward the kitchen, another second and his briefs hit the glass door to the patio and slid behind the coffee table.

For a long moment, he eyed her panties greedily. Then in one swift move, he shoved them down past her knees and sank his head between her legs.

She yelped in surprise, then delight, as his tongue went to work on the soft folds of her flesh, driving her well past sanity.

Pleasure, unbearable pleasure, rippled through her. She tried to hold back, but he was too skilled, too urgent. Release shuddered through her, making her whole body quake with bliss.

It had barely subsided when, he rose looking hungrier than ever. He hovered over her for a long moment, then plunged inside her.

Parker watched her blue eyes flash with surprise and desire and sensation. He loved her. Lord, how he loved her. He didn't dare say it now, for fear it would break the spell of this magic that had come over her. He closed his eyes and groaned aloud as he buried himself in that soft, sweet cocoon of flesh, willing this feeling to last forever.

He had wealth and power and a thousand PI tricks up his sleeve, but he was powerless when it came to Miranda Steele. He could never control her. Never rein her in. Not that he really wanted to. But he'd find a way to make her stay with him, even if he had to make love to her forever.

Not a bad idea.

Her breath coming in ragged pants, Miranda surrendered her body to Parker's powerful, greedy thrusts. His thighs pumped against her, peaking her passion, making her brain giddy, coaxing lusty groans out of her that mingled with his. Sweaty and throbbing, she let the sensation consume her. And felt only the tiniest twinge of guilt.

Nothing wrong with this, she told herself, as the pleasure mounted even higher.

They were married, after all. And deep down she knew, even if they couldn't stay married, even if it wasn't in the cards for them, she would always want him like this, always need him, always love him.

Once more her body convulsed. Parker uttered a deep, guttural growl and she cried out along with him as she felt his release.

Feeling suspended in air, she clung to his shoulders, digging in as if she were drowning in emotion.

She was.

CHAPTER TWENTY-ONE

They must have fallen asleep.

Miranda opened her eyes to a golden strand of light streaming in through the glass doors. The sun was setting.

She craned her neck and spotted her sports bra hanging over the marble counter of the kitchen area. "Hope the maid didn't come in to clean while we were out."

Parker stirred, lifted his head. "If she did, she took one look at this scene and left. Nothing's been touched."

He had an eye for that sort of thing. It took some effort to get up, and Miranda discovered Berber burns on her butt as she stretched and padded across the carpet to fetch the bra and pull it over her head. She turned back in time to see Parker rise in one graceful move.

The full-length view of that chiseled physique made her think of a Greek god. Not to mention going another round with him on the floor. Maybe not quite a Greek god. There was that scar along his abdomen and another on his right shoulder blade. But to her mind, those marks only made him more perfect. Besides, she had a few of her own.

Rubbing her fingers over the ones on her chest, she thought of Keola. Her brother. Time to get back to business. "How can we find this Jonathan Ha'aheo?"

Parker studied her a moment, as if assessing the state of her emotions. "Let's get cleaned up and do some research."

No argument. Glad he'd come over to her way of thinking, she nodded. "Sounds good."

They took a quick shower—separately to keep from getting distracted—then threw on underwear, jeans and T-shirts. Miranda picked up the clothes in the living room while Parker called room service for a very late lunch and set up his laptop on the coffee table, which was now back in its rightful place.

It didn't take long for the food to arrive, and they munched hibachi chicken sandwiches with avocado and Jack cheese and drank strong cups of the local Kona coffee while Parker went to work.

Miranda sat on the sofa and peered over his shoulder, watching him zip through websites and search screens. Some of his methodology didn't seem completely kosher but that didn't bother her. She was used to his tricks and they often came in handy.

After about half an hour, he gave a low chuckle. "Our suspect does indeed have a record."

"Yes, he does." Excited, Miranda scooted forward and studied the text on the screen. "Two DUIs and a misdemeanor for disturbing the peace."

"It seems he and a group of young men were fighting and harassing tourists on Front Street one night about a month ago. He spent only a night in jail for that."

"Not a model citizen, but not a hardened criminal, either. At least on paper."

Parker flipped to a new page. "And there are several recent police reports of vehicles that were broken into."

"Looks like the vehicles were rented by tourists."

"Yes. And the thieves took personal property from them but not the cars themselves."

"Harder to prove? Lesser sentence?" she offered.

"Possibly. None of the incidents are linked to Ha'aheo, though."

Miranda eyed him with suspicion. "Did you get those reports from where I think you got them?"

His lip turned up in a cocky smirk. "Ryo won't mind. Much."

"O—kay." Only Wade Parker could hack into a police database with so much self-confidence.

Ignoring the surge of admiration flushing her face, she leaned over and read the list of items reported missing from the cars. GPSs, watches, tickets to a local football game, cash, iPads, a laptop, a gym bag, jewelry. "Why do people leave those things in their cars?"

"They feel safe, I suppose. They have a right to."

That didn't make it a smart move. Rights and reality were two different things in her experience. "Those break-ins happened near here, didn't they?"

He scrolled through the summary. "All around the local luxury resorts."

"That sounds fishy. Like somebody's got people working for him, keeping tabs on the tourists in those hotels and what kind of stuff they've got."

"And who are likely to leave it in their cars."

"Some folks like to brag about what they have. Valets could watch out for the careless guests. Heck, valets could swipe the goods."

"Mm-hmm."

"You said you know where Ha'aheo lives?"

Parker brought up another document on the screen and scanned it. "He gave the address I know when he was arrested. His father's house. I assume he's still there."

Unless he lied. Miranda studied the screen and committed the address to memory. Might come in handy. "Wouldn't be hard to tail him. Maybe catch him going to a heist?"

"It would be quicker to flush him out." Parker sat back and rubbed a knuckle across his chin. "We could set a trap."

"What kind of a trap?"

Deep in thought, he rose and made his way to the bedroom. Wondering what he was up to, Miranda swallowed her last mouthful of coffee and followed.

She found him digging in a side pocket of his suitcase.

"I didn't think we'd have a need for these, but I brought them along just in case." He produced a small velvet pouch, opened it and drew out a long strand of pearls, accented with tiny diamonds.

"Whoa, Parker." Miranda shook her head at him. "Just in case?"

"In case we decided to take a side trip to Honolulu for the ballet or to Oahu for dinner at Benihana's."

Her eyebrow almost rose off her head.

"They're not real, of course. I wouldn't travel with genuine jewels."

That was a relief. Then she grinned. "But Ha'aheo doesn't have to know that."

"No, he doesn't." He put them back into the velvet pouch. "We'll take these downstairs to the concierge for safekeeping. If Ha'aheo has a contact he's working with in the Ashford-Grand, he'll know about them in short order."

She scratched at her hair. "Then what? He wouldn't steal them right out of the safe. The hotel would be liable. And it would be pretty easy to prove."

He gave her a sexy wink. "I have a plan up my sleeve. Would you like to go out for a drive?"

Now she was intrigued. "Sure."

With the pearls tucked safely in the pocket of Parker's jeans, they headed down to the concierge.

She had to admire Parker's style as she watched him make inquires about the hotel safe with just the right amount of tourist naivety. He asked how secure it was and explained that he had some rather valuable pearls he was taking with him into town where he planned to meet a local dealer who could appraise them. He then informed the clerk that he and his new bride were going to do a little shopping on Front Street, then meet the dealer at the Beach Café.

Parker leaned on the counter with a casual air. "I hear the beef satay is particularly good there."

The fawning clerk smiled and nodded. "At Beach Café? Oh, yes, Mr. Parker. It's excellent."

Dressed in the red-and-gold Aloha shirt that was the uniform for Ashford-Grand employees, the guy was short, young and bony. Asian. He had black hair and dark eyes that took in way too much, in Miranda's opinion. He looked barely twenty as he smiled under a thin mustache—that he must have been able to grow only yesterday—over an equally thin pair of lips.

Miranda didn't like that grin. Nonchalantly she glanced at his nametag. Cho.

"Now, I don't expect to make a sale tonight. You know, never accept the first offer." Parker winked as if he were letting Cho in on a business secret. "So I'll be storing the necklace in your safe when we return. Is that acceptable?"

Again the clerk smiled and nodded. "Whatever you wish, sir. I'm on duty all night. I'll see to it myself that your valuables are well taken care of."

"Thank you. That's a great relief." Parker laid a hand over his heart as if Cho had just done him a huge favor. "Uh, while we're out, they'll be all right locked in the glove compartment of my BMW until we meet with the appraiser, won't they?"

Cho gave him another oily grin. "Oh, they should be just fine, Mr. Parker. This is a very safe area."

Taking her cue from Parker, Miranda yawned and wrapped her arm around his, playing the giddy, spoiled wife, too interested in being wined and dined to care about the details of "business." "C'mon honey," she pouted. "You promised me a new dress and dinner."

Parker chuckled and patted her hand. "Very well, dear. Thank you again for your help," he said to Cho. "I'll bring the pearls back in a few hours, then."

"You're very welcome, Mr. Parker. I'll be waiting."

She just bet he would.

Two hours later they were sipping Chi Chi's on the outdoor patio of Beach Café and keeping a watchful eye on the BMW, which was parked in a side alleyway just around the corner. To a casual observer, it looked like they couldn't see it and weren't paying attention to it at all. But one shady move from a thief and they'd both be over the guardrail and at the car in two seconds flat.

Except there hadn't been a move.

Miranda leaned over her dessert menu and whispered. "There hasn't been a nibble."

"Patience," Parker murmured.

"We strolled up and down Front Street three times and nobody made a move for the glove compartment."

"It was a bit crowded, but you have a point."

"Something doesn't feel right about this, Parker."

He considered that a moment. "We could be missing something. Perhaps that wasn't the clerk who's working with our suspect."

"He looked pretty shady to me." If she wasn't reading into those overanxious grins.

"It may take some time for the information to trickle down—or up—to the person giving the orders."

"Ha'aheo."

"Or an underling he's delegated that power to." He took a sip of his coffee, avoiding the cocktail. It was just for show, since he was driving.

"Do you think Ha'aheo's that organized?" Miranda wondered.

"It's hard to tell at this point."

She drummed her fingers on the table. "It's getting late. Didn't you say we have to get up early tomorrow?"

"If you still want to check out that sea cave." His doubtful expression said he still wasn't sure the trip was worth the risk.

She caught his drift. "You don't think we'll find anything, do you?"

"I can't say. But if that is Jonathan's lair, he also may pay a visit to it early in the morning." He reached for the check. "Did you want anything else?"

She shook her head. The beef satay was good, but it was playing havoc with the nerves in her stomach. "Ha'aheo won't have your pearls to stash in the cave, but maybe his cohorts are busy hitting other cars tonight and he'll be carrying a big haul. Maybe we'll catch him in the act."

"That would be fortuitous."

"Yeah, wouldn't it, though?"

"And dangerous."

She closed her menu. "So we'd better get some shuteye. Want to be alert."

"Very well." He laid several bills on the table and rose. "We can continue this ruse tomorrow."

"If we still need to." She swallowed the last bit of vodka and got to her feet.

CHAPTER TWENTY-TWO

He opened the small fridge and peered inside, ignoring the food stains and the mold growing in the cheap containers. One freaking bottle of beer left? That was all? Shit. That was what happened when you lived with a drunk. He grabbed it and closed the door.

He opened the lid and leaned against the counter where the cheese-and-mustard sandwich he'd just made himself sat on a cheap paper plate. He ran the bottle over his brow. The coolness was a relief after eight hours at that lousy carwash. He hated coming home to this sweltering box. He liked it better along the beach.

The sound of the TV coming from the living room set his nerves on edge. As did the mangy yellow cat rubbing against his leg.

He kicked it off. "Go away, Bugs."

He held the bottle to his lips, about to take a swig when he heard the flop, flop of bedroom slippers in the hallway. The old man shuffled into the cramped little kitchen.

He was in his twenty-four-seven bathrobe and pajamas. Strands of stringy gray hair hung down over his dark, gnarled face and the stubble he rarely shaved. As usual, he smelled of BO and booze.

Those mean, beady eyes narrowed on him. "Give me that." He reached for the beer and jerked it out of his hand.

"Hey."

"Hey, what?"

Jonathan licked his dry lips as he watched his grandfather gulp down half the bottle. "Go easy. That's the last one."

He let out a loud belch and wiped his mouth with his sleeve. "Then you'll have to go buy me some more." He looked at the counter. "Is that for me?" He took the sandwich, too.

"That's mine." It was the last piece of cheese. Couldn't expect the old souse to go shopping.

"Not anymore."

"Give it to me." He took a step toward the old man, but he raised a threatening arm that halted him.

He swore if that old man backhanded him one more time, he might end up in a blowhole. And this time he'd make sure the body wouldn't be found.

He watched the old man chomp down on the sandwich, crumbs dropping onto the floor. Bugs lapped them up right away.

He was sick of living in this hellhole with his grandfather. But he'd get out of here one day soon. He had a plan. He already had his contact in Oahu and his first big delivery.

And once he was rich and powerful, he'd move to a nice house on the beach with A/C and a lanai with an ocean view where he could feel the tradewinds against his face. He'd leave the old man here to fend for himself.

His grandfather's sneer brought him out of his thoughts. The old man's thin lips parted showing those crooked, yellow teeth. "You no count son of a bitch. You're no better than your father was. Make yourself useful and do those dishes." Taking the food and the beer, he waddled back to the living room. Probably to jack off to a rerun of *Baywatch*.

He turned and stared at the grimy sink. Dishes, hell. He bent over, picked up the mangy cat and set the thing on the counter. He smirked as he watched the greedy bastard start licking the food off the plates. Bugs could take care of the dishes.

He grabbed a bag of chips from the cabinet and headed back to his room. He had important work to do.

After locking the door behind him, he stood and stared into space. It was a small room, but it was his. He had good sheets on the bed that he kept neatly made, a desk with a nice laptop he'd traded for the one Cho had taken from the Ashton-Grand, his workout equipment that he used religiously. He'd always kept things tidy and clean in here, but just now, as the memory of this morning came back to him, he had the urge to tear the room apart in a fit of rage.

He tossed the bag of chips on the desk and dug his fingers into his scalp.

He was getting too close. Wade Parker was getting too close. He'd been at the blowhole today.

Calm down. Think.

He recycled his anger into jogging in place for a few minutes, then lay down on the weight bench and picked up the bar to do his reps as he did every evening. He could press two hundred fifty now. His strength made him powerful.

Exhaling slowly, he lifted the bar and focused his mind.

He'd cruised by the site this morning to see if the cops were still there and spotted that fancy red BMW parked on the side of the road with the plates he recognized. He had to stop. He had to get out and see what was going on. His heart pounding, he hid behind a ridge and peeked over it. There was Parker and some frizzy-headed woman poking around the blowhole.

His place.

He'd watched them as long as he'd dared. Good thing. He saw them go to the other side and look over the opposite cliff. They'd seen his sea cave.

He'd panicked then, hurried back to his car, went to work. It was best to act normal, he'd told himself. Not vary his routine. Not raise any suspicions. But the question had pounded in his brain with every fender he'd buffed during his endless shift.

Did Wade Parker know...everything?

He was overreacting, he told himself. There'd been nothing on the news about Keola's death today. Nothing about any stolen goods or anything else. If Parker knew something, the cops would be knocking at the door.

The rap music ringtone on his cell sounded. It was Cho. He put down the bar, sat up to answer. "Yeah?"

"You were right. He's here."

Of course, he was right. He'd looked up the BMW's license plate in a database and learned it was owned by a local rental company. A few inquiries at the office had told him Parker was staying at the Ashford-Grand resort. Just where a stinking rich *haole* would stay.

"He's got a woman with him," Cho chuckled. "His wife. But she goes by the name Steele. Miranda Steele."

He smiled. Cho had done good work. "What's the room number?"

Cho rattled it off. He grabbed a notepad and pen off the desk, jotted it down. He already had Parker's cell number from his online search.

"And guess what?" Cho said. "They went out tonight and took a little trifle with them. Pearls. Diamonds."

His mouth watered. You didn't usually get really good high-end jewels from tourists. They mostly brought casual things along with their electronic toys.

"Be easy to nab. The dumb *haole* is leaving it in the glove compartment of his convertible. He asked me if it was safe. I told him 'sure.'" Cho snorted a laugh. "You still there?"

"I'm here." His mind was buzzing with excitement. So many ways to play it. It was tempting to rob the bastard blind. But that wouldn't be enough. Not nearly enough.

"I can boost the goods when they come back. They're in town shopping and seeing an appraiser. Or I can have Garcia hit them now." Garcia was a valet at the Ashton-Grand who'd proven to be a loyal underling with nimble fingers.

"Don't do anything." He couldn't give Parker a hint of his operation. Wait. "Did you say he asked you if it would be safe in his glove compartment?"

"Sure did, the dumb shit."

He didn't know a lot about him, but he knew Wade Parker was no dumb shit. He smelled a set up.

"Want me to hit their room while they're out for some extra bread?"

"Didn't you hear me? I said don't do anything." He had to think. Parker had been at the blowhole. He'd seen the sea cave. Did he suspect the truth about Keola? Wait a minute. That's why the cops weren't after him. There wasn't enough proof. Parker was setting him up to get it. That freaking sonofabitch.

But that meant there was still time to strike first. Visions of a plan came to him. A kidnapping in that fancy hotel room. Take the wife, too. Play with her a little until he got rid of them both.

He'd need help. Was Cho up to that? What to do with the bodies? No blowholes this time. He'd cruise out in his boat and dump them deep in the ocean himself.

He snapped out of his thoughts. Cho was babbling like a moron.

"Okay, okay, man. You know you can trust me."

Trust him? As far as he could any man working for him. Cho was a follower, but you could never be sure.

"I look up to you. You know what you're doing, man."

Now he was kissing his ass. "Don't. Do. Anything," he repeated in a low, raspy tone he knew would strike fear in the toady's heart. "Don't boost a toothpick. Until I give you the word, you're a model citizen. Understand?"

"Yeah. Sure, man. I got it." There was a pause. "What about my take for this week?"

Greedy bastard. He'd be losing money, too.

"Don't worry. I'll cover it." He'd have to pay him out of his stash. It was too risky to deal for money right now.

"Sure. Whatever you say." He heard the resentment in his tone. He might have to cut Cho lose. But that could lead to other problems. He had to take care of Parker first.

"Just stay clean until you hear from me." He disconnected and stared off into space.

It would be okay. He'd have enough to pay double for the loss after he started selling a little of the stuff in that sea cave. He just had to bide his time.

But first, Parker.

He'd be coming back. He'd be nosing around his place again. Telling the cops what he found. Had to take care of him soon.

He thought of his father, dying alone in prison from the bullet wound Parker gave him. He thought of his mother, her wrists slit and bleeding all over the bathroom where he'd found her. He'd sworn then to get back at Wade Parker. And now he would.

It was Fate. Destiny. His Destiny.

He'd already killed. Killing again wouldn't be so hard. He just had to cover his tracks.

CHAPTER TWENTY-THREE

Before the crack of dawn the next morning, Miranda came out of the oblivion of sleep to a low, irritating chirping sound.

Whoever invented that silly ringtone ought to be horsewhipped. She opened her eyes and found her limbs entangled with Parker's like a ballpark pretzel.

Trying not to disturb him, she extracted a leg, an arm. Then she saw he was already awake.

"Is that Wendy texting you?" he wanted to know.

"Who else?" She rolled over and grabbed the phone from the nightstand and swiped the screen. Sure enough. Three messages.

OMG!!! Mackenzie won the Regional!!! First place!!! She's the most amazing person I know.

Gee thanks, kid.

First place!!! Can you believe it? I'm tweeting about it every five minutes.

Yep, she could believe it.

Kaylee's giving Mackenzie a party when she gets home. She says there'll be boys, but Jordan says her father won't let her.

Groaning, Miranda indulged herself by shaking the phone. "Why can't she obsess over one of these other girls?"

"Other girls?" Parker got up and went to the closet.

"Kaylee and Jordan. Her new schoolmates. They seem nice." She hoped they were. "I'm just afraid Wendy's getting fixated on Mackenzie Chatham."

Parker pulled on a chocolate brown tank top that deliciously set off the well-shaped muscles that formed his chest and arms. "Oliver Chatham's daughter?"

She didn't know the man's first name. "You mean as in Chatham, Grayson, and McFee?" That was the law firm where Parker's surrogate son, Antonio Estavez worked.

"That's the Oliver Chatham I know." He slipped into an interestingly tight pair of indigo jeans. Perfect for boating, but she still couldn't get used to the casual look on him.

"Guess she's his daughter. Mackenzie just won a figure skating contest. A Regional."

"Impressive."

"Wendy's beside herself."

"Girls do have strong emotions at that age."

"Yeah, but worshiping a peer can't be healthy. Mackenzie's good. Really good. I saw her at the rink a couple of times. No doubt she deserves the awards she's winning."

"But?"

"But…I don't know. She's such a stuck up little snot. She treats Wendy like crap."

Parker came over to the bed, concern on his handsome features. He sat down next to her. "Are you worried this is like last time?"

When Miranda first came to Atlanta, she discovered Wendy had been mixed up in some very bad business. Partly because of the way some nasty schoolmates had been treating her.

"No. Mackenzie doesn't snub Wendy."

"Is she mean to her?"

"Not mean exactly. On the outside, she's nice. But she uses Wendy. Makes her do menial things for her like Wendy's her personal slave or something. Now she's got her cleaning her skates and Wendy acts like it's an honor. She adores the kid. It's not good."

His brow knit, Parker considered the situation. "Perhaps you could talk to Iris when we get home."

Miranda huffed out a breath. "Iris won't listen to me. I'm not supposed to even be in contact with Wendy."

That produced a deeper frown from Parker. "That woman has always irked me." He didn't like Wendy's mother or her golf pro father. "When is Shelby coming back?"

"Who knows? Wendy hasn't mentioned him in a while." Miranda was pretty sure Iris and Shelby's relationship was on the rocks again.

"Maybe I'll have a word with him when he's back in town."

"Yeah, he'll just jump at the chance to see you." Parker almost put Shelby Van Aarle in prison once. She sighed in frustration. "I don't know. It's like Mackenzie knows how good she is and thinks the other girls should worship her. That kid really needs to be taken down a notch or two."

"And are you the one to do that?"

If Mackenzie were an adult, she wouldn't hesitate. But she was a kid. And Wendy wasn't her child. "Maybe not."

Parker patted her knee and got to his feet. "We can discuss it more later. We need to get going if we're going to see that cave." He disappeared into the next room. To make coffee, she hoped.

She was exhausted. If only she could sleep just a few more minutes. Or hours. But the memory of pulling her brother out of that blowhole came back to her. She'd deal with Wendy later.

Rubbing her eyes, she pulled back the covers and forced her body up as she stole a glance at the clock. Four thirty. Geez Louise.

She plodded over to her suitcase, which Parker had placed on a folding rack, and searched for something appropriate to wear. She came up with an ash-colored tank top and an old pair of black jeans. That ought to provide some camouflage.

Thinking how funny it was that Parker had never picked out her casual clothes, she pulled them on, yanked on her sneakers. After whacking at her hair with a brush a few times, doing little good, she shuffled through the living room to the marble kitchen counter and plopped down on a stool. Something smelled awfully good here.

"Coffee?" she yawned.

"At your service." He handed her a cup.

Grateful, she held it in both hands and swallowed a gulp, savoring the rich flavor. Her gaze strayed to the front door. A large carrying case sat at the ready.

"What's that?"

"Equipment for our little excursion this morning." He slid a plate of scrambled eggs across to her, put a fork in her hand. Slices of jalapeños lined the side of the dish. He knew her way too well.

"When did you get it?"

"Last night after you went to bed." He set a bottle of hot sauce beside her plate. "You need to eat. Our trip will be strenuous."

Not to mention risky. She loved his talent for understatement. But he was right. "Okay." She reached for the sauce, doused her eggs and dug in.

Forty minutes later they were cutting through the waves along the Lahaina shoreline in a hard bottom inflatable motorboat—the only rig available that Parker thought would fit in the cave.

Miranda could only imagine how much he had to shell out for it.

Pulling her hair out of her face, she watched the sun coming up over the blue lava mountains in the distance, above a thick grove of palm trees. To the left of them, the island of Lanai sat still and motionless. A few other vessels were out, but they kept their distance.

Behind her, Parker manned the steering wheel, his face set on their mission.

After a few minutes, the coastline grew gray and rocky. A little farther a rocky wall rose up to greet them.

Parker cut the engine and grabbed an oar—smart not to broadcast their presence to anyone who could be around that bend. Miranda took an oar as well and paddled as she stared up at the jagged barricade of the cliff beside them.

The colors were amazing. Deep slates, dark greens, amber golds. Sunlight danced off some of the shapes, shadows hid others. A thousand spiky surfaces with not a smooth one to be found. She knew how sharp and painful those surfaces could be. They made for a strong fortress.

Overhead, a whoosh sounded and a stream of water shot into the air. "There's the blowhole." She pointed upward. It was in a dip in the wall, maybe twenty feet above them where the rocks jutted out farther into the ocean.

"I see it," Parker said. "We're close."

"It looks more like a bad water fountain at the park than a geyser."

"That's because the tide is low."

Made sense. She rowed harder. They rounded another corner, floated into shadow and…there it was.

The mouth of the sea cave yawned before them, dark and ominous.

Parker stopped rowing and stared at it. "Do you still want to go in?" His voice was steady, but she sensed his apprehension. And shared it.

But the image of Keola's dead body in her arms—right in the area overhead—drove out any fear. Without taking her eyes off the cave, she nodded. "Yes."

She heard Parker's oar dip into the water again and slowly they glided through the opening.

CHAPTER TWENTY-FOUR

The air was cooler inside the cave, more humid since it was trapped between the cave walls. The waves became choppy. The cavern itself grew dark.

Parker switched on the boat's anchor light and it cast eerie shadows along the jagged surfaces. Miranda was awestruck by the formations along the floor and walls. Masses of them. The light bounced over blobby columns of inky blacks, deep reds, shimmering golds. The ceiling, as high as a small cathedral, was like a giant pincushion someone had stuck a thousand golden needles into.

"I remember that old memory trick," Parker said, pointing up. "Stalactites hold tight to the top." He gestured downward. "Stalagmites might get to the top some day."

"That's cute."

"My father taught me that."

"You went spelunking with Mr. P?" It was hard to imagine Parker's father picking his way through a cave.

"I think he read it to me in a book."

"Uh huh." That sounded more like the sophisticated ladies' man who had raised her husband.

They rowed in farther.

It was like fording an underground river. Surrounded by the eerie glow of the rocky shapes, she felt like she was on Mars. Or maybe trapped in a sci-fi flick. Up ahead the cave wall curved. As they slowly floated around it, nerves danced in her stomach. Ha'aheo could be waiting for them around the corner.

The rig cleared the wall and from all appearances, they were still alone in here.

But the river narrowed and the rocky walls, along with their peaks and spikes, closed in a little more. The light glistened on the dark green surface of the water.

Then suddenly, the water stopped. Parker put down his oar and shined the light ahead of the bow. Waves washed over a stony surface.

"What is that? A shoreline?"

"The cave floor." Parker directed the light over the solid surface, making its boulder-like form glisten. "I don't think this is the cave that feeds the blowhole or there'd be more water in it," he said quietly. "There's not enough pressure."

"Really?" She didn't know if that was good news or bad.

"It'll be covered when the tide comes in."

"You mean this whole place will fill up?"

"Yes." His voice echoed ominously off the cave wall.

Bad news, she decided. "But that won't be for a while."

"Not for several hours."

Okay, maybe it was good news. "Good thing you dragged me out of bed so early. What do we do now?"

"Find whatever it is that we're looking for. Here, I have those flashlights." He handed her one.

Carefully, she got to her feet and stepped out of the boat and onto the uneven surface. It seemed to be made of large, flattened pebbles, a lot like the area around the blowhole above. Parker handed her a line and climbed out as well. They stood, sweeping their lights over the walls and floor.

The gray-gold floor rose as it went farther into the cave. Along part of a back wall lay a set of big, step-like shelves that reminded her of slabs of cement debris she and former coworkers used to produce after a couple of hours of jack hammering a sidewalk. A long dark patch in the wall indicated a small cavity. She hoped no one was hiding there.

The stalactites—the icicle-like formations hanging from the ceiling—were thicker here. The stalagmites—the columns on the floor that "might" get to the top someday—were crowded in clusters near the walls. Big blobby bases rising up to pointy, sharp spires. Might make a good weapon, if they needed one.

She gestured to one of the bigger ones. "Are those things sturdy enough to tie a mooring line to?"

Parker stepped over to it and gave the base a kick. "Seems to be. Here." He stretched out an arm and she handed him the line, helped him tether it to the stalagmite.

"You're good at this," he said with the admiration in his tone that always made her cheeks warm.

She shrugged. "I worked on a boat in Maine for a little while."

"Ah, yes. Harvesting crab." She was surprised he'd remembered that from her resume.

She busied herself with the line to hide the color on her face. "It's snug," she said, wiping her hands on her jeans.

"It'll do. Ready?" He reached a hand out to her.

With a nod, she took it and they made their way over the jagged surface, their flashlights shining against the bumpy, blackish-gold walls, making them glisten like jewels. It was awkward trying to avoid the spears jutting up from the floor while wending over the uneven boulder carpet, attempting to find whatever might be hidden in here.

"Not exactly in plain sight," Miranda muttered, her heart sinking. She dared to whisper her doubts. "What if we don't find anything, Parker?"

"Then we'll just call this a sightseeing trip."

"Very funny." She cast her light back and forth. And stopped. "What's that?" Her beam focused on a black surface just behind a cluster of stalagmites. It was smooth. Not at all like the jagged lava. She moved a little closer. "It looks like plastic."

"A plastic case." Parker's light swept the floor. "And there's another one."

She pointed the flash about a foot away. "And another. One. Two. Three. Four. Five of them in all." Each of them wedged behind the protection of the stalagmite fence. "Jackpot," she grinned.

Parker stepped closer to the first one. "They appear to be marine boxes. Waterproof, no doubt. They're secured as well."

She set her light down on a jutting piece of lava and bent to examine the first case. A heavy chain was wrapped around it and secured with a padlock. The other end of the chain was attached to a spike that had been driven into the rock.

"These look like the galvanized mooring chains we used to use on those crab ships."

"They are indeed."

"And the chains are held in place with padlocks. So when the tide comes in…"

"The containers don't float away."

Suddenly there seemed to be cold wind blowing in from somewhere that made her shiver. The hair on the back of her neck stood up. Odd since they were both sweating.

"Did you feel that?" she whispered.

"Feel what?"

And just like that, it was gone. "Never mind." She shook if off and squatted down to get a better look at the second box. It was bound as tight as a pirate's chest. "There must be something valuable in these containers."

"Stolen goods would be my guess."

"Like maybe some matches to the stuff listed in those police reports? Sure would be nice to get a look inside one of them."

A familiar cocky look spread over his good-looking face. "I have the tools for that."

She grinned up at him. "You brought them along?"

He reached into his pocket, drew out a small leather case and set it on one of the marine boxes. "Boy Scouts' motto. Always be prepared."

"Yeah, you're a Boy Scout, all right." She'd seen him use the B&E skills that went with those tools and she wasn't going to ask how he got them on the plane. But a problem crossed her mind. "Wait a minute. Won't you leave fingerprints?"

"Fingerprints will no doubt wash away when the tide rises, but just in case." He pulled two pairs of rubber gloves out of his pocket, handed one to her.

Her jaw dropped open. "You really did come prepared. Where did you get these? You didn't call room service, did you?" Ha'akeo could have underlings planted all over the hotel for all they knew.

"Of course not. I made a few stops this morning while I was getting the other supplies." His eyes sparkled with that sly Parker smile. "This may be a tropical island, but they do have drugstores."

"Uh huh."

She could only shake her head as she slipped on the gloves and watched him bend down, remove two long, thin instruments from his case and go to work on the first padlock. It didn't take long before something inside clicked and the lock was open.

"Voilà."

Smiling, she helped him remove the chains and lift the lid. "Well, lookie there."

"A hidden treasure."

Inside were neatly placed stacks of a variety of items, each carefully wrapped in plastic bags and taped. "Here's a bunch of cell phones."

"And a laptop. Watches. Jewelry."

"Look how straight this tape was placed on here. Oh, here's some cash. Wonder how much?"

"This might tell us." Parker lifted out a piece of paper and unfolded it.

"Wow." It was an itemized list of everything in the box, along with the estimated values. "This guy's really anal."

"He seems to have good organizational skills. Too bad he isn't putting them to better use."

"He's a planner. He doesn't make a lot of mistakes." That could make him all the more dangerous. Was Keola's death a mistake or planned? she wondered.

"We'll have to put everything back exactly as it was. A person this careful will notice if something is out of place."

"You're right." She got to her feet and scratched at her hair. "What do we do? Report this to Balondo?"

"This isn't exactly a motive for a murder."

She frowned. "Why not? If Keola found out about this place and threatened to tell the cops it would be."

"Those are a lot of assumptions and the penalty for this kind of activity is far less than for murder."

"You've got a point. So there must be something more valuable here." She heard the waves lapping against the shoreline where they tied the boat. It was closer than when they first stepped onto it. "How long do we have?"

"With respect to the elements? Several hours at least. The tide won't be fully up until just before noon.

With respect to when Ha'aheo might happen by to check on his loot, neither of them could predict. But the more evidence, the better. "Let's keep looking."

"Agreed." Parker picked up his tools and moved to the second case.

Watching those lovely, moist shoulder muscles flex under that tank top, Miranda put a hand on her hip and pursed her lips. "You know, I don't remember having a class in that particular skill at the Agency."

The side of his mouth turned up. "Would you like to learn now?"

Could come in handy. You never knew. "Sure." She bent down beside him.

He handed her one of the tools, which was L-shaped. "This is the tension wrench. You use it to keep the cylinder in place." He put it into the lock to demonstrate, pulled it out again. "Try it."

She took the tool and copied what he had done.

"Excellent. This is the pick." He placed the wire-thin instrument in her free hand. "Insert it into the keyhole and push all the way to the back."

She did as he said. "This is awkward."

"You'll get used to it with a little practice. Now drag the pick slowly forward. The object is to push the pins inside the lock up. They're held in place by springs."

"Okay." She dug away.

"Not too much pressure. Try to feel what's going on inside."

She lightened up and tried to sense what she couldn't see but after a minute, the pick slid out. The top of the lock hadn't budged. "You make this look so easy."

"Patience. It just takes practice."

With a grunt, she put the tools into the keyhole and tried again. This time she came closer.

"Turn the wrench."

"Too late." She tugged the lock and nearly fell over on her backside. The padlock was still tight as a drum.

"One more time." Parker always had more patience than she did.

But she took a deep breath, gritted her teeth and jammed the tools in again.

"Gently."

"Okay, okay." She lightened up. She worked the pick carefully, but just as she almost had it, she lost a pin. Livid, she jammed the pick in, shoved it up and zipped it out again. This time, she did fall backward and as she did, the lock came open in her hand. "Hey, I did it."

"That's another method." Parker reached out a hand to help her up, pride beaming on his face. "Let's see what's in this one. You do the honors."

She put her hands on the marine box lid and lifted. Her breath caught.

"Motherlode."

Parker's voice was a low reverberation. "Now that is worth killing for."

Five large bags of white powder lay along the top of the box. There were more beneath. "I bet that's not Hawaiian sugar cane."

Parker picked up a bag, gingerly opened it. He gave his gloved forefinger a lick, dipped in and took a taste. "It's the real thing all right."

And he wasn't talking about the soft drink.

"Looks like he's following in his father's footstep." Parker almost seemed sorry for the guy.

She opened her mouth, about to say they should go straight to the police, when she heard the waves churn and the chopping sound of a boat motor. "Oh, my God, Parker. That's got to be Ha'aheo."

"Go back behind that wall." He meant the back part of the cave beyond the shelf-steps where there was a dark recess.

"You're coming, too, aren't you?" she whispered. But it was too late.

"Hold it right there," a voice boomed through a megaphone.

A floodlight blinded her. She raised her hands to shade her eyes. "Hey, put that light down."

"Who are you?" Parker demanded in a threatening tone.

The light dipped and Miranda blinked, trying to see. The first thing she could make out was the white hull of a midsize speedboat—with the word *Police* stenciled on it. Relief rippled through her. "Sergeant Balondo?"

"It's Officers Andrews and Yamagata, Mrs. Parker." Now she recognized that Brooklyn accent. "Someone reported they'd seen a boat come in. We came in to check it out. Didn't know it was you."

She grinned giddily at Andrews as he grabbed a flashlight from Yamagata, splashed across the water and stepped onto the rocks.

"Actually, we want to speak to an officer," she told him.

Andrews pulled up the belt on his uniform and swept his light over the spiky columns, casting long shadows on the knobby wall. "Uh, that's good because Sergeant Balondo asked me to have you come in for—" His eyes grew wide as he spotted the open marine box with the cocaine bags. "What in the Sam Hill is that?"

"That's what we want to discuss with the Sergeant," Parker said, firmness in his tone.

"Really now?" Andrews gave Parker a suspicious look. Then he strolled over and took the bag Parker was still holding. He gave his finger a lick and took a dip to taste. "Damn." He turned to Yamagata.

Yamagata gave him a knowing nod.

Andrews expanded his chest and went into full authoritarian mode. "I'm sorry, Mr. Parker. But the Sergeant wants me to bring your wife in for questioning in the Keola Hakumele case."

Miranda took a step toward him. "Does he realize it was murder now?"

"There's been some new evidence and…I'm sorry, but you're a person of interest."

"Me?" That didn't make any sense.

"And with this additional…evidence," he gestured to the bag, "I'm going to have to arrest both of you."

CHAPTER TWENTY-FIVE

"Tell me again what you were doing at the blowhole the other night when you found the victim's body?"

Victim? Now Keola was a victim?

Miranda sat back in the hard chair of the narrow interrogation room in the Lahaina police station and watched Sergeant Balondo pace up and down, peering at her with dark, suspicious eyes. It had to be past seven. Way past his usual shift and he seemed pretty grouchy about it.

She wasn't feeling too peachy herself. Did he really think they were drug dealers? That she was involved in Keola's death? She'd never heard of anything so ridiculous.

She couldn't help curling a lip at him. "Didn't we go over that the other night?"

He slapped his legal pad down on the table and took a seat at the opposite end. "I'd like to hear your story again."

She folded her arms. "You did make a report, didn't you?"

The little man's eyes grew even darker with annoyance. "Humor me."

She drummed her fingers against her arm. Better cooperate or this would just go on longer. She drew in a breath and went over the details again. Her late night run. The blowhole. Finding Keola and dragging him out of the water, giving him CPR, realizing he was dead. "And then I called 911 and you and your team showed up."

"Are you sure that's all there was to it?"

"Of course, I'm sure."

Balondo's soul patch swayed back and forth as he pursed his lips and considered her reply. "Mrs. Parker, we found nothing at the crime scene but Keola's fingerprints and yours."

Yeah, and what about those bloody handprints on the sign? She thought of how neatly those marine boxes had been packed. Ha'aheo had to be too anal to leave evidence behind.

"And today we find you and your husband in the vicinity of the crime scene. In a sea cave with stolen goods and drugs. I don't know about you, but to me that looks a little too coincidental."

She opened her mouth, shut it again. How could he even imply that?

"Do you have an explanation as to why you were there?"

She raised her palms "We're investigating the murder?"

He gave her a smug little smirk. "Don't private investigators usually have a client?"

"Not always."

He got up and strolled to the wall. "Yesterday you call me to tell me there's new evidence in the Keola Hakumele case—"

"Yeah, what about those prints?"

He cut her off, raising his voice. "And today we find you and your husband near that spot with twenty kilos of cocaine. Plus assorted stolen goods. And you can't tell me why."

She glared at him, resisting the urge to shake the little man. "We have a suspect."

"Oh, you do, do you? And who is he?" he plopped himself down in the chair again and ran his fingers over his soul patch.

She thought of those police reports Parker had accessed online. Better not mention those. Her mind raced. Suddenly she remembered the detective Parker knew. "There's an officer here. Actually, he's on vacation. Officer Nakamura. My husband knows him. He trained at the Parker Agency."

Balondo's eyes went wide. "What did you do? Pick up a card in the lobby? Answer the question, Mrs. Parker."

She gave him a sassy smirk. "No, I didn't pick up a card in the lobby."

His eyes flashed. "Not that question. Why were you in that sea cave today?"

She ran her tongue over her teeth. Best to be the one to act like a professional here. She and Parker were going to tell him about the cave anyway. "We noticed the sea cave when we were at the blowhole yesterday. We suspected there might be a clue to Keola's murder down there. Turned out we were right."

"So it was just a hunch? Intuition?"

"That's right. Don't you use intuition at times? Or is it all just dull facts with you?"

She could have sworn his face twitched. "You're frustrating me, Mrs. Parker."

"Likewise."

Grinding his teeth he stared down at the table a moment then slapped his hands on it and shot to his feet. Picking up his pad he waved a finger at her. "You're in deep trouble, Mrs. Parker. Now you sit here and think about that while I go talk to your husband and see what kind of story he gives me." He turned to go.

She wanted to tell him to engage in a lewd act with himself, but she'd only be digging the hole she was in deeper. Maybe it was time for the truth. Part of it anyway.

"Sergeant Balondo," she said in the most somber tone she could muster.

His hand already on the door, he turned back. "Yes?"

"I went to speak to Keola's father yesterday. I met his son, Mikaele. He told me Keola was involved with a man named Jonathan Ha'aheo."

Balondo turned around with a satisfied look that told her she'd just made a big mistake. "Mikaele is your brother, isn't he? Well, your half brother anyway."

How in the hell did he know that? "I—"

"His father goes by the name of Pumehana, but his real name is Edward Steele. And Steele is your maiden name. Still your legal name, right? And Keola's last name."

Miranda swallowed. If she'd thought Balondo was the type who didn't do his homework, she'd been wrong. He'd run a background check on her. She felt a sweat drop slither down her back. "I only found out about my father yesterday."

Balondo chuckled. "Are you sure about that?"

She stared at him. She sure didn't want to air her dirty laundry in front of this guy but apparently, she had no choice. "My father abandoned me when I was a child," she admitted. "I didn't know he was here or I never would have come to Maui."

His lips formed a who-are-you-trying-to-kid smirk as he folded his arms over his square torso. "Are you sure you didn't find out about him when you were in the states? Your PI husband has been poking around looking for him, right?"

Her mouth opened.

"And when he found him and told you your father had a new family and other children, maybe you went a little ballistic. How dare your father go off marry someone else? You were going to show them who you were, right?"

She felt like he'd just punched her in the gut. "That's crazy."

"It would be pretty farfetched." He leaned over and put his face close to hers. "If there just wasn't so much evidence against you."

She bared her teeth. "What evidence?"

He straightened and chuckled to himself. "Those bloody prints you pointed out on the warning sign on the blowhole?"

"What about them?"

"There were two sets. One Keola's. The other yours. No one else's was there."

What? How could that be? She thought back. She must have drifted over to the sign and leaned against it while she was waiting for the cops to arrive that night. It was the only explanation. But not one this hardheaded cop would buy.

"If I were guilty of killing Keola, why would I call it in that night? Why would I call you about those fingerprints?"

He shrugged. "Maybe to look innocent. Maybe you want to rub it in the dumb cop's face. Maybe you've got self-destructive tendencies. Psychology isn't my department, Ms. *Steele*." He sounded like he relished saying her real name. "All I know is that all my evidence points to you."

She pressed both hands to her temples. What would Parker do? Think. Then she knew. Lifting her chin with an air of confidence she barely felt, she uttered the words she'd thought she'd never say in her life. "I want a lawyer."

Balondo looked like he was about to do a victory dance. "Do you have one you want to call?"

Estavez, she thought. But he was back in the states. He might know someone here, but that would take too long. "Not really."

"You'll be assigned a public defender then." And with that he turned and left the room.

CHAPTER TWENTY-SIX

"Well now, Mr. Parker, private investigator, what do you have to say for yourself?"

Parker turned from the corner of the small interrogation room where he'd been staring at the walls and gave Sergeant Balondo his most ingratiating smile. "Sergeant, I'm so sorry to have inconvenienced you and your men. There seems to have been a terrible misunderstanding."

Balondo's lip curled as he laid a notebook on the small table in the room. "Oh, you're good, aren't you?"

"I beg your pardon?" The refined approach would work better if he were in a suit rather than a tank top and jeans, Parker thought.

Balondo scratched at his cheek and shook his head. "There's no misunderstanding, Mr. Parker. My men caught you and your wife red-handed."

"You mean you caught us just as we had discovered illegal drugs and stolen goods. You do realize there's no cell phone signal in that cave, don't you? We would have called you as soon as we left. Just as we did yesterday at the crime scene to report the evidence we found."

The sergeant put his hands behind his back and chuckled. Odd reaction. "And how would I know this?"

Parker eyed the square-bodied man, recalling Ryo's words about his stubbornness. He had hoped it wouldn't be necessary to pull his trump card, but apparently it was. "Sergeant," he smiled. "As you're probably aware, I'm quite well acquainted with Detective Ryo Nakamura. I believe he's your boss?"

Balondo's expression told him Miranda must have mentioned the name as well. "Who my boss is isn't relevant to this investigation."

"On the contrary, it's extremely relevant in this case. If you call him, Ryo will vouch for me."

"I can't do that, Mr. Parker. Officer Nakamura is on vacation."

"Oh, I'm aware of that. He mentioned it to me when I came to see him two days ago. In fact, it was just before he left. You see, Ryo is a former student of mine and I dropped by to catch up and chat about old times with him." He gave him another one of those society smiles that he'd learned from his father.

He watched Balondo's hands ball into fists before he put them behind his back and stared at the floor. He was weighing the choice of calling his boss and disturbing his vacation over nothing and looking like a fool, against the evidence he had. If he were as by-the-book as Ryo had said, Parker could guess the decision before he made it.

Balondo raised his head. "Okay, Mr. Parker. We'll call the Detective." He took his cell phone out of his pocket and speed dialed the number. He laid it on the table and pressed the speaker button.

It rang three times before Ryo picked up. "Yes, Sergeant?" Ryo didn't sound pleased.

"Sir, I'm very sorry to disturb you, but we picked up a person of interest in the Keola Hakumele case and he claims to know you. I need to verify."

The sound of muted voices and clattering dishes trickled through the phone. Around ten a.m. in LA. Ryo must be having a late breakfast with his family. "And who is it, Balondo?"

"His name is Parker, sir. Full name, Wade Russell Parker the Third."

Parker was relieved to hear Ryo's chuckle over the speaker. "Yes, Balondo. I know Mr. Parker. I attended his investigative agency. It's one of the best in the country."

The look of chagrin on Balondo's face was something Parker would relish for a long time. "And what about his wife, sir? Do you know her as well?"

"I can't say I've had the pleasure of meeting her. Did you say you picked Mr. Parker up?"

Balondo did a little hemming and hawing before he thought of a reply. "It was just routine, sir. I simply needed to verify his identity."

Parker stepped toward the phone with a smile. "Ryo, it's good to hear your voice again."

"Parker, are you getting into trouble with my men?"

Parker gave an easy laugh. "I'm trying to keep my nose clean, but you know how difficult that can be for me."

"Well, just try to behave yourself in the future."

"I'll do that."

Balondo cut off the friendly banter. "Thank you for your help, sir. I won't keep you any longer."

"That's quite all right." With another chuckle, Ryo hung up.

Balondo pursed his lips back and forth for a few moments. Finally, he stiffened his shoulders. "Very well, Mr. Parker. I stand corrected. You're released." He picked up his notebook from the table.

"And my wife?"

Balondo's jaw went hard. "You heard Detective Nakamura. He doesn't know her."

"She's my wife. She's also my employee. The Parker Agency will vouch for her."

"She's got a rap sheet."

Parker winced. Of course Balondo would have run her background. "Misdemeanors."

"And she's related to the vic."

The man was as methodical as Ryo had described him. "She didn't know that until yesterday."

"Maybe, maybe not."

Parker raised a brow. "Are you calling me a liar, Sergeant?"

Balondo opened his notebook and shuffled through a file until he found what he was looking for. "Yesterday morning you rented a second BMW because your first rental was missing. Is that true, Mr. Parker?"

Parker tensed. "Yes it's true, but what does that have to do with anything?"

"Your wife took the first car, didn't she?"

"Yes, she came to see you that night."

Ignoring the point, he kept his gaze on his notes. "But you didn't rent the second car until the next morning. It looks like she didn't come home."

Parker frowned. "What are you saying?"

Balondo shut his notebook with a snap. "Just that you wouldn't be the first husband not to know everything his wife was up to."

He laughed. "I assure you, Sergeant. I know my wife."

"Like I said. Maybe, maybe not. In my book, she's got motive. And that's all I can say to you about it right now."

Anger pounded in Parker's temples. Time to play his other trump card. "Sergeant I have reason to believe one Jonathan Ha'aheo is responsible for the contraband found in that cave."

There was no sign of recognition in Balondo's expression at that name. He didn't know the case. "Thanks for the tip. We'll look into it."

"Sergeant, Jonathan Ha'aheo's father was a dangerous criminal. Jonathan may be following in his footsteps."

"As I said, we'll look into it. Now if you'll excuse me, Mr. Parker, I have work to do. You're free to go."

Parker felt the pulse in his neck quicken. Free to call Ryo back. This time the call wouldn't be so friendly. This time he'd have Balondo's job.

Giving up the argument with the dense sergeant, Parker stepped past him and through the open door. As he did, another thought struck him. He turned back. "Has my wife asked for a attorney?"

Balondo nodded stiffly. "She'll be assigned a public defender."

"I'll take care of her attorney." If she still needed one after he made that call.

Summoning all his control, Parker turned away and marched down the hall to the small waiting room. He glanced at the clerk on duty at the reception desk. He seemed oblivious enough. Parker strolled to a potted palm tree in the corner, pulled out his cell and dialed Ryo again.

"Parker? What's going on?"

"Your sergeant let me go, but he's still holding my wife."

There was a groan of annoyance. "I apologize, Parker."

"There's more. I have reason to believe Jonathan Ha'aheo is involved in the Keola Hakumele case."

There was a long pause. For a moment Parker thought he had lost the connection. "Do you mean Robert Ha'aheo's son?" The son of the man they'd chased down together four years ago. The man who had almost shot Ryo. The man Parker had killed to save the detective's life.

"Yes. We haven't got enough to prove it yet, but our evidence is leading that way. I told Balondo about the younger Ha'aheo, but he brushed me off."

There was more than annoyance in Ryo's voice now. "Give me a minute. I'll straighten the sergeant out. I'll call you right back." He disconnected.

The next few minutes seemed like an eternity. Parker paced to the potted palm across the room and back again. He thumbed a magazine on the small coffee table, then returned to the palm. He'd made several trips before his cell rang.

"Yes?"

Ryo didn't speak right away, but when he did, Parker felt his whole body quake. "Bad news."

"What do you mean?"

"Balondo's got evidence on your wife."

"The drugs and stolen goods we found today?"

"No. There were bloody fingerprints on the warning sign near the blowhole."

Stunned, Parker blinked. "Yes, we discovered those yesterday. We reported them to the sergeant. I don't understand what—"

"One set of them was your wife's."

Parker had to sit down in one of the metal chairs at that news. They thought they'd found Jonathan's fingerprints but, of course, he wouldn't have been so sloppy. Parker's mind raced. "That could have happened the night she found the body."

"I'm sure there's some explanation but there's no other evidence right now. Nothing to point to Jonathan Ha'aheo. I ordered Balondo to investigate Ha'aheo, but that will take time. Meanwhile, I talked Balondo into letting your wife see a lawyer before he books her. A good one might get her released temporarily. That's the best I can do."

Of course, Ryo couldn't order his sergeant to let Miranda go. Not without a shred of proof on Jonathan.

"Do you need the name of a local attorney?" Ryo asked softly.

Parker wiped a hand over his face. "I'm going to try Mr. Estavez first. I'll call you back if I need to."

"Please do. I'm so sorry, Parker. I wish there were more I could do for her."

"It's all right, Ryo. Thank you for what you have done." He hung up and sat there, his mind reeling. Then he shook himself out of it. He got to his feet and dialed Antonio's number. The best criminal defense lawyer in Atlanta ought to be able to think of something.

He breathed a sigh of relief when Antonio picked up. "Hello, son. Are you in the office?"

There was a pause. He knew Antonio would be surprised to hear from him. "I am," he said in his Hispanic accent. "I just got back from an early lunch with a client. You aren't back in town, are you, Papa?"

"I'm still in Maui." He didn't bother with pleasantries. "Son, I need an attorney."

"What's wrong?"

"It's Miranda. She's been arrested."

"Again?"

She did have a habit of getting herself into trouble, but this wasn't her fault. "This time, it's serious."

"It was serious last time."

Parker ignored the comment. "There's been a local murder. I'll explain the details when I get home." When that would be was anyone's guess. "Do you know an attorney in Maui? Someone good?"

He was surprised when Antonio didn't pause to consult his Rolodex. "I do. Zabel Garcia. We dated back in law school. She took a job in California after graduation, but she moved back home to Maui a couple years ago. Her father owns a coffee farm there."

"Is she good?"

Antonio uttered a smug laugh. "She almost beat me for the first slot in our graduating class. She has an excellent win record as well. I'll be glad to give her a call."

Parker exhaled a sigh of relief. "Thank you, son."

He disconnected, sank back down onto one of the chairs and waited for what seemed like years. He was vacantly staring at a photo of a surfer on the cover of a magazine when his phone rang again. "Wade Parker."

"Mr. Parker, this is Zabel Garcia. Antonio Estavez asked me to call you?" She had a lovely, confident voice that made Parker breathe easier.

He glanced at his watch. It had only been fifteen minutes. "Yes, Ms. Garcia. Thank you for getting back to me so quickly. My wife needs a defense attorney. She's being held on drug possession charges and a possible murder." Briefly he explained a few of the pertinent details.

"Where is she being held?"

"In the Lahaina police station. I'm in the waiting room. She's been allowed a visit with her representation before she's booked. Can you help?"

"I'll have to look at the case, but I can talk to her."

The twisted knot in his stomach began to loosen a bit. "How soon can you get here?"

"I'm on the other side of West Maui. Give me an hour."

"I'll be waiting for you."

CHAPTER TWENTY-SEVEN

The funky beat of Cho's rap tune ring tone woke him. Irritated, he opened his eyes and reached for his cell. "What is it?"

"Hey, Bro. Wazzup?"

"*I'm* not up," he growled, glancing at the clock on his nightstand. Not even eight yet. He'd been awake half the night coming up with a plan for Parker and his frizzy-headed lady. It still had too many holes in it. "You know I told you never to call this early."

"Chill out, man. I got something to say." His words were slurred. Fucking douchebag was high again. He'd better not ask for money.

"Make it fast."

"Sure, sure. I was like, out fishing early this morning, you know." The idiot sounded nervous. He should be.

"Of course, you were." Cho was supposed to guard the sea cave during the early hours when the tide was low.

"Yeah, well anyway," Cho whined. "I was drifting along and I see a boat heading toward the stash spot."

He tensed. "What?"

"So I move in a little closer, watch them through my binoculars. It was Parker and his bitch."

He dug a hand into his scalp. "What are you talking about?"

"They went into the cave."

He sat up on the bed. "What?"

"I waited for a while. You know, to see what would happen? And pretty soon...oh, man. Pretty soon a cop boat comes by."

His breath turned solid in his lungs. "The cops? Did you call them, Cho?"

"No, man. I wouldn't do that. Why would I do that? Some jerk on the water must have called them. There's always some goodie-goodie out there. Must have thought Parker and his bitch were lost in the cave or something."

Okay, okay. That didn't mean anything. "What did the cops do?"

"Th—they went in." Cho sounded like his teeth were chattering. If he were here, he'd knock them down his throat. He was sick of this pussying around.

"Dammit, Cho. Spit it out."

He could have sworn he heard the coward whimper. "Bad news, man. They got the stash."

He shot to his feet. "The cops got our stash?"

"I—I kept watching and after a little bit the police boat came out again. They were carrying boxes. One by one. I counted them. Five, man. Oh, man they took everything."

He paced to his desk, leaned on it. He felt numb. Sick. His whole body throbbed. His brain pounded in his skull like he was on a bad acid trip.

Everything? The fucking cops had everything? Emotions tore through him. Everything gone? Rage pulsated through every muscle. He picked up a chair ready to smash it against the wall. He would kill that fucking Wade Parker. Kill him with his own two fucking hands.

Cho's voice was in his ear again. "But there's a bright spot."

Slowly, he strolled to the end of his bed and put the chair down. Maybe he'd kill Cho first. "What bright spot?" he sneered.

"They had Parker and his bitch in handcuffs."

Suddenly dizzy, he steadied himself with the chair. "What did you just say?"

"Handcuffs, man. Parker and his wifey."

"Are you sure you aren't tripping?"

"Course not. No lie. The cops arrested Parker and his woman."

"What are you on, Cho?"

"Nothing, man. The dumb pigs must've thought the stash was theirs." He dared to squeak out a laugh.

He stood there, frozen. It was Fate again. Twisting things his way.

"You still there, man?" Cho squeaked. "What do you want me to do?"

"Don't you do anything," he barked. "Don't you do a fucking thing. Until you hear from me...just...just lay low."

"Yeah, man. Good idea. I can do that."

He hung up, tossed the cell on the bed. Wade Parker arrested? And that nosy wife of his, too?

The anger dissolved into a joy so sweet it was painful. He let go of the chair and sank onto the bed. He began to laugh. He giggled. He cackled. He laughed until the tears came.

Wade Parker arrested.

Then his laughter stopped. Those charges wouldn't last. Parker knew the cops. He was connected. He'd be out in a heartbeat. Might be out already. And then the cops would start looking for him. How much did that sonofabitch PI know? What did he tell the pigs?

He couldn't take any chances. He had to get out of here.

He'd saved back two bags of blow in case of an emergency like this. He could get to Oahu, sell the dope on the street and get enough for a ticket to New Zealand. He'd get lost in a city like Auckland. They'd never find him.

Hurrying to the closet, he grabbed a backpack and started stuffing clothes in it.

But what about Parker?

He thought about the sea cave. He thought about his stash. The rage began to pulse again but his head was clear. An idea came to him. The cops had to break open the locks on the boxes they confiscated. They saw what was in them. Why else would they make an arrest? That meant most of the chains would probably still be there.

A smile spread across his face. Yes, that would work. That was it.

He glared at his alarm clock. It would take a couple of hours for the timing to be right.

Could he risk waiting?

If he didn't, he'd have the ghost of Wade Parker haunting him the rest of his life. He couldn't live with that, no matter what it might cost him. Even if the cops caught him before he could get away, it would be worth it to know he'd paid Parker back for what he'd done to his family.

The satisfaction of giving Parker a horrible death was worth jail time. He'd do it.

He pulled on a fishnet shirt and the tight-fitting pants that showed off his muscles. In the bathroom, he slapped some gel on his black hair and ran a comb through it. Returning to his bed, he zipped up his backpack, reached for his phone and stuffed it into his pocket.

Time to get busy. He had work to do.

CHAPTER TWENTY-EIGHT

Parker sat in the Lahaina police station waiting room staring at his cell phone. There was one more call he could make before the attorney arrived. If Edward Steele could get his son to make a statement about Jonathan Ha'aheo, Balondo would have no cause to hold Miranda.

Two days ago he wouldn't have hesitated to make that call. But now?

Miranda was innocent. Any decent lawyer could get Balondo's flimsy charges dropped. Would it be worth it to contact her father when he knew perfectly well she wanted nothing to do with him?

What would that do to their relationship?

Before he could decide, the door opened and a tall, well-dressed woman in her early thirties stepped into the room.

She took one look at him and moved toward him, hand extended. "Wade Parker? I'm Zabel Garcia."

He shot to his feet. "Ms. Garcia, thank you so much for coming."

A striking woman, she smiled warmly with a well-formed mouth as she shook his hand. Her dark, auburn hair was pulled back in an elegant chignon and she wore a lightweight double-breasted herringbone suit of pale gray. Her expensive briefcase and attire would have marked her as a professional, if her demeanor hadn't done the job all by itself.

"I'm sorry I couldn't get here sooner," she said. "Is your wife still here?"

"As far as I know."

"If you don't mind, I'll get the details of the case from her."

"Not at all."

He watched her stride with confidence over to the reception desk, hand the clerk her card and address him in a crisp, businesslike tone. "I believe you're holding a Ms. Miranda Steele here? You may have her listed as Mrs. Parker."

The clerk eyed the card, then the woman. "Maybe."

"She's my client. I'd like to see her as soon as possible." Her tone wasn't demanding, yet it subtly implied he didn't want to find out what might happen if he failed to comply with her request.

"Yes, ma'am." The clerk sat up straight, dialed a number and muttered into his phone. After only a moment he hung up. "Sergeant Balondo will have someone take you to her right away."

"Thank you."

It only took about thirty seconds for the side door to the hall to open and an officer to appear. "Ms. Garcia."

"Yes."

"Please come with me."

And the young woman disappeared into the hall.

Hope rose in Parker's heart as he sat back down. Antonio was right. She was good. This shouldn't take long at all.

Miranda plodded back and forth in the little holding room they had stashed her in, frustration eating a hole in her duodenum. What would Jonathan Ha'aheo do when he found his stolen goods and drugs gone? Would he kill again? She was certain that sea cave was connected to Keola's murder, but she couldn't prove squat.

Dammit.

She came to a halt at the wall, ran her hand over the beige painted cinder blocks. They reminded her of the first time she met Parker. She'd been arrested and had been locked up in a Fulton County cell in Atlanta.

And she'd thought she'd come so far since then.

Parker. She remembered the way he looked that night, all dressed up in that silly tuxedo. His satin vest and wingtip collar, his expensive leather shoes. That well-formed physique beneath the cut of his elegant clothes. The stray wisps of his salt-and-pepper hair falling flirtatiously over his forehead. Those piercing, gray eyes that could see right through her.

She smiled, in spite of herself. If only things could have worked out between them. But it wasn't possible. Not for the long term.

She really had come a long way since her arrest in Atlanta, thanks to Parker. He'd gotten her out of jail, even after she'd told him to go to hell. He'd hired her as an investigator at his Agency and trained her. She had a whole gamut of PI skills under her belt now.

And she knew the law better. Because she did, as soon as that attorney got here, she'd have Balondo's balls in a sling.

"Mrs. Parker?" The cell door jangled open and an officer Miranda didn't recognize appeared. "Your lawyer's here to see you. Come with me."

That was fast. She got to her feet and followed him back down the hall to the interrogation room she'd been in before. Inside a woman was waiting for her.

She held out her hand as soon as Miranda entered. "Mrs. Parker, I'm Zabel Garcia. Your husband contacted me."

Miranda waited for the officer to leave the room and close the door before she turned to the woman with a raised brow. "He did?"

"I'm a friend of Antonio Estavez."

"I see." Miranda eyed the woman. Pretty. Auburn hair swept back in a no-nonsense style, expensive-looking heels and a matching light gray suit, a simple strand of pearls around her neck. Parker's surrogate son always had good taste in women.

And she'd thought Antonio wouldn't be able to do anything. She should have known better. Should have known Parker wouldn't sit idle while she was being held. Miranda didn't know whether that made her happy or uncomfortable, but for now she'd go with it.

"I spoke to the sergeant just now. He told me he's going to book you on charges of drug possession and accessory to a murder."

"Accessory, huh?" That was the best Balondo could come up with?

Ms. Garcia opened her briefcase and pulled out a legal pad and pen. "Why don't you tell me your side of the story."

Miranda pulled out a chair, sat down and went over it all again while her new attorney took notes.

When she finished, Ms. Garcia, who Miranda was calling Zabel by now, sat back and studied her pad. "Balondo's case isn't very strong. Evidence is circumstantial at best."

"I know. But it's strong enough for now."

She tapped her pen against her pad. "You mentioned a lead on this Jonathan Ha'aheo?"

"Keola Hakumele's younger brother. His father thinks he's involved in a gang. They call themselves Huaka'i Po."

Zabel nodded. "The Night Marchers. I've heard of them. They named themselves after that old island legend. That is a good lead. And Balondo didn't buy it?"

Miranda studied the calm expression on her attorney's face. She looked into her steady, dark brown eyes. They say you should always come clean with your lawyer. Besides, this woman was no idiot. "I should tell you…"

"What is it, Miranda?"

Miranda drew a circle on the tabletop with her finger. "Keola's father is…my father, too."

The lawyer almost gasped. That tidbit sure rattled her composure. "I'm sorry."

No choice but to spit it out. What did she have to lose now, anyway? "My father abandoned my mother and me when I was five years old. I had no idea he was here until I sauntered into his tiki bar yesterday during my investigation." She snorted wryly. Why of all the tiki bars in all the towns, in all the world, did she have to walk into his? "It just so happens he's my father."

"And so the murder victim is your…half brother?"

Miranda raised her hands. "I had no idea about that when I found the body."

Zabel dropped her pen and sat back. "So that's why Balondo's holding you."

"That about sums it up."

Zabel stared at the notes on her legal pad. The wheels in her head seemed to be turning. After a moment, she picked up her pen, tapped it against the paper. "What's the name of the bar?"

"Coconut Rum. The owner, my father, goes by the name Pumehana."

She sat back, surprise on her face. "I know that place. And the owner. I always thought he was a fun guy."

"Oh, he's a lot of fun all right. If he's around."

Zabel got to her feet and pulled out her cell. "Let me see if I can make a phone call. Excuse me a moment." Before Miranda could answer, she stepped outside the door.

What was she going to do? Call good old Pumehana? Yeah, he'd come running right over here to her rescue, all right. She hoped her new lawyer could come up with a better idea than that.

CHAPTER TWENTY-NINE

Parker paced from the potted palm in one corner of the waiting room to the potted eucalyptus tree in the other corner yet again. By now he thought he could count the fronds on each bough.

He glanced at his watch. Quarter of ten. How long did it take to get some trumped up murder charges dropped? Perhaps Ms. Garcia wasn't as good as she appeared to be. Perhaps Antonio's memory had been overshadowed with old affections. Perhaps the situation was worse than he thought.

Once more he stared at his cell phone and considered calling Edward Steele.

He was about to look up the number when the ring tone sounded. He didn't recognize the caller.

"Hello?" he answered cautiously.

"Hello, Wade Parker." The voice was low and raspy and had a slight pidgin lilt. He couldn't identify it, but he had a feeling he knew who it was.

He played dumb. "Who is this?"

"Can't you guess, man?

Irritation tightened the back of his neck. "I'm not in the mood for games."

"This is no game, Parker."

"Who are you?

"Ha'akeo," the voice whispered.

So the feeling was correct. "Jonathan Ha'akeo?"

"Ah, you know my given name."

The coldness of his tenor chilled the blood in Parker's veins. Jonathan Ha'akeo was contacting him? He didn't ask where he'd gotten the number. Now he had an idea of the young man's online search skills. "Why are you calling me?" he asked, hiding the wariness raking through his gut.

"I heard you raided a sea cave this morning."

"Who told you that?"

"A little seagull. I wanted to let you know that you didn't get it all."

Warning bells went off in Parker's brain. "What do you mean?"

"Just what I said. You didn't get it all. There's more."

The warning bells grew louder. "Why are you telling me this?"

"Because you have an in with the police."

He chuckled, trying to sound casual. "Do I?"

"I know you do. You and Nakamura. You were part of the task team that was formed four years ago."

To hunt down his father. The young man had to have a grudge. This couldn't be good. "What do you want?"

"I want…to turn myself in."

Parker stiffened. "Then you should. I assume you know where the police station is."

"I can't. Not without an advocate."

"They do have public defenders here."

"I need you, Mr. Parker," he pleaded. The warning bells turned into full-blown sirens. "If you could tell the police—explain to them that I came to you voluntarily and turned in the rest of the drugs, they'd believe you. I might get a lighter sentence."

"Why should I believe you?"

There was a pause, then something that sounded like a stifled sob. Was Ha'aheo actually crying? "You shouldn't, I guess," he said sadly. "But this is all I've got. Please, Mr. Parker. I'll tell you everything."

He was feeling him out, Parker decided. Trying to learn how much he knew. "Everything?"

"Everything," he repeated before uttering another whimpering sound. "I know I'm in trouble. I'm scared. I don't have a father or a mother to guide me. Please help me, Mr. Parker."

Parker didn't believe him, but there was always an outside chance he was telling the truth. After all, it was his fault the young man didn't have his mother to be a better influence in his life. Guilt stung him. And if he did confess, Miranda would go free.

Parker rubbed the back of his neck and blew out a breath. "What do you want me to do?"

"Meet me at the sea cave in half an hour. I'll tell you everything you want to know and I'll give you the rest of the drugs. And then I'll come with you and turn myself in."

The sea cave. Parker had put in too many years at this game not to see through a trap. Odds were that's exactly what this was. "Not the cave. Somewhere public."

"I can't. I can't risk anyone seeing me now. I'm so afraid." There was a low moan of pain.

There wasn't time to talk him into meeting somewhere else. And if this were a trap, Jonathan wouldn't budge on that point. Parker had escaped from traps before. If there were even a fraction of a chance he could get Jonathan to confess to the police and save Miranda from criminal charges, he had no choice but to take it.

But he would hedge his bet. "All right, Jonathan. I'll meet you at the sea cave. Half an hour."

"Oh, thank you, Mr. Parker. You won't regret it."

Parker clicked off and slipped the cell into his pocket. He crossed to the counter.

The clerk at the desk was more than oblivious. He was snoring behind a boating magazine. His youthful face and buzz cut only accented a pair of protruding ears and betrayed the fact he was a rookie. Glancing at the desk, Parker spied a photo of the officer with a young woman holding a newborn. That explained the fatigue. He felt for the young man.

Spotting a small steno pad, he tore off a sheet, grabbed a pen and wrote down a message.

The poor clerk snoozed through it all. Parker tapped him on the hand. "Officer?"

He snorted, opened his eyes, rubbed his face and put down the magazine as if he had just realized he'd been caught. "Yes? What do you want? I mean, how can I help you, sir?"

Parker held up the piece of paper. "Do you see this?"

The officer scowled. "Of course, I do."

"I have to run an errand, but I need you to deliver this note to Sergeant Balondo right away. Do you understand?"

He frowned that semi-condescending cop frown. "I not an idiot, sir."

"I didn't mean to imply you were. But I need your help. Can you do that for me?"

"Sure." He put the note down and picked up his magazine again.

"Did I not say right away?"

Grimacing, the clerk picked up the phone and dialed a number. "Sergeant Balondo's not at his desk."

"Can you take that to him?" Parker pointed at the note.

"Yes, sir. I'll take it to him as soon as he gets back."

Parker glanced at his watch. If he spent any more time giving directions to this rookie, he'd miss Jonathan. "Don't forget, officer. It's very important."

"I'll take care of it, sir."

Parker turned and left the station. Outside, he called for a cab, had it take him to where his BMW was parked at the dock since this morning. He'd have to make a short detour before he rented another boat.

He paid the cabbie, got into the rental and headed for Napilihau Street.

After about ten minutes, he turned into the parking lot of a small strip mall, got out of the car and strolled into the little storefront that provided mailing services. He still remembered the number of his box. Four-twenty-eight. He reached into his pocket, pulled out his keys and selected the one he'd slipped onto his key chain four years ago.

The one he'd thought he'd never need.

He'd thought of this box this morning. He'd considered stopping here before going to the sea cave with Miranda. But when they were arrested, he'd known that would have been a mistake.

This was a different situation.

He opened the mailbox, drew out a rectangular container, closed and locked the box again. He left the store and went back to his car. He drove around to the back of the strip mall and parked beneath the trees for cover. He didn't really need it. There wasn't a soul around. But it paid to be cautious.

Carefully, he opened the package. There it was.

The Glock nine millimeter he'd used four years ago. He only prayed he didn't have to use it again. He pulled back the slide, examined the chamber, loaded the clip and slapped it into place. Then he slipped the weapon under the belt of his jeans.

Steadying himself, he turned the car around and headed back to the dock.

CHAPTER THIRTY

Parker had to bribe the boat owner with three times the price he'd paid this morning to get the inflatable back. Not that he was concerned about the money. What did concern him was the wind, the choppy water and rising tide that were slowing him down. By the time he reached the meeting place, he wondered if Jonathan would still be there.

But at last he rounded the cliff where the blowhole was spewing overhead and once more beheld the yawning mouth of the sea cave.

At the entrance, he cut the motor. Nerves taut, he reached for an oar and paddled inside.

As soon as the light was gone, he switched on the anchor light and immediately saw that the cave's ceiling, with its myriad of sharp, needle-like stalactites was much closer than before. Because the water was higher now, he knew, but it gave the place an even eerier feeling than it had earlier.

The boat floated along until he reached the bend in the river. He glided around it and spotted a speedboat up ahead. It seemed to be moored to the spot where they'd docked the inflatable this morning but the stalagmite was nearly underwater. He squinted toward the rear of the cave. A dozen light sticks had been positioned in various locations, making the area glow and casting odd shadows along the walls.

What a festive welcome party.

Parker peered over the shadowy transom of the speedboat. Backpack, cooler, general supplies. Looked like the owner was about to go on a trip.

He didn't dare take his own rig in any farther for fear of tearing its bottom out with these rocks. He maneuvered the inflatable to a stop, stepped out and sank to his knees. He tied the line next to the other vessel, steadied the flashlight in his hand and proceeded inward. The new shoreline was about fifteen feet or so beyond the one they had climbed on this morning, the choppy water lengthening the distance with each wave.

His apprehension rising like the tide, Parker swept his light over the dark parts of the cave walls. The water had nearly reached the spot where they found the hidden marine boxes. The chains that had held them in place rattled as the tide went in and out.

No sign of Ha'aheo.

He had a bad feeling about this. He switched the flashlight to his left hand and with the other drew his gun.

Noiselessly as he could, he moved to the cave's wall, the moist air in his nostrils, the sound of the waves in his ears, his steps tentative on the stony floor. The clusters of sharp, knobby spires threatened below and above as he crept along. Jonathan could be hiding in any gap or fissure. Parker could walk right past him and not see him.

Forward was the best choice, he surmised. He crept along, inching toward the cave's rear. Then just beyond a set of rocky slabs that reminded him of ancient Greek ruins, he spotted a large cleft he'd seen this morning. No light there, the rift was as black as night.

That was where Ha'aheo was hiding.

His Glock pointed straight at the opening, he moved silently toward it. Keeping his flash down, he decided to use it only at the last moment to startle the killer with a beam in his eyes. He was no more than ten feet away when Jonathan stepped out from the crevice. He wore a hungry smile. And he had a .45 in his hand.

"So this is the famous Wade Parker," he sneered in that raspy pidgin lilt.

He must have seen Parker coming and had decided a frontal approach was his best option. That meant he wasn't stupid.

"Wade Russell Parker the Third," Parker corrected, slipping the flashlight onto his belt to put both hands on the Glock.

"That's right. You're one of those well-bred assholes." Not the same attitude he'd had on the phone.

Parker took in the sight of the man who was half his age. His jaw and forehead had a square shape. He'd slicked back his black hair with gel. Thick black brows, dark narrow eyes. He was his father's son. But at six four and possibly two hundred twenty pounds, he was bigger than his father. More muscular. He wore a black fishnet muscle shirt and tight black slacks. The shirt was made to show off his admirable physique as surely as the tattoos that littered his deltoids and biceps were meant to intimidate.

He must spend a lot of time working out. And in the tattoo parlor.

Parker ignored his insult. And the gun. "I'm here, Jonathan. Are you ready to talk?"

His eyes on the Glock, Ha'aheo shrugged as if he didn't know what Parker meant. "What do you want to talk about?"

"Don't you have something to tell me?" He needed a confession. He wasn't about to leave without one.

"You're really asking for it, aren't you?" The young man laughed. Not quite a cocky laugh. He wasn't as sure of himself as he pretended.

Parker dared a step toward him and tried a gentle approach. "Jonathan, why don't you put that weapon down?"

Ha'aheo backed away, a flicker of alarm on his face. "Why should I do that?"

"So we can have a conversation."

"About what?"

Parker's store of patience was nearly empty by now, but he drew on it once more. "You can start by telling me what happened to Keola Hakumele."

"I have a better idea, PI. You put your weapon down."

"I'm sorry, Jonathan. I can't do that. It looks like we have a standoff." Just like with his father. Parker really didn't want to have to shoot the boy.

"Let me put it this way. If you don't put down your gun, I'll fire. I won't ask again."

Parker clucked his tongue. "Jonathan. Do you really want a gunfight with all these jagged surfaces? So easy for a bullet to ricochet and hit the shooter."

He watched him weigh the pros and cons of that. "Tell me what happened that night," he pressed.

"Why do you want to know that?"

"It's my job." Casually, Parker moved another inch closer to the young man. This time Ha'aheo didn't seem to notice.

"That's right, you think you're one of the good guys." He said it like it was a disease.

"Was Keola one of the good guys?"

"He was a nosy asshole who should have minded his own business."

"Did he find out about your 'business'?" Without taking his eyes off the boy, Parker nodded to where the marine boxes had been."

"I thought he had." Something in the young man seemed to snap. "I hated that prick ever since high school."

"You knew him for a long time, then?"

"We were freshmen together. Before I dropped out. Everybody in the whole school worshipped him because he could toss a lighted stick around. Especially the girls. I thought it was stupid. He was always so high-and-mighty."

"You would have liked to kill him back then."

"No. Hell, no. I forgot about the dumb shit. He called me and wanted to meet me that night. I told him to come to the blowhole."

"What did he want to talk about?"

Ha'aheo fisted his free hand and glowered at him, but he had a faraway look in his eyes, as if he were reliving that night. "His little brother."

"His brother?" Parker feigned surprise. "What did his brother have to do with you?"

"He works for me. Yeah, that's right. I recruited the kid for my business. So what?"

Stay on point. "And so you met Keola at the blowhole that night. What did he have to say?"

"He told me to leave his brother alone." He waggled the gun as he spoke. Couldn't have much experience with weapons.

"And that upset you?"

Jonathan snorted as if the question were ridiculous. "I asked him to join me."

"And?" Parker inched a little closer.

"What do you think? The snob refused. He thought he was too good to work with me. He was such a stuck up prick."

Too bad Miranda wasn't here. Those words would make her beat the young man to a pulp, .45 or no .45. Parker preferred a subtler way of dealing with this hoodlum. "And so you threatened him."

He shifted his weight from foot to foot, seething over what had happened. He had to get it out. "I told that sonofabitch that his brother was lost to him and if he ever betrayed me he'd find himself in a ditch somewhere."

"And that was all?"

"It would've been. But the fucker swung at me." His passion rose and the shift turned into a sort of hip-hop step. Suddenly, despite his size, his tough talk and even the grisly action he was describing, he seemed like a lost child.

Parker dared to take a full step toward the young man. Ha'aheo didn't seem to see him anymore. "So it was self defense?"

"Sure as hell was. What could I do? I swung back. I socked him hard in the face. He fell over and hit his head on the rocks. It was an accident."

"Keola had more than one head wound."

"He wouldn't stop. He told me I couldn't have his brother. That he was going to the police. So I went a little crazy. I grabbed him by the throat and bashed his head into the rocks. He passed out. I thought he was dead."

Parker waited for him to go on.

Waving the gun, Jonathan began to pace. Parker moved in a bit. He was just a leg's length away. "Things had been going so good. I couldn't have him messing it all up. I couldn't have a murder rap now. So I picked him up and tossed him in the blowhole. I figured the tide would suck him out to sea, like some of the dumbshit *haoles* who come here."

"But it didn't."

"No. Somebody found him and pulled him out. Maybe he wasn't dead when I put him in. Maybe he drowned in the hole. All I know is it all went to hell after that." He fell silent.

Parker didn't move. He let the stillness between them stretch for a long moment before he quietly spoke. "My wife found him."

"What?" With a look of crazed alarm, Jonathan turned to him, blinking, his gun forgotten.

Now.

Parker took a step, kicked hard and hit the boy's wrist at just the right angle. The .45 flew from his grip and clattered onto the cave floor.

It didn't take long for Jonathan to recover. "You freaking cocksucker." He bent down to scoop up the weapon.

Parker moved fast. In one fluid movement, he jammed his Glock under his belt, flexed his knees and swung hard.

The uppercut landed nicely on the young man's jaw, pulling him up and away from the gun and sending him flying against the cave wall.

Jonathan caught himself, scraping his back and looking more shocked than a moment ago. Shaking his head as if he was seeing stars, he glared at Parker. "Now you're really asking for it, motherfucker."

"I thought I was asking for it before."

Propelling himself off the wall, he came at Parker. Parker danced away and threw a jab, missing his target by a hair's breadth. Jonathan struck out and landed a punch to the shoulder. Parker moved with it, but it stung like hell. The boy was quick and strong.

He didn't let the pain show. He returned with a leg kick to Jonathan's shin. "I can go on like this all night. You won't last forever."

"Wanna bet?" He gave Parker a knee to his ribs that would have knocked his breath out if he hadn't dodged the full force.

Parker returned with another shin kick and a jab.

Jonathan faked with his left. It threw Parker off. Before he could duck, the boy's right landed with a smack just below his eye. He staggered back, nearly cutting himself on one of the stalagmites. He felt blood on his cheek. His vision blurred. This young man had recently killed someone with his bare hands, he reminded himself. It was time to stop holding back.

He sauntered forward and began to pummel the young man's stomach hard. Jonathan took a few punches, blocked another, countered. Left. Right. Left. Right.

"Tired yet?"

"You should see your face, PI," Jonathan sneered.

Parker had had enough of this game. Perhaps what the boy needed was, in the words of his grandfather, a good, old-fashioned ass whooping. He took aim, reared back and let go with a hard jab to the nose. He connected and felt the cartilage break beneath his knuckles.

Jonathan fell back barely missing one of the rocky spears. Blood spurted from his face.

Parker watched the young man for a while as he held his nose, whimpering, reminding him of a wounded puppy.

He strolled toward him, leaned down, extended a hand. "That's enough, Jonathan. Let's go see Sergeant Balondo."

Jonathan gave him the look of a demon from hell. "You must be out of your fucking mind."

It must have been the guilt that made him drop his guard. It was a lucky punch. A sucker punch. Parker saw the young man's bloody fist shoot up. He tried to dodge, but the boy was lightening fast, his rage giving him the power of a steam engine.

With the force of a sledgehammer, Jonathan's knuckles landed square on his bleeding eye. Pain exploded into him.

Parker fell back, tried to catch himself. He felt the back of his head bounce off lava rock, felt the sharp edges slice into his back and hands as he slid to the floor. It felt as if the whole cave had shifted in an earthquake. He could no longer see. He felt his body go limp.

And with Ha'aheo's raspy laugh ringing in his ears, he lost consciousness.

CHAPTER THIRTY-ONE

Edward Steele opened the door of his beloved Coconut Rum and stepped inside the empty space. Letting his eyes grow accustomed to the dim light coming in the windows, he thought of the good times he and his customers had enjoyed here. Would there ever be good times again? He wasn't sure.

He crossed the room, checking for what needed repair or cleaning as he headed for the back.

He hadn't felt this much anxiety since…Well, maybe he'd had too much anxiety lately. And in the middle of all this anguish and pain, a spark of joy.

Miranda. He regarded the barstool where she'd sat.

His own daughter, back from the dead, as it were. Or maybe she thought he was the one in that state. He still couldn't believe it.

A private investigator. Fancy that. Pride rippled through him. She'd been a bright little girl. He always knew she'd do well for herself. And married to the boss? Now wasn't that something. But she hadn't come here to look for him. It was obvious she hadn't known who he was when she walked in or she wouldn't have come. Once she did know, she didn't even want to speak to him.

He couldn't blame her for that.

Leaving his little girl had been one of the deepest regrets of his life. But at the time, he'd had no choice. Or so he'd told himself.

He made his way to the back of the bar and stepped into the narrow hallway. He paused before the door of the back room.

Last night after Olina and Daniel and the kids had left the house, he'd broken the news about Miranda to Leilani. Oh, he'd told her years ago when they were dating. He couldn't risk the fact that he had been married before and had a daughter coming out later and wrecking his marriage to the girl of his dreams.

And she, just as she had the first time he'd told her about Miranda's existence, had listened in her kind, patient way. Just as he knew she would. No jealously, no recrimination or disapproval. Just acceptance. She'd even asked to meet her. Leilani's kind and gentle heart never ceased to amaze him.

He hated having to tell her his first-born wanted nothing to do with him.

Mikaele would be a different matter, but Leilani was right. It was time for the truth.

He rapped his knuckles on the door.

No answer.

Edward grunted. The boy was in there. He could smell the recently cooked French fries. After a moment, he opened the door. "Mikaele?"

He found his youngest child on the cot he'd put into the small storage room when Leilani kicked him out of the house. Even his patient angel couldn't abide the boy's recent activities.

His thin body was sprawled across the bedspread, his arms folded tight. In an oversized T-shirt and baggy drawers, he stared at the wall, as if he didn't know his father was standing right here. Though how he could see through that hair, Edward couldn't imagine.

He was awake, but he didn't look up. He didn't have his earbuds in, so he certainly knew his father was there. Edward was glad the boy wasn't listening to that awful music.

"Mikaele," he repeated.

"The phone rang a little while ago," the boy said on a bored exhale without moving his gaze.

"Who was it?"

"I didn't get it."

"You couldn't be bothered to get up and answer the phone?"

He gave him a sour face and turned over toward the wall. "The answering machine picked it up."

"Never mind. I have something to tell you. Can I sit down?"

He shrugged the shoulder that wasn't pressed to the mattress. "It's your place."

Edward suppressed a grunt of annoyance. There was no chair in the small room, so he lowered himself onto the end of the bed. "I have a confession to make."

Mikaele didn't move.

"That woman who was in here yesterday?"

"The nosy one?" he sneered. "What about her?"

How could he say it? Better start back a bit. Edward stared at the supplies on the shelf against the wall and gathered his thoughts. "You know I came from the mainland."

"Yeah, so?"

"Years ago, back there…"

The boy expressed his lack of interest with a yawn.

Edward sighed. "I had another family back then. Another wife."

That got his attention. He turned his head around. "You were married before Mom?"

Feeling guilty at his son's surprise, Edward nodded. "I had a child. A little girl. And I did something terrible."

"What?"

"I left them."

"What do you mean, 'left them?'" The anxiety in Mikaele's youthful voice only added to Edward's guilt.

"I took off. Packed my bags, left and never went back."

"Just like that?"

"Just like that. I was young and headstrong and I wanted to see the world. I wanted to come here to the islands."

The scowl returned. "What's that got to do with anything?"

"That woman in the bar yesterday…" No easy way. Just blurt it out. "Is my little girl."

Now he turned all the way around and leaned up on an elbow. "No way."

"Way," Edward said, in the vernacular of the young. "Miranda's my daughter. Your half-sister."

The boy brushed his hair out of his eyes and Edward saw they were wide with curiosity. "Did she come here to find you?"

"No, she's here looking into Keola's death, like she said." He couldn't explain how she'd gotten involved in that, but Edward thought it best not to go into details. Especially about Miranda's reaction to him.

"Wow. Does Mom know?"

"Yes. She's always known I had another family before. I told your mother last night that Miranda was here in Lahaina. She and I agreed we should tell you. After all, you're a man now."

He blinked at that as if he didn't know how to take that remark. "Does Olina know?"

Edward knew the boy was testing his sincerity, but he had nothing to hide. "No. I wanted to tell you first. I'll tell your sister when she comes to the house tonight."

"Wow," he said again and sat back against the plank that served as a headboard.

"There's something else."

"What?" Suspicion was back in his eyes.

"I just got a call from a lawyer. Miranda needs our help. Your help."

"What do you mean?"

"Earlier today she and her husband were investigating around the blowhole where they found Keola. The police arrested her."

He sat up. "What? Why?"

"The attorney said something about a sea cave in that area. They were in it. There were boxes of stolen goods and 'illegal substances,' as she called it. A police boat came by and spotted them. They confiscated the boxes and took Miranda in. They think she's involved in Keola's death."

His dark eyes glowed with what looked like terror. He shot to his feet. "No, no, no. That can't be. It just can't be."

"What do you know about that cave, son?"

He hugged himself and paced to the end of the bed, the only spot in the room to go. "This can't be right. It can't be happening."

"Mikaele, you have to tell the police what you know. You don't have to tell me, but we have to help Miranda."

He glared at him. "I can't, Dad. I just can't."

"Why not? What are you afraid of?"

"You don't get it, Dad. You just don't get it."

"What don't I get?"

Mikaele began to moan. He eyed the door.

Edward rose and moved to block his son in at the end of the bed before he could bolt from the room. "Tell me," he demanded. "This has to do with Jonathan Ha'aheo, doesn't it?"

The boy covered his face with his hands. "Dad, please."

Edward grabbed him by the arms, resisted the urge to shake him. "You're a man now, Mikaele. You have to face the consequences of your actions. Did Ha'aheo threaten you?"

"It was more than that."

"Tell me what he said."

He held his straight dark hair back and glared at him. "You really want to know?"

"Yes, I do."

"He threatened to hurt you."

"Me?" Edward almost wanted to laugh.

"And Mom. And Olina and her kids. He knows where they live. He told me if I didn't do what he said, something terrible would happen to one of them. Or all of them."

Anger pounded in Edward's chest like a pahu drum. "That sonofa—"

"He said if I didn't join him, or if I ever ratted him out to the cops, he'd kill one of you." The boy began to weep.

Now everything made sense. He should have known. "Come here."

He took his son in his arms, let him cry against his chest. Edward's heart went out to the boy. He was frightened and lost and alone. Keola must have known about this. He must have tried to save him somehow. But he'd failed. If only his sons had come to him. But he'd been too busy enjoying life and good times in his tiki bar. He'd never neglect Mikaele again.

"Mikaele, listen to me. You have to tell the police about Jonathan."

"No." He tried to pull away, but Edward held him fast.

"You have to. You have to help Miranda."

"I want to help her, but you can't expect me to—"

"Listen to me, son. If you tell the police about Jonathan, they'll have the evidence they need. They can go after him. They'll let Miranda go free."

He stared at his bed and slowly shook his head. "I can't, Dad. I—"

"Miranda is a detective. She and her husband can help bring Jonathan in. Your testimony will help put him away."

Edward felt the tension in the boy's body ease. He was thinking it through. He spoke softly, letting the impact of his words sink in. "Mikaele, if you don't do this, the man who murdered your brother will be out there running free. He will come after you then. Or us. And the police will lock Miranda up."

He jolted from his arms. "That's not fair."

"But it will happen, nonetheless."

Edward could almost smell the fear on Mikaele's face. "What if they put me in jail? I'm scared."

Edward hadn't considered that. He had no real idea what his son had gotten himself into. He wasn't going to make idle promises. He reached out and put a firm arm around him. "I can't answer that, but I know it's the right thing to do. I'll stand by you no matter what. I think your mother will, too."

The boy looked up at him with big, tear-stained eyes. He'd missed his mother most of all.

"Will you go with me to the police station?"

"Now?"

It was time to act before Mikaele lost his nerve. "Right now."

Mikaele wiped his face and slowly nodded. "Okay."

"Come on. Let's get in the car." Gently he took his son by the arm.

Relief mixed with trepidation washed over Edward as they trudged down the hall and out of the bar.

CHAPTER THIRTY-TWO

"C'mon, Parker. Wake up."

Something was knocking against his ribs. Parker's legs were wet, as if he were standing in water. His backside was pressed against a hard surface. He opened his eyes and saw he'd been propped up on a surfboard. It floated on the water near the cave wall, its nose was banging rhythmically against his chest.

In a haze, Ha'aheo's angry form appeared in the distance.

"That's it. That's how I want you. Awake." The young man was holding the far end of the board. He had it wedged between the cave wall and one of the stalagmites.

Parker put his hand to the side of his head. Blood. Jonathan had knocked him out. His vision was still blurry. His eye must be swollen from the young man's punch.

He shook his head. Pain spiked through his skull. But he was fully alert. Miranda. He had to save Miranda. He forced himself to focus on Ha'aheo. "Will you go with me to the police station now?"

Jonathan stared at him a moment, then rolled his head back and guffawed. "You really think you have the upper hand, don't you?"

He wasn't getting anywhere with him, was he? "You're only going to get into more trouble, Jonathan. It's only a matter of time before you're in jail or dead."

"Like my father, right?" Jonathan jerked the surfboard out from under him.

Parker reached out for it, but its surface was too slippery to hold onto. He slid into the water. The waves were waist deep. He reached behind him. His Glock was gone.

The young man hoisted his large body onto the board. Globe lights were connected to the far side of the board with a rope. So was Parker's flashlight. He assumed the Glock was on the boy's person. He began to paddle away.

"Jonathan." Parker took a step to follow him. Something heavy weighed down his leg.

The boy paddled faster. The board drifted out of reach.

"Jonathan," he shouted, taking a few more steps. Something pulled his leg back. "What in the world?"

Jonathan stopped in the water. He held his board with one arm, his side with the other as he laughed. "Oh, this is sweet. I've finally taken care of you, Parker. I finally have my payback for what you did to my father and my mother."

Parker's head pounded with the words. "What?"

"I chained you up. Just like the stash you took from me. Consider this payback for that, too."

"Jonathan, this is no time for games."

He spat saliva out of his mouth as he snorted in delight. "It's no game, you dumb PI. I say you have about, oh, half an hour before the water's over your head. I left you another few feet of chain for extra entertainment." He reached his speedboat, untied the mooring line and tossed it onto the bow. "I only regret I can't stay here and watch you struggle for your life the way my father did for his." He climbed aboard the boat, hauled up his surfboard.

The impact of the words and the weight around Parker's ankle sank in. This was ridiculous. He forced himself to sound menacing. "Jonathan. Do you really want two murders on your hands, son?"

"The dumbshit cops will never find me. I'm going to Oahu." He reached for an oar then turned and paddled his boat away, taking the light with him.

"I wouldn't be so sure."

"You just don't understand family, do you?" he called out as he drifted toward the crook in the cave. "I don't care if the cops catch me. I would risk anything to pay you back. You can't imagine how much I hate you." The bitterness in his raspy voice echoed the sentiment.

And then he turned the corner and was gone. Lost.

Parker stood staring into the darkness in stunned shock. Then he shook himself out of it. He had to deal with the situation.

He got to work.

Sucking in his breath, he dove under the waves and felt his way along until his fingers touched the surface of the large stalagmite. He swam down to its thick base and found the chain that had held one of the marine boxes. He worked his way back toward the other end of the chain. It was bound around his foot, secured with a padlock.

Not such a problem.

He shot back to the surface. All he had to do was get his tools and open the lock. It wouldn't be easy underwater and in the dark, but he could do it. He patted his pockets, feeling for his pouch.

Where was it?

He always kept it in his right pocket. He struggled to slide his fingers between the soggy denim of his jeans under the moving waves. At last, he got his hand inside the pocket. He twisted this way, that way. Nothing there.

Was it in the other pocket? He pulled his hand out and tried the left side. Nothing there either.

And then he remembered. He'd left the pouch on the last marine box. It was still there when the police boat arrived. His tools must be at the station with the contraband.

He fought down the knot of fear forming in his belly. The waves lapped against the cave walls, against his body. It wouldn't be long before they were up to his chest. He'd have to think of something else.

And he'd have to think of it fast.

CHAPTER THIRTY-THREE

"What do you mean, Sergeant Balondo is busy?" Edward Steele glared into the glassy eyes of the youthful, large-eared clerk behind the front counter of the police station.

"He isn't answering his phone, sir. He must be away."

"Don't you have an intercom?" They'd already waited over twenty minutes. They had to see the sergeant before Mikaele lost his nerve.

Mikaele tapped his arm. "C'mon, Dad. Don't make a scene."

"Scene? I'll show you a scene." Edward turned and marched down a little alcove with a door at the end of it.

The clerk got to his feet. "Sir, you can't go in there."

"Watch me." Edward grabbed the handle, yanked open the door and bellowed as loud as he could. "Sergeant Balondo? Are you back there? We need to speak with you."

A tall, dark-skinned uniform popped around a corner. Before he could speak, a door near the back opened and Balondo stepped into the hallway. "What the hell is going on?"

Edward blew out a breath of relief. "I apologize, Sergeant. We—my son—needs to speak with you."

The sergeant's face softened when he recognized Keola's family, but he still looked annoyed. "Now?"

Edward had a love-hate relationship with cops, but Balondo had seemed genuinely concerned when he came to the house to talk to the family yesterday as a follow-up to the first officer. And just now, he couldn't be picky. "Yes, sir. Right away," he said. "We have important information you can use." His voice nearly broke as he uttered the words. He couldn't explain any more here in the hall.

"All right." Balondo gestured for them to come ahead. "Let's go to my office."

As he stepped forward, Edward whispered to his son, "Don't say anything until we see Miranda."

Miranda lifted her head from her balled fist and stared at Zabel, who had been quietly jotting down more details of her honeymoon adventure. She knew that booming voice. Had her new lawyer really pulled it off?

"Is that who I think it is?"

Zabel looked up and grinned at her as she rose and moved to the door. "I think so. And if everything goes right with the sergeant, in a little while you'll be out of here." Then she knocked on the door for an officer to open it.

When he did, she glided through with even more confidence in her step than before. "I'll be back as soon as I get this straightened out," she called out just before the officer shut the door and locked it behind her.

CHAPTER THIRTY-FOUR

The water was almost to his shoulders now.
Breathe, Parker told himself, forcing back the panic. There was always a way out. It was just a matter discovering it.
In time.
A thought came to him. He still had his shoes on. That should do it.
He drew in another breath and bent his knees to sink down below the surface. In the dark, he used his leg to find the chain and followed it to where it was attached to the stalagmite. He let the chain go and felt his way up. The rock grew narrower as he went.
His head popped over the water and he drew in air. His fingers touched the spiny top. He let his hands travel down again several inches to a narrower place. There. That ought to do it.
Now for some leverage.
Once again he found the chain and held onto it while he angled his body. He raised his free leg and pushed back, his heel coming down against the rock with as much force as he could muster. He plunged forward again, groped for the top. It was still in place.
He needed more force.
He repositioned himself and gave the stalagmite another kick. He dove in. Still there, but partly broken now. One more try.
He repeated the movement, thrust out his leg with all his might.
He felt the rock give way, heard it plop into the water. He propelled himself toward the spear. "Oh, no you don't." His hands found the jagged piece just before it floated out of reach. It was the perfect size.
The next step would be a tad more difficult. He took a quick breath to calm himself. Then he sucked in all the air he could and dove below the surface once more, the rock pressed to his chest.
Once again he found the chain with his free hand. He pulled it away from his ankle. It barely budged. He was afraid of that. The chain was too tight, the padlock too close. If he tried to break it, he'd shatter bone. Next idea.

He followed the chain down to the base of the stalagmite, felt for the place where it was attached to the rock. It seemed to be connected with a heavy bolt, held in place with another lock. Jonathan had done a lot of work to secure it. If only he had put his efforts to better use. Parker ran his fingers over the surface. Sturdy, not a speck of rust. Must be stainless steel.

This was his best bet. The weakest spot in the chain.

He held the chain taut against the base of the stalagmite, gripped the piece he'd broken off the top in his other hand and rammed it down against the bolt with all his might. The vibration stirred the water, kicking up silt, but overhead the waves were already restless.

He gave the bolt another hard smack. It shook again, but the hard steel wouldn't give. He struck it again.

Still intact. Time for some air.

He stood and stretched to his full height, until his head broke through the surface. The water was to his chin. No time to rest.

He took a quick gulp of air and plunged in again. Once more, he maneuvered the chain against the spear's base and pounded it. Over and over. The makeshift hammer cut into his palm. His hand started to bleed and he hoped no sharks would find their way into the cave.

On the last strike, the rock gave way and crumbled in his hand. The pieces floated away. He took the chain in both hands and pulled, ignoring the pain of his cuts. No give at all. The link hadn't loosened one bit.

He rushed back to the surface and gasped in air, his chest heaving.

A wave splashed against his face. He shot up, floated.

The back of the cave. The water would be shallower there. He forced himself to regain composure and got his bearings. That way.

He swam as hard as he could, but he didn't get far before the chain went taut and jerked him back. The links bit into his ankle.

He put his legs down. His head was still above water here. At the bottom of his neck. There was still time before he had to swim. Think, dammit, think.

But nothing came to him.

CHAPTER THIRTY-FIVE

Miranda thought she must have been dreaming when the door to the interrogation room opened and her father strode in with Mikaele, Sergeant Balondo and Zabel following behind.

She watched them assemble themselves around the cramped little table.

"Is this satisfactory, Ms. Garcia?" Balondo said, sounding as grouchy as ever.

Zabel nodded. "Yes, it is, Sergeant."

Balondo plopped down into a chair, slapped his notepad down and clicked his pen. "All right, young man. What do you have to say?"

Mikaele blinked at the faces the room. He looked as if he'd like to turn and run away and hide somewhere.

Edward Steele, her father, put a steadying hand on his shoulder. "It's all right, son. Tell the sergeant everything."

The boy stared down at the floor, his dark hair falling over his eyes, and swiped at his nose. "I was at the blowhole the night my brother was killed."

Balondo raised a brow.

"And?" her father prompted.

"Jonathan Ha'aheo was there. My brother went to meet him there."

Balondo made a note on his pad. He was trying to look objective and authoritative, but Miranda could see he was surprised to hear the same name she had given him. "Why did your brother go to meet this person?"

"He's the leader of Huaka'i Po. The Night Marchers."

That got Balondo's attention. He raised his head. "The gang? How do you know about them?"

"I'm a member. Jonathan recruited me."

Miranda hugged herself, her stomach in a tight knot. Gang affiliation. She knew it. Mikaele's baggy T-shirt and droopy drawers only added weight to his words.

"Go on, son," Balondo prompted.

"Jonathan promised me lots of money and that I wouldn't have to finish school. He took me to his lava cave. He showed me drugs and goods he had stolen from local hotels. He said I could steal stuff like that for him, too, and make lots of scratch. He threatened to hurt my family if I told anyone." The boy pulled his hair out of his eyes. There was real fright in them.

"Did he hurt them?" Balondo wanted to know.

"Not until Keola found out about Jonathan. That I was hanging around with him, at least. He went to the blowhole that night to tell Jonathan to leave me alone."

Balondo put down his pen and folded his arms. "And what happened?"

"Jonathan laughed at him. They talked a while. Argued, really. And then my brother swung at Jonathan. He shouldn't have done that. I could've told him that. You don't rile that hot head."

"You saw what happened?"

Mikaele nodded. "Keola came to see me before he went there. He told me he was going to meet Jonathan. I got scared and followed him. But there was nothing I could do." His eyes began to well up with tears.

"Your brother got into a fight with this Jonathan Ha'aheo?" Balondo asked to keep the boy on the facts.

Again he nodded. "Like I said, Keola took a swing at Jonathan. Jonathan wasn't gonna stand for that. He hit back. Really hard." Mikaele's voice broke.

"And then?"

"Keola fell back on the ground. Jonathan jumped on him. He pounded him. Really pounded him. He took his head in his hands and smashed it against the rocks." He made a sickening gesture to mimic the action. "Those sharp lava rocks. I saw the blood spurt out of him." The tears were streaming down his face now.

Balondo pulled out a chair. "Sit down, son."

Mikaele sank into it and swiped at his face. Zabel produced a tissue from her briefcase and handed it to him. The boy took it and blew his nose.

Her father stepped up behind the boy and laid comforting hands on each shoulder. "It's all right, son. You're doing fine. Go on, Sergeant."

Balondo leaned forward. "Did Keola fight back?"

"He tried to. But he couldn't fight that maniac. He got up and ran. He almost got away."

"Did he make it to the warning sign?" Miranda wanted to know.

Mikaele nodded. "He tried to grab onto it, but Jonathan is so strong. He dragged him back, threw him on the ground again. I heard his head hit the rocks this time." He put his hand to his mouth like he was going to be sick. He wiped his eyes with the tissue again.

"What happened then, son?" Balondo's voice was the gentlest Miranda had ever heard it.

Mikaele took a deep breath. "After that, my brother…didn't do anything. I couldn't see him moving any more. Jonathan got to his feet and picked him up. Keola's head and arms fell back…like he was dead." He pressed the tissue against his eyes. "I thought he'd killed him. Jonathan carried him over to the blowhole and threw him in."

"What did you do?"

"I ran. I ran like hell and got out of there. I went to a tattoo parlor and got this." He held up his arm with that tattoo of the fiery torch. "It wasn't for the Night Marchers. Yeah, it's their mark. And I was scared of Jonathan and thought it would prove my loyalty. But it wasn't really for him. It was for Keola. Because he was dead. Because Jonathan had killed him and I couldn't stop him." Breaking into deep sobs, he got to his feet, turned to his father.

Edward Steele held him as the boy buried his face in his chest and wept. Miranda watched the tears flow from her father's eyes as well. She couldn't keep them back herself. These were her brothers. Her family.

Everyone sat in silence for a long moment.

At last, Balondo brought them all back to reality. "So Jonathan Ha'aheo is the drug dealer and the killer. Do you know where he lives, son?"

"No, I don't."

Miranda sat up. "I do. Or I think I do. Jonathan's father, Robert Ha'aheo, was a career criminal as well. My husband and Detective Nakamura chased him down four years ago. Parker told me where Ha'aheo used to live. He thought Jonathan still lives there." She gave him the address she'd memorized.

Balondo made a note on his pad, snapped it shut and shot to his feet. "I'll get my men on it right away."

"Parker and I will go with you."

"This is police business, Mrs. Parker. You're free to go. Now if you'll all excuse me."

Miranda gritted her teeth as the sergeant brushed past her and out the door.

Zabel laid a gentle arm on hers. "Let's go, Miranda."

"Yeah, okay." Miranda's head was spinning as she hurried down the corridor. She'd get Parker and they'd beat the police to Ha'aheo's house. If she caught that bastard, she might be back here on charges for murder. Real ones this time. But as she reached the alcove that led to the waiting room she came back to the present.

She turned to her attorney. "Thank you so much, Zabel."

"Just doing my job."

"And you, too." She took the boy's hand. "Thank you, Mikaele." She meant it with all her heart.

"You're welcome...sister." He reached around her with his thin arms and gave her a hug.

She hadn't expected that. Or the tears stinging her eyes as she reached out for her father's hand. "And thank you, Dad."

He squeezed her hand, a sad smile on his face. "Keola's memorial is tomorrow. Will you come, Miranda?"

She opened her mouth, not sure what to say.

"Please come. He would have wanted you to be there. You and your husband. Please?"

Holding Mikaele's hand, she stepped through the door and into the open area. Husband.

She spun around, scanned the waiting room. "Parker?" Where was he?

She trotted across the room and peered through the window. He wasn't in the parking lot. She ran to the desk where a young clerk sat. "Where's my husband?"

He looked up from his magazine, a blank expression on his face. As if coming out of a trance, he scanned his desk, ran a hand over his face. "He left a little while ago."

Miranda felt as if the floor had dropped out from beneath her. "Where did he go?"

"I don't know. He gave me this note. I was supposed to give it to Sergeant Balondo."

At the sound of his name, the sergeant appeared in the aisle in front of the divider behind the reception desk. "What is it? Something else?"

"This is for you."

Miranda snatched the note out of the clerk's hand before Balondo could get it. She read it aloud.

I'm going to meet Jonathan Ha'aheo at the sea cave. He is Keola's killer. If I haven't brought him back in forty minutes, send someone after me.

"When did he leave?"

The clerk looked up at the clock. "About an hour ago."

"Oh, my God. Parker's in trouble."

She turned to Balondo. "We've got to get to that sea cave. Now."

This time, he gave her no argument. "We'll take the police boat." He shouted toward the back. "Yamagata, Andrews, you're coming with me."

The instant reply came over the divider. "Yes, sir."

Balondo turned to Mikaele. "What kind of boat does Ha'aheo have?"

"A Hustler Rocket," the boy said without a beat. "Red and black."

Balondo nodded and gave Miranda a somber look. "I'm sorry. There's not enough room in the police boat for you civilians." Then he disappeared.

Miranda pulled at her hair. "What do we do now?"

"We've got a boat," Mikaele offered.

She spun around to him. "Is it fast?"

"Our Stingray cruiser? It can do eighty."

That would do. "Let's go."

CHAPTER THIRTY-SIX

It seemed to take forever to get down to the dock and get the two vessels launched, but it was only about fifteen minutes before they were zipping over the water toward the cave.

Praying they weren't fifteen minutes too late, Miranda held onto her seat with a white-knuckle grip.

The waves were choppier now and more people were out but Balondo cleared the way in the police boat with his megaphone.

Finally, they neared the cliffs.

"Is this the cave near the blowhole where Keola was found?" Pumehana shouted.

"Yes. It's just beyond it." She gestured overhead. "You can see the blowhole from here."

"She's right, Dad," Mikaele said. "Jonathan showed it to me once."

"You said he took you there?"

"Yes. He said now that I'd seen the secret spot, I could never leave him. He threatened to slit my throat if I ever told anyone about it."

"We've got to get to that bastard," Miranda grunted from the back seat.

She saw concern mixed with pride flash in her father's eyes as he nodded in agreement. He was at the wheel, his dark hair and open Aloha shirt blowing in the wind. His strong, tan arms steered the cruiser around the cliffs with ease.

Mikaele sat next to him, a sharp eye on the police boat.

Miranda glanced in that direction. Over the roar of the motors, she couldn't be sure, but it looked like Yamagata was on the radio. He said something to Balondo. The sergeant nodded then picked up his megaphone and turned it toward them.

"A red-and-black Hustler Rocket was spotted heading toward Moloka'i. We're going after it."

As they passed the mouth of the sea cave, the police boat spun away and kicking up water, headed out to the ocean.

"We should follow them," Mikaele said.

Miranda gasped out loud. "What about Parker?"

She'd never seen her father's face so grim. "Ha'aheo could have him with him." He meant kidnapping.

"Or he could still be in that cave." And if he were, he was most likely dead.

Considering that, her father nodded. "The tide's up now. And didn't you say the police got everything Jonathan had?"

"Yes, they did."

"What do you think we should do, Miranda?"

An ominous heaviness came over her heart. Either way could be bad news. The worst news. She turned and stared at the yawning mouth. Parker, where are you? And suddenly, she knew. She couldn't explain it, but she knew. "We've got to go check out this sea cave. I think Parker's in there."

"The sea cave it is." He maneuvered the cruiser around, though the choppy waves slowed them down.

With what seemed like a sea snail's pace he motored toward the cave's mouth. After another eternity they were inside and in darkness.

"Do you have a light?"

"Several."

He switched them on and just as before that same, suffocating feeling came over her. This time more intense. She peered over the water. No sign of a boat.

She felt sick. The waves rocked the cruiser. The water was higher by several feet now and more active. You could almost touch the stalactites and the top of the stalagmites stuck out of the water like figurines on a lawn.

Then she saw the curve in the wall. "We're almost to the bend. Just around there is where we found the loot."

"I can't go any farther," her father said. "These rocks will tear the hull apart."

She leaned forward and shouted. "Parker. Are you in here? Parker." Please, dear God. Let him answer.

"Parker," she called again.

At last a voice echoed in reply. "Miranda. Thank God. I'm over here."

He sounded weak but that didn't stop a flood of relief from pulsing through her. "We're just around the corner. Past the curve in the wall. Can you see the light?"

"Yes, I can see it."

"Can you get to us?"

"No. I'm chained to the rock where we found the marine boxes."

Chained? What had Ha'aheo done to him? Panic turned her insides to ice. But sudden rage thawed it fast. "Wait here," she said to her father and threw her legs over the side of the boat.

"Be careful, Miranda. Those lava spears could go right through you."

"I'll be careful." She let herself down sucked in her breath and dove under. A wave rose over her head, and she had to rotate and butterfly her way down before her feet touched the cave floor. Once there, she stood and fear gripped her. The water was at least a foot over her head. And rising. If she didn't get to Parker fast, he'd drown.

She squatted, pushed up again. "I need a light," she said as soon as she her head popped through the water.

"Here." Mikaele tossed a lighted globe into the water. "It's got a strap."

"Thanks." She grabbed it, slung the strap over her shoulder and began freestyling as fast as she could toward the bend.

"Watch out for the rocks," her father warned again.

She slowed a little, fighting her panic and feeling for the sharp spears as she went. It seemed to take an hour before she made it around the corner, but at last she did.

She couldn't see anything beyond a few feet. "Parker," she called.

"Over here."

She swept the light over the water in the direction of where they had spotted Jonathan's marine boxes. In the dark shadows, she could make out a figure. There was Parker, treading water. He must be exhausted.

"I see you. I'm coming."

"Be careful. The lava rocks."

"I know. I'm fine." She felt her way, like a blind man through an obstacle course of sabers and daggers. Just as she thought the slow pace would drive her insane, she reached him. "I'm here."

"Thank God." He gasped air and reached for her.

She ran her hands over his arms. As she pulled one across her shoulder she thought nothing had ever felt so good. "That's right. Hold onto me."

He rested on her shoulder moment. His head was bleeding. "Must've been one hell of a fight."

"It was at that."

One of his eyes was dark and swollen. She wondered what Ha'aheo looked like.

"How did you get here?"

"Speedboat. My father's."

He looked surprised but there was no time for explanations. "Ha'aheo's on his way to Oahu," Parker told her. "He confessed to killing Keola. But he wanted revenge for his father's death at my hands. And for his mother. He chained my ankle to the rock. One of the chains he used for the marine boxes. It's padlocked. I tried to break it open at the base, but it was too strong."

"Good thing I happened along." She tried to sound cheery, but at the moment she wanted to wrap that chain around Ha'aheo's neck.

"The police must have confiscated my lock picks when they took the loot. Does your father have a bolt cutter?"

He probably had some tools, but it would take forever to swim back to the cruiser and get them. "Wait a minute."

"What?"

Her mind raced. The police had taken Parker's leather pouch when they found him here. But she'd still had the picks in her hand. She'd slipped them into her pocket without thinking. Good thing Balondo's man had missed that corner when he searched her at the station.

"I think have them. I just need to get to them." She looked around but there was nowhere to pull her butt out of the water. "Hold on to me. Can you do that?"

"Of course."

He held onto her shoulders and she let her body float up and turned on her side. The exposed pocket of her jeans was soaked through. She held it with one hand and carefully dug in with the other. It wasn't easy, but at last her fingers touched the long, thin metal pieces.

Wanting to shout for joy, she eased them out of her pocket. "Got 'em."

"Don't drop them."

"I won't." The force of the current was getting stronger, but stubbornly she held onto the picks.

"Give them to me." His hands were cold. He had a black eye, a bloody noggin and he looked totally spent.

She shook her head. "You're too tired. I'll be right back."

Before he could respond, she opened her mouth and inhaled the deepest breath she'd ever taken in her life. She secured the picks between her teeth and dove under the surface just as Parker began to protest.

As hard as she could, she paddled downward. The current was strong. The silt had kicked up and the water was murky, making it almost impossible to see. But remembering Parker had been in the dark all this while, she forced herself to concentrate. She could do this.

Stubbornly she felt her way along the surface of the thick spear of lava until her fingers touched the chain. She pulled herself along it, being careful not to yank it down and drag Parker under the surface.

His legs were moving. Part of what was kicking up the silt.

His shoes were off. And the ankle that was bound was bloody where he'd pulled against it. Heartbreak swelled inside her, but she knew she couldn't afford to give in to it.

She found the padlock, picked it up and focused on the keyhole.

Slowly, carefully, she slipped the L-shaped mini-wrench out of her mouth and inserted it. She turned it clockwise. That seemed right.

Holding it in place, she took the pick out of her mouth and was just about to put it into the keyhole when the force of a wave overhead pushed her back against the stalagmite. She held on tight to the picks and the padlock.

She could see Parker had come below the surface. He was holding his breath, thank God. He frowned at her as if to ask what the hell was going on. She gave him a look to tell him she was doing the best she could and gestured for him to go back up. He seemed to get the message and swam upward.

She followed his movements, pulled the chain upward to give him as much space as possible. By some miracle she was still holding onto the picks.

One more time.

She got the lock in place, took the wrench and forced it into the hole. Summoning patience she didn't possess, she inserted the pick. She could barely feel the pins with the water, but she tried. Come on, come on. She eased the pick out and gave the lock a tug.

Nothing.

If only she wasn't such a newbie at lock picking. Why hadn't Parker taught her this trick before?

She tried again. This time she thought she almost had it, but the lock wouldn't budge. She was running out of air. Her heart breaking, she removed the wrench, put both tools back between her teeth and swam to the surface.

She broke through the water and grabbed the picks out of her mouth in time to gasp for air.

"No luck?" Parker was trying to look suave and cool.

"I'm working on it. And you can drop the nonchalant act."

"Do it your way," he said in a deadly calm voice.

She frowned at him. "My way?"

"The way you did before."

Now she remembered what she'd done to get the marine box open. "Got it."

She took another deep breath and dove down. She found the padlock more quickly this time, but the water was getting rougher. Time was running out. There was almost no slack left for the chain. If she didn't get him out of here fast he'd be underwater.

Forcing herself to stay calm, once more she took the wrench out of her mouth and shoved it into the keyhole. That part she could do. It was just this next part she was having trouble with. The part that actually opened the lock.

Once more, she eased the pick into the end of the cylinder, felt for the pins. Her way. It was her last chance. Could she do it? She had to try. Here goes nothing, she thought, and jerked the pick back out.

The U-shaped part slid up and the lock opened.

It took a second for her to realize he was free. She put the tools back into her mouth and carefully pulled the lock off the chain. She slipped the shackle off Parker's ankle. He was free. She couldn't believe it.

He was free.

She swam back to the surface as fast as she could, pulled the picks from her mouth. "I did it."

"So I see. Did I ever tell you how much I love you?" He drew her to him and gave her a kiss so hot, it might have evaporated the entire Pacific Ocean if she'd let it last.

Instead she pulled away. She wouldn't be satisfied until they were on dry land. "No time for that, Parker. I've got to get you back to the boat. You're too tired to swim. Hang onto my shoulders. And be careful of these rocks."

Her heart almost broke at the sound of his laugh in her ears. "Yes, ma'am."

CHAPTER THIRTY-SEVEN

Miranda inhaled and reached for Parker's hand to let him help her out of the BMW. As handsome as he was in his navy swim trunks and robe, the black patch over his swollen eye still made her wince. He had a concussion to match hers, cuts on his hands and a slight limp, but he'd insisted on coming with her today.

An easy silence between them, they strode across the packed parking lot and down to the beach.

Along the shoreline a crowd of people milled about.

They were all ages, from children to the aged. A few were in black, some in white, others in the bright Hawaiian colors people wore here for mourning. Many wore leis and carried surfboards. A few had canoes or kayaks.

The sun had just come up and the golden colors played over sky and water. Somewhere someone was playing a lovely, sad tune on a ukulele.

Miranda made her way over the sand in her flip-flops, gazing at the spectacle. "There must be a couple of hundred people here."

"Keola was well loved," Parker observed in that quiet way of his.

She spotted Dominic Wainani, the creative director from the luau, and Nahele, Keola's replacement, and even Minoaka. The tough-talking luau boss must have a soft spot, after all. Of course, there was a hoard of girls, Keola's fans, all gathered into small groups and grieving with much pomp and show, in the way young girls do.

As they strolled along, she noticed a small shrine with photos of Keola in full costume performing with his fiery torches. The pictures were nestled among palm fronds and lilies. Several leis completed the memorial.

Wrapping her arms around the light T-shirt that covered her swimsuit, Miranda studied his intent, good-looking face.

She pressed her lips together as emotion rolled over her. "I wish I could have saved him."

Parker touched her shoulder and put his mouth to her temple in a soft kiss. "You did all you could."

She nodded, despite what her heart was telling her.

She took a few breaths and thought she'd gotten herself under control when a gentle hand touched her arm.

She spun around and saw a small Polynesian woman in a flowing blue swim robe with an expression on her face as wise as a sensei. A deep red lei hung around her neck. In her hand, she held four white long-stemmed peace lilies.

Her long black hair was tied back in a colorful ribbon and had a touch of gray at the temples. She must have been in her late forties or early fifties, but her delicate features made her seem younger.

She was, in fact, stunning.

Her deep brown eyes were tinged with red and bloodshot from recent crying, but they brimmed with compassion and tenderness. "I'm so sorry to startle you. Are you—Mrs. Parker?"

"Yes," she answered cautiously.

"I'm Leilani Steele." She made a short, cordial bow to her and Parker. "Thank you both for coming. It means so much to Edward."

Miranda opened her mouth, not knowing what to say.

Parker spared her the awkwardness by extending a hand. "It's so good to meet you, Mrs. Steele. Though we're both very sorry for the occasion."

"Mahalo. Thank you." She shook with Parker then took both Miranda's hands in hers. "Thank you both for finding my son's killer."

Parker accepted her gratitude with a gracious nod. "And my thanks to your husband and son for helping to save my life. I'm sure you know the police caught up with Jonathan Ha'aheo at Molokai when he stopped to refuel his boat."

"Yes, at Kaunakakai. Sergeant Balondo called us last night and told us."

"Did he mention the fight Ha'aheo put up?" Parker asked.

"No, he didn't."

"It took three officers to subdue him, but they finally got him in handcuffs. He's threatening to sue for abuse."

Miranda had heard all of that when Balondo called them at the clinic where she'd taken Parker to get patched up, but she still had to smirk. "You're the one who ought to be suing," she said to Parker. "I guess he's going to prison for a long time." She couldn't be sad about that.

"His sentence won't be a light one."

They fell silent.

Leilani took advantage of the pause to change the subject. "Miranda—may I call you Miranda?"

"Sure." The woman still held her hands, but for once, she didn't feel like pulling away.

"I know this must be very awkward for you, but I want you to feel as welcome with us as any other family member."

Miranda didn't know what to make of that. She stared into Leilani's warm, motherly eyes and knew why her father had married her. She must have been awfully good for him.

"Thank you," she said at last, dropping her hands.

A young woman touched Leilani's arm. She was in a bright yellow swimsuit and wore a pink hibiscus lei around her neck. She carried several more on her arm.

"Mama, is this her?"

Leilani turned with a cautious smile. "Yes. This is she."

"I'm Olina. Keola was my brother."

Miranda couldn't help staring at the pretty face.

Another pink flower sat behind her ear, holding back her dark, wavy hair, which had just the right amount of natural curl. She was probably in her mid-twenties. Round cheeks ending in an angular jaw similar to her own. And big blue eyes the color of hers. She remembered her father had mentioned another daughter.

"Hi," she squeaked out after what seemed like a year.

"We're happy to meet you, Olina." Parker shook hands with her as he had with the mother.

"You don't have leis. May I?"

"Of course," Parker answered for both of them, aware of how awkward this was for her.

Miranda watched the young woman drape the garland over Parker's head, then bent and allowed her to do the same for her.

"Thanks," she murmured.

"You are so welcome. Mama, did you tell them how grateful we all are to them? For what they did for Keola?"

"Yes, I did."

The pretty face took on a somber expression as the dark brows knit together. "I didn't want to believe my brother had been…murdered. But now that the killer's behind bars…At least that part is over."

Sadly, she hugged herself with her free arm and studied Miranda with an expression that said she was having as much trouble coming to terms with the idea of having a half-sister as Miranda was.

Silence hung in the air until Leilani broke it. "Do you know where your father is? The ceremony is about to start."

Olina turned to her. "He's talking to all the customers who came out. Isn't it wonderful so many people are here? Mikaele is with him. Oh, Mama." She laid her head against her mother's neck and the woman embraced her. "Thank you for letting him come home to us. I just couldn't lose him, too."

Leilani stroked her daughter's arm. "I know, dear. I know."

A warm, loving family. Miranda felt touched and tempted with jealousy at the same time. But she was glad for the boy—her half-brother—and that he had straightened up.

She needed some space, but before she could step away, a lanky man in a dark wetsuit appeared and put his arm around Olina. "Are you doing all right, honey?" He kissed her cheek. He appeared to be Asian and there were two young kids at his side.

And a baby in his other arm.

"I'm fine."

The little girl tried to hide behind the man's leg while the boy jumped up and down. "Mama, Mama. When do we go in the water?"

"Soon, sweetheart." She turned to Miranda. "This is my husband, Daniel. And my son Makaio and daughter Kye." She took the baby from Daniel. "And this is our youngest, Lanakila. Lana for short."

The little thing was wrapped in a pink blanket and had her eyes closed and her tiny fists balled.

There was more handshaking. Miranda couldn't swallow. Must be the sand clogging her throat. She had a half-brother-in-law? And two half-nieces and a half-nephew? Or whatever you called such relations.

Just before she thought she might pass out from shock, a conch blew and everyone turned toward the beach.

"Oh, it's the priest. We're starting." Olina handed the baby back to her husband.

"Mother's going to watch the children while we go in," he told her.

"We can't go in?" the little boy whined.

Olina bent to stroke his hair. "You're going in the boat with Gramma and Grampa."

Leilani took the boy's hand. "Come, Makaio. Come along," she said to Miranda and Parker.

Daniel turned to Olina. "You go on ahead. I'll catch up to you."

"All right."

Mikaele ran up from the crowd and wedged himself next to Parker. "Dad's got your surfboards right over there." He waved toward the water.

CHAPTER THIRTY-EIGHT

They followed the family and found her father at the edge of the shore, standing next to five boards and a kayak laid out on the sand. He had his thick, dark locks tied back with a strip of leather and wore pure white swim trunks, exposing the tan and hair of his large belly and chest, adorned only with a lei.

He looked perfectly at home on the beach.

"There you all are," He smiled as they reached him. "Miranda, Mr. Parker, I'm so glad you're here. You've met...the family?"

"Yes," Miranda murmured, arms tucked around her waist.

Sensing her discomfort, her father dropped the subject.

At the edge of the crowd the man in a bright blue robe raised his hands. "We are gathered here this morning to celebrate the life of Keola Hakumele Steele. Family and friends, please feel free to join me in the traditional farewell to this beloved artist."

The people began to move toward the water.

"Let's get going." Her father bent down, lifted a blue and white board, handed it to her. "I assume you know how to use this. You're a pretty good swimmer."

"Guess so." She took it from him, and he gave the next one to Parker.

"Thank you, sir."

"You're welcome. Oh, we're having food at our house afterward for anyone who wants to stop by. Please come."

"We'll see," Miranda said, picking up her board.

With a sad look, he swiped a hand across his brow as if forcing himself not to pressure her. Then he waved his big arms. "Let's all stay together, now. You too, Miranda. You and your husband are part of us."

She nodded, kicked off her flip-flops and waded out into the ocean.

When they were waist-deep in the water, she lay down on the board and paddled, following the others.

She glanced over at Parker. His face was stern and set with determination, his muscled beauty glistened in the sunlight as he swam. How he could go out in the water again after yesterday, she'd never know. But Parker always surprised her.

On the other side of her, Mikaele paddled with vigor, intent on the meaning of the ceremony they were about to participate in. Beside him, Olina and Daniel made their way over the waves on their boards while her father rowed the kayak and Leilani sat behind him, holding Makaio in her arms.

They went out about a hundred feet or so and the crowd formed into a huge circle, the priest in the center. Everyone righted themselves, some sitting on their surfboards, and held hands.

Miranda felt Parker's strong grip on one side, Mikaele's mild one on the other.

Once again, the priest raised his arms, chanted in Hawaiian, then spoke in English. "Keola Hakumele was the beloved son of Edward and Leilani Steele. Many of us know Edward as Pumehana. I know he loved his son very much." He turned to her father. "Edward, does your family have any words for us?"

Her father turned to Leilani. She took one of the white peace lilies she'd brought and held it over the water. "I named him Keola, 'the life' because he was my first-born son. I named him Hakumele, which means 'to weave a song.' He lived up to that name. He was a poet of the fire dance." She tossed the lily onto the water.

"Yes, Keola was a poet," Edward said, taking a second lily from his wife. "A moody temperamental, artistic type. I didn't always understand him, but I loved him with all my heart. And I will miss him." He tossed the flower on top of the first one.

Olina took the next lily. "I was so proud of my brother. Yes, he was an artist, but he cared about others, especially his family. We all loved Keola very much. And all his friends loved him, as well." She tossed in her lily and handed the last one to Mikaele.

The poor boy was sobbing and Miranda couldn't help but reach out to touch his shoulder. "Just speak from your heart," she whispered.

He nodded, his hair over his eyes. "My brother died trying to save me from a very bad man. I love him for that and will miss him...so much." He tossed his flower into the water and put his hands over his eyes.

The priest began to softly chant. He drew a white urn from under his robe, raised it up and poured its content into the ocean.

Keola's ashes. Her brother.

And then everyone took off their leis and tossed them into the circle, close to the ashes. Miranda did the same, her heart breaking.

People began splashing and the performers from the luau started to sing the most beautiful song she'd ever heard.

Her throat went tight and tears welled up in her eyes.

"*I ke ala i ho'i 'ole mai.*" She didn't understand the words, but as her tears rolled down her cheeks and dropped into the ocean, she knew they must be something about the body returning to the earth from whence it came and the spirit rising upward to Heaven.

And deep in her heart, she felt assured that whatever God there was, He would take care of her brother and perhaps from time to time let him look down upon her and smile.

CHAPTER THIRTY-NINE

Miranda couldn't get out of going to the house. So after they'd showered and changed into jeans and T's, they followed the procession to a two-story bungalow on a peaceful residential street of Lahaina.

In the backyard Miranda's father manned the grill while Leilani made sure her plate was full of roasted pork, guava barbeque chicken and grilled vegetables and her glass was filled some sort of mango drink. She and Parker were introduced to all of Keola's friends and everyone who'd ever been in Coconut Rum.

For an hour or two everyone gorged on the delicious food and told stories about Keola. The awards he'd won, his girlfriends in high school, how he'd begun fire dancing at the age of ten and knew he had found his passion.

Miranda learned that Olina's husband was an intern at the medical center in Wailuku when he insisted on checking Parker's eye and made sure his ankle was elevated. He said he only wished he could have treated him yesterday.

Her father, in full, gregarious Pumehana mode, told the tale of how Parker hunted down and battled Ha'aheo and nearly beat him. And how his ace detective daughter had braved the inky waters of the sea cave to rescue her ace detective husband. He made it sound like an ancient island legend.

Embarrassed, Miranda slipped into the kitchen where Leilani and Olina were doing dishes.

"Need any help?" Miranda offered.

The women turned to her with welcoming smiles.

"No, you're a guest," Leilani said. "Please, just sit down over there." Her hands in soapy water, she nodded to a small kitchen table in the corner.

"Thanks." Miranda saw homey wooden booths had been built into either side and slid into one of them.

"Did you get enough to eat?"

She rubbed her midsection. She was as stuffed as the roasted pig. "More than enough." There was a long moment of silence while the women worked. "It was a beautiful ceremony today," Miranda said at last.

Leilani turned on the water to rinse a dish, then stuck a pot in her dishwasher. "Yes, it was. Keola would have been pleased."

"He would have loved the singing." Olina said.

They chatted awhile about the various people they'd seen today while Miranda listened.

Olina put the plate she was drying into a cabinet, then came to sit down in the booth across from her. "May I ask you something?" There was caution in her tone.

Miranda's stomach tensed. "Sure."

"How did you know Keola had been killed? The police thought it was suicide."

She didn't know how to answer that. She thought of the dream she'd had of someone calling to her for help. "I saw his last performance."

Her pretty eyes went wide. "Really?"

"I didn't know who he was but there was a point in the show where he stopped and looked at me."

"He did?"

"It was as if he knew who I was, and I felt some kind of…connection. And after I found him, I just knew it wasn't suicide or an accident. I know that sounds silly."

"No, it doesn't. Keola was intuitive like that. Sometimes he could sense things before they happened."

She wondered if they had the same gene. "Maybe he did this time."

"I will miss my brother so much. We were close."

"I wish I could've known him."

Olina looked up at her with those wide inquiring eyes. "I should have said 'our brother.' Oh, Miranda, you must hate me. You must hate all of us. All this time we've had your father and you've had nothing."

That was the last thing Miranda expected her to say. What did she feel? She barely knew. "I don't hate you. I just…it's a lot to process."

"Yes, it must be."

A low moan of grief came from the other side of the room and Miranda looked up to see Leilani leaning over the sink, weeping.

Olina shot up and went to her, put her arms around her mother and wept with her.

Quietly, Miranda got to her feet and slipped out to leave the grieving women to their sorrow.

In the living room she found her father saying good-bye to the last of the guests. He closed the front door and reached for a trash bag to clean up the empty cups and plates some of the kids had left.

There was no one else here now.

"Where's Parker?" she asked.

Dressed in flip-flops, cutoff jeans and a red Aloha shirt that gave his tanned skin a ruddy glow, he deftly shoveled paper plates and cups from the coffee table. "Out back with Mikaele. I think he's giving him a pep talk."

"He's good with kids." Miranda reached for a gooey plate on an end table and stuffed it in the bag he held open for her.

"Thanks." His brow furrowed. "By the way, why do you call him by his last name?"

Another question she didn't know how to answer. She shrugged. "Guess I just got used to it."

"Sorry. It's none of my business." Shaking his head at himself, he tied up the bag, put it near the door, then moved behind a small bar in the corner. He washed his hands and reached for a glass from an open cabinet on the wall. "Would you like a real drink? I'm a little tired of mango and ginger ale."

"Was that what that was? Yeah, I guess so." She could use one after today.

He set two tumblers on the counter and picked up a bottle. "Jack Daniel's good?"

"Sure." She slid onto a stool.

He poured two fingers and placed the glass in front of her.

Miranda took a swallow. It had a stinging punch but was just what she needed. She set the glass down. "Your wife is a wonderful lady."

"The love of my life," he said with a tender smile, pouring a drink for himself.

"She's very nice. And so is Olina. And Mikaele seems...content."

"First time I haven't seen a surly scowl on his face in I don't know how long. He told me last night he wants to work on his surfing. Maybe compete professionally or teach when he's old enough. And he's determined to get back into school. Says his brother would have wanted him to."

"That's great." She looked at him a moment, took in that big frame, that familiar face, then dropped her gaze.

They were silent for a long while. Miranda was thinking it was time to find Parker and get going when her father cleared his throat.

"There's something I need to say to you, Miranda."

Her shoulders tensed. So much for the Jack Daniels. "What?"

He wrinkled his bulbous nose and took a swallow from his glass. "I want to explain why I left your mother."

The liquor suddenly felt like it had scorched her stomach lining. "Dad, you don't have to—"

He shot up a big hand. "Please. I need to say this." He took a deep breath, followed it with another swig of booze. "Your mother and I—I married her because I thought she'd be good for me. But—hell, she was always so serious. Don't think the woman cracked a smile the whole time we were together."

Miranda couldn't remember her ever cracking a smile, either.

He grabbed a rag and began wiping the top of the bar, even though it didn't need cleaning. "Whatever I did was wrong. Do this, don't do that. I'd just gotten out of the Army. I was young and headstrong. Didn't want to put up with that kind of crap. Didn't want to fight over everything. I got fed up. Life's too short to be so grim all the time." He took another drink, put his glass down on the table with a slap. "In short, Miranda, your mother was a bitch."

She gave him a bitter smirk. "Call the news station."

"Yeah. So I left. That's the long and the short of it."

She watched him wipe the rag across the bar until she thought he'd rub a hole in it. Then dared to ask the question that had burned inside her for three decades. "Why did you leave me with her, Dad? Why didn't you take me with you?"

He stopped wiping and raised his head to stare at her. His deep blue eyes glowed as if he'd never thought of that before. "Take you with me?" He shook his head. "I—you were five years old. I went on the road. I didn't even know where I was going. I couldn't take care of a child."

"Where did you go?" she asked softly, hoping her voice wouldn't break.

"I worked my way to California. I cooked in any restaurant that would take me, then switched to bartending because the money was better."

She had a sudden flash of her father's big arms reaching out for her when he'd come home late at night from work, smelling of smoke and char-grilled steak.

"Finally, I made it to LA. After a year or so, a fellow looked me up and served me with divorce papers. Your mother had hired a detective to find me."

Miranda reached for her drink and took another gulp. "She never told me that. She never allowed me to mention you."

He nodded, his face lined with sorrow. He wiped the counter some more. "I decided what I'd always wanted was to see Hawaii, so I worked and saved and finally had enough for a one-way ticket. I came here, settled in West Maui because I heard it was a hotbed for wealthy tourists. They're good tippers. Easy to get a bartending job. And that's when I met Leilani. Fell in love at first sight. I worked some more, saved some more, finally bought my own place and asked her to marry me. So that's my story, such as it is." He looked up at her with an apologetic grin.

She didn't smile back. "You left me with her," she said in a hoarse croak.

"Aw, honey." Tears started to fill his eyes. "I screwed up. I was wrong. I know I hurt you."

"You never wrote. I thought you were dead."

Tears fell down his cheeks and onto the bar. "I know. I was a lousy father. That's really what I wanted to tell you. I'm sorry, Miranda. Can you ever...forgive me?" His watery blue eyes tore at her heart.

She opened her mouth but couldn't find her voice. She felt as if a noose were tied around her throat. Forgive him? After all the pain he'd caused her? The sense of loss and abandonment?

Three days ago, she would have kicked him in the balls and walked out. But now?

"I—I don't know, Dad."

"Well, I didn't think it was possible. But I had to ask."

The deep sorrow in his voice twisted her insides. If he hadn't gotten her released at the police station, if he hadn't helped her get to Parker yesterday, she'd be a widow right now. And he'd just lost his son. Her brother. How could she add more pain to what he'd already been through?

Once more she remembered those big arms holding her when he came through the door. They'd always felt so good.

She took a deep breath and somehow got the words out. "I don't know if I can forgive you, Dad. But—I'll try."

He looked up, sheer joy on his ruddy face. "Sweetheart." And then those big arms were real and here now. They slid around her in a bear hug.

She hugged him back, overcome with emotion and wept against his shoulder while he wept against hers.

At last, he pulled back and swiped at his cheek. "That felt good after everything that's gone on lately."

"Yeah, it did. You have a tissue?"

He found a box under the bar and set it down before her. She grabbed a sheet and blew her nose.

Watching her, his face grew somber. "Isn't it funny how life sometimes hands you joy and sorrow at the same time?" He had a faraway look in his eye.

"Yeah." She had a feeling he was talking about something else.

"I haven't told Leilani, but…"

She froze. "What?"

"Just before Keloa…passed."

She reached for his hand. "What is it?"

"I went to the doctor. I hadn't had a checkup in a long time. She's been nagging me to go forever, so I finally did. The news wasn't good."

"No?"

"Congenital heart disease. Hardening of the arteries."

Miranda felt as if a volcano had erupted beneath her feet and was about to swallow her up any second. She'd just found her father, halfway made up with him, and now…this? "That can't be right."

"It's not as bad as it sounds. It's in the early stages. I still have a few years. More if I take care of myself. The doc gave me some meds. And I need to start watching my diet. Laying off the pork." He forced a chuckle, then shook a forefinger at her. "You need to take care of yourself, too. It's hereditary, you know."

The shockwaves just kept coming. *Hereditary disease?* "I—I will. Uh, Dad."

"Yes, honey?"

Honey. She scratched at her hair, trying to find the right words. "I need…a favor."

"What? Anything. Or maybe I should hear it first." He chuckled.

"Do you have any documentation for that disease? And that it's hereditary?"

He looked puzzled. "I guess the doctor has."

"Could you get a copy for me?"

"Sure. Why?"

She couldn't tell him about her daughter. It was too much. "I can't tell you. It has to do with…a case I'm working on." That was close enough to the truth.

He gave her a suspicious glance. "Okay. I can get it in a few days. Will you still be here?"

She was supposed to be on her honeymoon but that had been shot to hell. Parker would probably want to cut his losses and head home. "We're only here for a little while. We have to get back to the Agency. I can give you my address in Atlanta."

"Okay." He turned around to find a pen and a notepad on a shelf. He handed them to her. "Here."

She took them, scribbled down the information and slid them back to him.

He stared down at the pad for a long moment. "Can I…write to you?"

She'd longed for him to write to her for thirty-one years. "Sure."

He wrote something down, tore off a slip of the paper and handed it to her. "Here."

"What's this?"

"The phone number here at the house. Call any time."

She heard the back door open. Before she could say anything, Parker came around a corner. "Would you like to stay a little longer?"

"No, I'm ready to go." She slipped the paper into her pocket and got to her feet.

With a look that said he was satisfied with what she'd given him, her father came around the bar and walked them to the front door.

"Say goodbye to Leilani and Olina for me. And tell Mikaele to keep his nose in the books."

He gave her a radiant smile. "I will."

Parker extended a hand to him. "Thank you, sir. For everything."

Her father patted his arm. "Sir? Call me Pumehana. Or, if you don't like that, Dad."

"All right, Dad." Man, did that ever sound strange coming out of Parker's mouth.

He gave her another one of his bear hugs and she drank it in, knowing she'd cherish the memory of it. "My PI daughter and her PI husband. I couldn't be prouder of you. Aloha, Miranda."

She stepped out the door and waved good-bye. "Aloha, Dad."

CHAPTER FORTY

They drove in silence down the Honoapiilani Highway, heading back to the Ashford-Grand. Before they reached the garden entrance, Parker glanced over at the stretch of beach that ran along the other side of the road.

"Would you like to take a walk?"

She leaned toward him and gave his foot a glance. "Don't you think you should give that ankle a rest?"

"It'll be all right."

What was he up to? She was afraid to guess. "Okay."

He pulled over and they got out and made their way across the street, under the palm trees and down to the shore. Miranda took off her flip-flops and let her toes sink into the warm sand. They strolled for a while, with no sound but the foamy waves and the sea gulls overhead.

Miranda knew Parker was getting ready to say something ominous. Well, it was a day for that.

He shaded his good eye and gazed out over the water. "I don't think I'll ever look at the ocean the same way after today."

"Me, either."

They walked a little more. From the corner of her eye she watched his gait, which was fairly steady. She took in his stone-washed jeans and form-fitting shirt. The man wore casual clothes with the same swagger he wore a tuxedo. Maybe it was that patch. It did give him the air of a pirate.

Nerves swam around in her stomach. At last, she couldn't stand it any longer. She stopped short and turned to face him. "Look, Parker. Why don't you just say what you have to say?"

"You're getting to be a bit of mind reader yourself." He smiled, but somehow that seemed all wrong. You shouldn't be smiling if you're about to break up with someone.

"Go ahead, get it over with."

His expression changed and she recognized that all too serious look in his eye. The one she could see. "This isn't easy for me."

Why should it be? "I can handle it." She put her flip-flops back on, shoved her hands into the back pockets of her jeans and raised her chin.

"Very well," he said slowly. "I want to ask your forgiveness."

She snorted out loud. "What? You, too?"

One dark brow rose. "Who else wanted your forgiveness?"

"Never mind. What do you want me to forgive you for?"

"For looking for your father behind your back."

She gave him a scowl. "Didn't I already do that?"

"You said you guessed you had to. And you were upset at the time."

She stared at him. He wanted to know if she'd really meant it. She lifted her hands in a shrug. "You were doing what you do. I know you were trying to help me. And…you did."

"That's not the way you reacted when you saw that message from Ryo on my phone," he said stiffly.

"So? A lot has happened since then."

He drew in a breath and shifted his weight. "I still need your genuine forgiveness. I don't want ill will between us." Or anything buried in her heart.

Ill will, huh? She put a hand to her head and thought back to Parker sitting in the BMW waiting for her when she first saw her father. The thought still touched her heart. "When I came out of Coconut Rum and saw you hadn't rushed in to rescue me…it meant a lot."

He nodded slowly, like a judge who didn't quite buy the defendant's alibi. "That's gratifying. But I need to hear the words."

He could be so noble at times, so formal. And so stubborn. "Okay, I forgive you. Feel better?"

"Yes, as a matter of fact." He seemed truly relieved.

Okay, so that was square between them. Now he'd hit her with the big guns, right?

They walked on, following the curve of the shore and were greeted by the laughter of children playing in the water.

"Who else did you forgive today?"

She kicked at the sand with her big toe. "My father."

"That's wonderful."

"Well, I sort of did. He said he was sorry for abandoning me. I told him I'd try to forgive him. I don't know if I can, but at least I had to say it." She turned and began to walk again, rubbing her arms. "And then he told me he has a hereditary disease."

Parker came to a halt. "What?"

"It's a heart condition. He doesn't know how long he has."

"That's awful."

"Yeah, a real kicker. But it's in the early stages. He's in pretty good shape. He's probably got years." At least she hoped so.

"Miranda…do you want to contact the judge in Chicago? About Amy? No pressure. Just a question."

She stopped walking. She was at the shoreline and the frothy white water washed over her feet. Listening to the tide going in and out, she stared at the ocean. The blue expanse of sea and sky, the fishing boats along the horizon, the wispy white clouds hovering over the neighboring island.

Funny, a few weeks ago she would have jumped at the chance to find Amy. But now? Now she had a family. And back home, she had friends. And Wendy. The girl was so fragile. Her parents still ignored her. Miranda cared about the kid. She couldn't desert her.

And what if she discovered Amy was living in bad circumstances? She couldn't stand knowing that. If she were with a good family, she'd be jealous and angry that she had never been able to give her daughter that kind of life.

Most of all, what if Amy...hated her?

But how could she go on not knowing anything about her daughter? She'd had these doubts before. They'd nagged at her the whole thirteen years she'd searched for her. How could she throw away this chance to find out where Amy was? Who she was? How could she not use the information her father had given her?

"I never wanted to interfere in Amy's life. I have to believe she's got people she knows and loves as her parents."

"I know that," he said gently.

"I just want to know she's...safe."

"And so...?"

"I asked my father for documentation of his disease from his doctor. He's going to send it to Atlanta."

She heard him exhale the breath he'd been holding and knew she'd surprised him. "Would you like me to handle the details from there?"

Feeling numb, again she nodded. She reached for Parker's hand, squeezed it. "Yes, I want to see what the judge says." He still might not open the adoption records but this was the best chance they'd ever have.

"I'll file the papers as soon as we get back home."

She almost laughed. She couldn't believe how un-pushy he was being. It felt a little weird. She turned to study that gorgeous, middle-aged face. The distinguished lines, the salt-and-pepper hair, the one intense gray eye she could see. She was really going to miss him.

She took a deep breath. "Okay. Now will you say what you have to tell me?"

His good eye narrowed at her. "What do you think I have to tell you?"

Was he going to make her spell it out? "That you've finally realized I'm right. That our relationship will never work out."

His brow furrowed in masculine confusion. "I thought you just forgave me."

"For looking for my father. For being you." She frowned at him. "Saying 'I forgive you' doesn't mean things will work out between us, Parker."

"And why not?"

"Why not?" He didn't see it? Now he was making her mad. "A thousand and one reasons. We're from different worlds. You come from a stable family, I don't."

"You like spicy food and I prefer it blander."

She scoffed at him and marched away, kicking up sand.

He caught up to her, reached for her arm, turned her to face him. "Miranda, haven't we been over all this before?"

"So?"

"So you married me anyway."

She folded her arms and rolled her eyes. "Parker, we had a fight on our honeymoon, for Pete's sake."

He seemed bewildered. "And your point is?"

Tears of exasperation stung her eyes. Good Lord, she was sick of crying. She raised her hands to the sky. "Even Leon and I didn't fight on our honeymoon."

"Oh, so that's it."

"Yeah, that's it."

He rubbed his chin and studied her with the air of a psychologist. "So you believe a fight on the honeymoon means the marriage won't last."

He was driving her nuts. "How can it, Parker? If you can't keep from fighting on your honeymoon, it will only get worse later on."

Parker looked at the woman before him and thought she'd never been so beautiful. Those gorgeous eyes as blue as the water beyond them. That wild, sensual hair. Even in flip-flops and jeans, she seemed regal to him. His heart went out to her. She'd never had a decent relationship with a man. She didn't understand the first thing about healthy disagreements.

He dared to step toward her and take her hand in his. That hand had saved his life yesterday. Along with that fiery spirit and determination and resilience he could never stop loving. "Would a marriage of twenty-two years disprove your theory?"

Slowly, she narrowed her eyes at him. "What are you talking about?"

"Sylvia and me."

"You two fought? On your honeymoon?"

"Yes, we did."

Miranda glared at Parker's way too good-looking face. How could he keep it straight and tell that bald-faced lie? She pulled her hand out of his and slapped both fists on her hips. "How long did it last? A minute?"

He put a finger to his lips to keep from chuckling. "All night. We shouted at each other. She locked herself in the bathroom and wouldn't come out until morning."

She couldn't help blinking at him in shock. "Really?"

"Really. I swear it." Held up his right hand.

She folded her arms and cocked her head at him. "Okay, then. What was the fight about?"

His smile disappeared. He frowned, rubbed his brow. "I can't remember."

She pursed her lips in disbelief.

"Really, I can't remember for the life of me. I'd bet Sylvia couldn't either. We made up, forgot about it and went on."

She stared at him.

"Oh, my darling. Fighting doesn't tear you apart as long as you fight fair. And if you make up afterward."

Did she dare believe that? She wanted to. She really wanted to. After all, she loved him more than her own life. "Well, I'm not saying I buy that…"

"Yes?"

"But I guess…"

"Yes?"

She caved. "I guess it's worth finding out if you're right."

"A wise decision." He stepped to her, put his arms around her, drew her to him and placed his sexy lips against her own.

The kiss was warm and sensuous. He moved his mouth over hers with that incredible skill that never failed to turn her knees to pudding and fill her body with a throbbing need.

Now that was more like it. Her heartbeat kicking up, she pulled away from him before they ended up rolling around naked in the sand in broad daylight.

She cleared her throat. "I was thinking…"

"Yes?" he said in a wicked tone. He leaned his forehead against hers and toyed with her hair.

"Our honeymoon got kind of wrecked."

"I'll admit it wasn't what I had in mind when I planned it. But we still have more than a week of vacation."

She laid her head against his strong chest, listened to his heartbeat, relieved that she could still hear it. She thought of the paper in her pocket. She would call her father and she would come back here to see him. But right now she needed to process everything that had happened. As magical as this island was, it wasn't the romantic getaway it had been when she and Parker first arrived.

"I can't stay here," she murmured.

"No, I didn't think so." His fingers were in her hair again, his lips kissing the unruly tresses. "How about we go to Paris?"

She had to laugh. "Paris? Because of my acute fashion sense?"

He smiled an understanding smile. "Where would you like to go?"

She thought about it. Before she met this man, she never thought she'd get out of the country, so she'd never let herself dream about going anywhere. But maybe… "Don't they build Ferraris in Italy?"

"There was a plant in Maranello. I don't think it's still in use, but I believe there's a sports car museum there."

Her blood began to pump with excitement. "I thought we could pick one up and drive it around the countryside."

That made him chuckle. "I'm sure we can find one to rent."

"Is Maranello near Rome?"

"It's in the north. Rome is in the south."

She dug her fingers into his thick mane of hair. "But it's a small country, isn't it? I've always wanted to see some of those ancient ruins."

"We can take a tour of the entire nation, if you like."

"It sounds like a dream vacation."

"It does sound good."

She let him go. "C'mon. Let's go get packed."

"All right, but I'm warning you, we may not get to the packing right away."

"That's okay," she laughed. "I've never made it with a pirate before."

The trade wind in her hair, she closed her eyes and breathed in the sea air. She had her father back. She had a family. And she had a husband who loved her so much, she couldn't get rid of him no matter what she did. For the first time since she'd met him in that jail cell, she thought it just might work between them.

Feeling lighter than she had all week, she took Parker's hand and helped him hurry up the bright, sandy beach to the hotel.

THE END

ABOUT THE AUTHOR

Writing fiction for over fifteen years, Linsey Lanier has authored more than two dozen novels and short stories, including the popular Miranda's Rights Mystery series. She writes romantic suspense, mysteries, and thrillers with a dash of sass.

She is a member of Romance Writers of America, the Kiss of Death chapter, Private Eye Writers of America, and International Thriller Writers. Her books have been nominated in several RWA-sponsored contests.

In her spare time, Linsey enjoys watching crime shows with her husband of over two decades and trying to figure out "who-dun-it." But her favorite activity is writing and creating entertaining new stories for her readers.

She's always working on a new book, currently books in the new Miranda and Parker Mystery series (a continuation of the Miranda's Rights Mystery series). For alerts on her latest releases join Linsey's mailing list at linseylanier.com.

For more of Linsey's books, visit **www.felicitybooks.com** or check out her website at **www.linseylanier.com**

Edited by
Donna Rich

Editing for You

Gilly Wright
www.gillywright.com

Printed in Great Britain
by Amazon